WILD IRISH ROOTS

MARGARET & SEAN

TRICIA O'MALLEY

LOVEWRITE PUBLISHING

WILD IRISH ROOTS: MARGARET & SEAN

BOOK 5 IN THE MYSTIC COVE SERIES

Copyright © 2015 by Tricia O'Malley
All Rights Reserved

Cover Design:
Alchemy Book Covers

All rights reserved. No part of this book may be reproduced in any form by any means without express permission of the author. This includes reprints, excerpts, photocopying, recording, or any future means of reproducing text.

If you would like to do any of the above, please seek permission first by contacting the author at:
info@triciaomalley.com

Dedicated to all those who take a little extra time finding their way. Sometimes the more difficult road ends up being the better one.

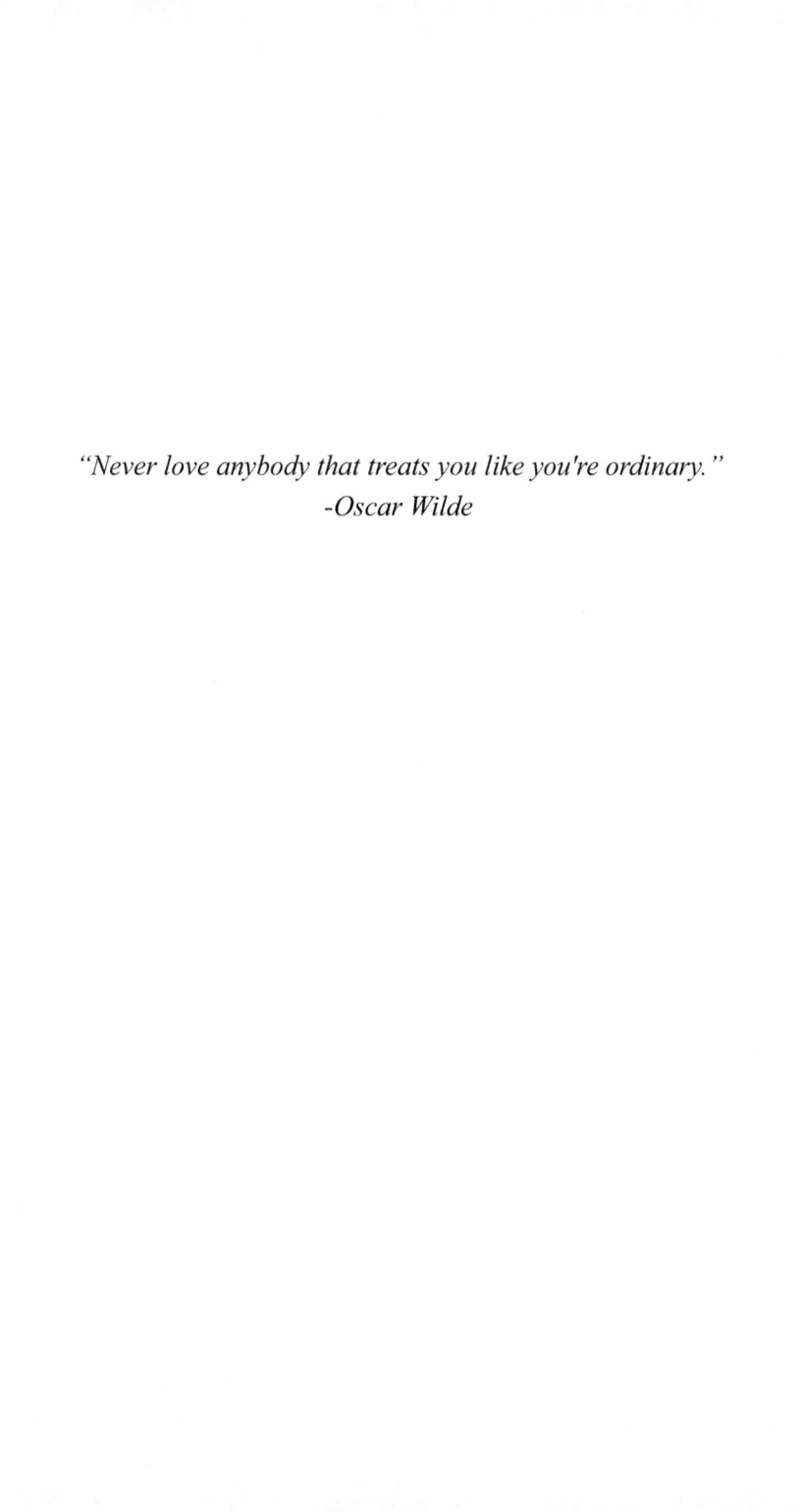

"Never love anybody that treats you like you're ordinary."
-Oscar Wilde

CHAPTER 1

"Mum, that man is lying." Margaret Grainne O'Brien tugged on Fiona's hand and pointed. At nine years old, Margaret was a precocious, intelligent child. She watched people closely and often offered her unfiltered opinions of their behavior.

"Shh, Margaret. Just because you can see that about him doesn't mean that other people can," Fiona said gently to her daughter. Margaret looked up at her quizzically.

"But, he is," Margaret insisted.

The man in question was, luckily, too far away for Margaret's small voice to reach him. He leaned across the table and held the hand of a blonde woman, looking searchingly into her eyes.

"Yes, he is. But some things we must allow to unfold naturally," Fiona cautioned and pulled her daughter away.

Margaret looked over her shoulder at the man as Fiona dragged her from the small restaurant. If someone had asked her, she would have been unable to explain why she knew when people were lying, in love, or hiding something. It was just how she saw the world. She'd never been told that she was different.

"Margaret, honey, let's get a cup of tea and sit outside, okay?" Fiona asked and stopped at a coffee shop next to the restaurant. She ordered cinnamon scones for the both of them and a pot of tea, motioning for Margaret to pick a table outside. Margaret picked one where she still had a view of the restaurant. Her nine-year-old brain was a curious one and she wanted to know what happened with the lying man.

Fiona came to join her at the table. Margaret smiled up at her mom, admiring her strawberry-blonde hair and sherry-brown eyes. Margaret took after her mother in that respect and she loved having Fiona braid her long hair. Even at this age, she had some vanity with her appearance.

Fiona smiled at Margaret and poured her a cup of tea, before spooning some clotted cream onto a scone for her. Together, they sat in silence for a moment as the small village of Grace's Cove bustled around them. A lovely spring day, the air was gentle with the promise of summer. The sun warmed the colorful buildings that jostled for attention on the main street that led to the harbor. At the bottom of the hill, the water spread out, the waves dancing in the sunlight.

"Margaret, honey, we need to talk," Fiona began.

Margaret tensed up. She could already tell that Fiona had something serious, if not scary, to tell her. She could read her mother's emotions and sensed her trepidation. Margaret put her scone down.

"What? What did I do wrong?"

"No, nothing like that. I want to talk to you about that man in the restaurant," Fiona said.

"Oh. Do you know why he was lying?" Margaret asked and took a bite from the cinnamon scone, letting the flavors settle over her tongue before taking a small sip of her tea.

"No. And, most people don't know that he is lying. It's time that we talked about your ability," Fiona said carefully.

Margaret felt her stomach knot up. She wasn't sure what was going on, but could tell that Fiona was tense.

"What do you mean?"

"Well, do you know how the other little girls that you play with sometimes get upset when you say things? Like how you know if they have a crush on a boy or if they are keeping a secret?"

Margaret shrugged her shoulders and looked stonily at her plate. Lately, she'd been having more and more trouble with her friends. It was hard for her to keep her mouth shut about the things that she saw. She didn't mean to blurt out the things that she knew; Margaret thought that she was helping her friends.

"Are they mad at me? Did their mums say something to you?" Margaret whispered.

"No, honey, not at all. First, I want you to know that I love you very much and always will. But, it is time to learn the truth about yourself. About us. You are an extra special girl. Just like me. Just like all of the females of our family." Fiona smiled warmly at Margaret and Margaret couldn't help but smile back even though her stomach was in knots. She could feel the love radiating from her mother and felt safe.

"What do you mean extra special? Like, because I can do math so well?" Margaret asked, deliberately steering the conversation around where she sensed it was going.

"No, because you have a special ability that other people don't have. But, if you don't learn how to keep quiet about it, people may treat you differently," Fiona said and patted Margaret's hand. "Honey, you're empathic. It is a very special gift that allows you to see other people's feelings even if they don't say anything. That man that you saw in the restaurant? Well, nobody else would know he was lying. Not even the woman that he was talking to. Most people can't see what you see."

Margaret felt heat creep through her as she began to understand all of the awkward moments she had been having at school. She *was* different.

"But you said that you could see he was lying!" Margaret said, accusation in her voice.

"I can. I did. But, see, I'm different too." Fiona smiled at her.

Margaret knew this to be true. She'd heard whispers of it on the playground and around the village. Fiona O'Brien's healing skills were both revered and feared. Margaret had always wondered why someone would be scared of Fiona, when she brought so much good to others.

"So, we're weird?" Margaret asked and crossed her arms over her small chest. Shame began to build within her.

"Margaret O'Brien, stop that. Immediately." Fiona's harsh tone jerked Margaret's gaze to her face. "We are not weird. We are special. Not everyone gets to have these types of gifts. They have been handed down from a very famous woman."

Her interest piqued, Margaret toyed with her scone before looking up at Fiona.

"From who?"

"Well, none other than the famous pirate queen, Grainne O'Malley. Grace. Just like my middle name. Just like yours."

"We're related to a pirate queen?" Margaret said excitedly. She'd always loved the water and spent many a happy hour down in the cove with Fiona.

"That we are...the best one, at that. Grace ruled the seas with a steel fist and wide-open heart. She helped to maintain much of our Irish culture. When it was time for her to pass on, well, she chose the cove as her final resting place."

Margaret's hands stilled on the plate. "Our cove?"

"Yes, our cove. The cove is where she chose to die. In doing so, she protected it. And, through whatever powers that be, she also gave everyone of her bloodline special gifts. You're lucky to have it," Fiona said fiercely.

Margaret stared across the road sullenly. She didn't feel lucky. She felt different now.

"I don't want it," Margaret said stubbornly.

Fiona laughed at her and reached across the table to cup her chin.

"That's something you'll have to come to terms with, my love."

CHAPTER 2

TEN YEARS LATER

MARGARET DUMPED THE rest of the teacups into the sink and powered the large sprayer over them. Her mind was on her date with Sean tonight, so she almost missed the cups and sprayed herself. Laughing, Margaret stepped back from the sink and went to lock the front door, calling to Sarah, the other server that worked at Grace's Cup, a small teashop in downtown Grace's Cove.

"Sarah, I'm closing up. I have a date to get ready for. You can go." Margaret smiled with anticipation as she locked the front glass-paned door and wound her way back through the small tables that cluttered the floor of the small restaurant.

"Alright then, see you later this week," Sarah grumbled as she left from the back door. Margaret rolled her eyes and moved through the small kitchen to twist the lock on the back door. Sarah always had one complaint or another. Shrugging it off, Margaret went into the back room to pull her garment bag from the closet. Smiling, she unzipped the bag to reveal a deep purple dress. She'd saved it just for this date with Sean, knowing that they would move their relationship forward soon.

Margaret changed quickly, slipping the purple dress over her curvy frame. On the taller side, Margaret held her curves well and she'd often received compliments on how she filled out a dress.

Always from the wrong people, Margaret thought. At nineteen, Margaret was still a virgin, having rebuffed all of the fumbling attempts by the inept boys that she had gone to school with. Until Sean. Sean had moved to Grace's Cove two years ago, just as Margaret was finishing school. A few years older than her, Sean had caught her eye immediately. He was everything that the boys at school weren't. Tall, muscular, and with a confidence that most guys her age had yet to cultivate. Dark brown hair, brown eyes and a bright white smile completed the package and Margaret's heart had been lost ever since.

A month ago, Sean had casually bumped into her at the pub. They ended up talking for quite a while that night. Margaret smiled as she thought about how their friends had faded away into the background as they grilled each other about their lives and their dreams for the future. Since then, they had been stealing moments with each other—a cup of tea, a walk by the water. Slowly, they had begun to reveal their true selves to each other.

Margaret stiffened as she ran a comb through the strawberry-blonde hair that fell halfway down her back. Except she hadn't been fully truthful with Sean. She hadn't told him about her gift. Margaret never talked about that side of herself. To anyone. Ever since Fiona had taught her how to place shields between herself and the world, Margaret had lived behind a barrier, never slipping up — never wanting to be different.

Since the night at the pub, their attraction to each other had grown rapidly. Margaret was already lost and could feel that Sean was on his way to loving her. Tonight was their first real dinner date. A trickle of excitement ran through Margaret. She'd never felt so connected to a boy – a man – before.

Leaving her hair to fall down her shoulders, Margaret leaned in to look in the small mirror that hung in the back room. Grabbing her makeup bag from her purse, she outlined her sherry-brown eyes with a navy pencil and smudged the makeup into the lash line. Smoothing on a lipstick shade in soft rose, Margaret dropped her hand and smiled at herself in the mirror. The touch of makeup made Margaret look older, her face edgier, as though she held a wealth of womanly secrets.

And what secrets she did hold, Margaret thought.

Brushing off her nervousness, Margaret took one last look in the small mirror, craning over her shoulder to look at the back of her dress. Satisfied, she picked up her small bag and went to meet Sean at a local restaurant down the street where they had both agreed to meet after their workdays. Knowing that Sean probably didn't make much money as a fisherman, Margaret had picked an easygoing restaurant. Though she was probably overdressed for dinner, Margaret wanted to feel beautiful.

Sean had haunted her dreams for months now. She wasn't going to let anything mess this up. With a solemn oath to herself never to speak of her gift to Sean, lest he be disgusted by her, Margaret left for dinner.

CHAPTER 3

*S*EAN WAITED FOR Margaret outside of the local fish and chips pub. He scratched beneath the collar of one of the few nice dress shirts he owned. Sean felt awkward standing here with a simple clutch of wildflowers in his hand, while people passing by on the street eyed him with a smile.

Sean did a mental groan as he thought about the town gossips. Although he'd lived in the small town of Grace's Cove for a couple years, he'd yet to grow accustomed to the nosey ways of the locals.

Sean leaned back against the brick wall of the building and thought about Dublin. He'd loved the big-city life and longed to run a successful fishing operation out of Galway or Dublin. But, he was also prudent. Coming to Grace's Cove where some of the most prized seafood in all of Ireland rested was a smart decision on his part. Here, he was learning the intricacies of the different ways of fishing, from gathering mussels to spearing larger fish.

A flash of heat zipped through him as he saw pretty

Margaret O'Brien step from the front door of the teashop down the road. His stomach knotted in lust as he watched the sway of her hips under a purple dress with a hem that was just short enough to make his mouth water. He'd watched Margaret for over a year, never having a chance to really talk to her until that one night at the pub.

The night that had changed his life.

He'd never fallen for a girl so hard before. There was just something...*different* about her. It was like she had known him, not just the person he pretended to be. In just a few moments she had broken through his barriers and he'd found himself confiding his dreams to her.

Was he love struck? Oh yeah, Sean thought. The stars were crowding his eyes, no doubt. He could all but see little birds chirping around Margaret as she walked up the street. If he didn't get a taste of her soon, Sean was quite certain he would die. Holding the flowers up in the air, he moved down the sidewalk to greet her. As she laughed at him and his poor little bouquet of flowers, it seemed like nothing in his world would ever go wrong so long as pretty Margaret O'Brien kept smiling at him.

CHAPTER 4

MARGARET LAUGHED AT Sean's outstretched hand, where wildflowers wilted around a twine bow. Her heart clenched as she took the flowers and looked up into his warm brown eyes.

"Thank you," Margaret said, twinkling up at him. She saw the moment that Sean leaned in a little, almost as if he would kiss her, before stepping back. She wanted to stamp her foot into the ground. She'd been aching for his kiss for months now.

Margaret smiled as he held the door open for her and whisked her into the small restaurant. She inhaled the scent of sea and man as she brushed past him and had a sudden urge to kiss the skin that she glimpsed from the opening of his shirt. Swallowing against the heat that rose inside her, Margaret wound through the restaurant as the hostess directed them to a small table in the corner. A fat candle sputtered in the middle of the table and the waitress pointed to a chalkboard on the wall.

"Food's listed there. Drinks?" She raised an eyebrow at the both of them.

"Um, a glass of your red, please," Margaret said.

"No wine, hun, beer or cider."

"Oh, a Bulmers please," Margaret said.

"Guinness," Sean requested before scanning the chalkboard. "I suppose fish and chips would be best as that seems to be what they are popular for."

"Aye, that's fine with me," Margaret said even though her stomach was in knots and she was quite certain that she wouldn't be able to eat a thing. She breathed out a small sigh and smiled as the waitress dropped their glasses onto the table with a thump, before sashaying away.

Margaret laughed as Sean raised an eyebrow at the waitress and used his napkin to wipe the table where their drinks had sloshed over the rim.

"Sorry about that. I guess I thought that this place would be nicer," Sean said.

"It's no big deal. So, how was your day?" Margaret said and settled in to listen to him talk about being out on the boat. His eyes lit up as he talked about his passion and Margaret wished that he would look at her this way. Sipping on her Bulmers, she allowed her shields to slip and let his emotions slip into her.

Happiness and a strong punch of lust washed over her. Margaret's eyes widened as she realized just how much Sean was interested in her. Knowing this, feeling this part of him, made her heart sing. Never having felt confident with boys before, Margaret watched this man who was clearly enamored with her and decided then and there that she would give him every part of herself.

Well, except for one thing. Nobody would ever know that. She'd always been careful to conceal that part of her and after awhile, it had just become second nature. Margaret didn't see any reason that Sean would have to know that side of her. The less she used it, the less she thought about it. It had become easier and easier to distance herself from Fiona's curious reputation, and it wasn't long before people forgot that Margaret might be touched with something extra special too.

Margaret took a bite of her fish and savored the melted butter and freshness of the daily catch. Thinking about Fiona made her stomach clench a bit. The older she had gotten, the more her mother had pressed her to explore her gift. She'd refused more times than she could count. Although she knew that Fiona was a renowned healer and that people traveled from all over Ireland for her services, Margaret had staunchly refused to ever attend a healing session. Guilt had led Margaret to help her mother collect herbs and flowers for various ointments, but her involvement in her mother's world stopped there.

It had to, Margaret thought stiffly, and brought herself back to the table.

"So, it's just you and your ma, huh?" Sean asked as he shoved a chip in his mouth. Margaret jumped as she realized that she had gotten a little engrossed in Sean's emotions and had stopped listening to him. She took a sip of the crisp cider and nodded, hoping to deter any more questions.

"What happened to your dad?"

"He died when I was young. My mother never remarried," Margaret said with a shrug. She remembered that time of her life in colors and emotions more than anything. The grief that Fiona felt almost dragged her daughter's sensitive soul under. It was only when Fiona realized her emotions were harming her empathic daughter that Fiona closed that part of herself off to Margaret.

"I'm sorry to hear that," Sean said with a gentle smile. Margaret could tell that he meant it and she shrugged her shoulders at him.

"Just something that can't be changed, I guess," Margaret said.

"Is it true," Sean hesitated, "what they say about your mum?"

Margaret stiffened and leaned back in her chair. She knew this was going to happen. It always did. People invariably questioned her about her "witch" of a mother.

"Hey, I'm sorry, I didn't mean it like that," Sean said and reached across the table to catch Margaret's hand. She jumped as a shiver of heat ran up her arm from where he traced his thumb over the sensitive skin of her palm.

"Um, yeah, it's okay, I get it." Margaret blew out a breath. "No, she's not a witch. She's not even Wiccan or anything like that. She just practices the centuries-old tradition of Celtic healing. You know, herbs and ointments —all made the old way, is all. I can't knock it either, to be honest. She seems to really help people."

"That's kind of cool. My mum just raised us kids while my dad worked. Nothing special. It must be neat to see your mom help people," Sean said eagerly.

Margaret tilted her head and considered his words.

"I suppose it is pretty cool that she helps a lot of

people. She certainly bucks traditional medicine," Margaret said.

"Do you want to learn to heal, like her?" Sean asked.

"No, I really have no interest. I…" Margaret let her voice trail away. She'd almost let out her secret dream.

"Tell me. What do you want to do?" Sean asked, excitement lighting his eyes.

"I want to move to the city and work in real estate. I know that may seem crazy, a small-town girl like me, but I really think that I'd love it. The hunt for the best properties, helping to match people with their new homes. I think that I'd love that," Margaret said softly. She had never told anyone this as she didn't think it would happen for her.

Sean leaned over and grabbed her other hand. Margaret stared longingly into his handsome face as he brushed a kiss across her hand.

"I want to move back to the city too, after I learn all that I need to know about running a fishing business here. We—" Sean stopped abruptly.

"Yes?" Margaret said, her voice husky with need.

"We could go there together. You know, start a new life, away from here," Sean suggested, his heart in his eyes.

Margaret gulped against the emotion that clogged her throat. She simply nodded, drowning in her love for him. She'd known. From the minute she saw Sean, she knew he was her destiny.

CHAPTER 5

*S*EAN PULLED MARGARET from the restaurant, her hand all but disappearing in his wide palm. Turning his head, he looked up and down the street and groaned.

"I want to kiss you so badly right now," Sean whispered down at her.

Margaret, her heart knowing what she wanted, smiled up at him and tugged his hand to have him follow her down the street. Looking both ways down the street, she waited until it was clear before ducking behind the teashop and pulling Sean into the small, sheltered courtyard that was tucked behind the shop.

Sean smiled as he saw the private yard and in one motion he backed Margaret against the wall, his tall frame making Margaret feel dainty.

Margaret gasped as he pressed his body against hers and slid his muscular leg between her thighs. Bracing his hands on either side of her head, he looked at her, his eyes heavy with lust. Without a word, he lowered his mouth to hers, laying a whisper of a kiss across her lips.

Margaret's heart, quite simply, sang. The touch of his lips on hers shot lust straight through her and she moaned into his mouth. Liquid heat pooled low in her stomach and she jerked against the hardness of his leg pressed to her. He still didn't touch her with his hands, and led the kiss with his lips only. Softly, slowly, he opened her mouth with his tongue, tasting her heat.

Margaret shuddered against his mouth and brought her arms up to wind them around his neck, threading her fingers through his thick hair. Sean's kiss was demanding, a question and an answer.

Finally, finally…he touched her, running his hands down her waist and pulling her tight against his body. His heat burned into her, and Margaret's skin felt sensitized to his touch as he drew a hand up her waist and cupped a breast in his hand. Shock popped Margaret's eyes open and she arched her back, pushing her breast into his palm as his finger toyed with her nipple through her dress. Sensations pounded through Margaret and with no shields up, Sean's lust washed through her, doubling her own pleasure. Unable to help herself, she writhed against Sean's leg, and gasped as he caught her mouth in a heady kiss. The combination of his hand on her breast and the heat of his mouth proved to be too much for Margaret and much to her embarrassment, she found herself shattering over the edge into a blissful wave of pleasure.

Sean's hand stilled against her breast and he pulled her closer, burying his face in her neck. His breathing was heavy against her neck and Margaret was glad that he couldn't see the heat that stained her cheeks. Uncertain of what to do, how to handle this, she stayed still.

"We can't do this here. You deserve more," Sean said gruffly against her neck. Margaret shuddered at the movement of his lips against her sensitive skin.

"Sorry about that," Margaret whispered in embarrassment.

Sean drew back and met her eyes. He brought his lips to hers ever-so-gently and Margaret almost fainted from the kiss.

"Never. Don't be sorry. You want me as much as I want you. But, not here. Not like this. Saturday? Can I see you Saturday?" Sean breathed against her mouth.

Margaret did a quick mental calculation. It was only two days away. She could wait two days to start the rest of her life. Nodding happily, she smiled up at him.

"Saturday it is."

CHAPTER 6

*M*ARGARET AWOKE TO Fiona singing softly in the kitchen. At nineteen, Margaret supposed that living with her mother was probably frowned upon, but she just never found the right time, or enough money, to move out on her own.

Until now. A little thrill shot through Margaret as she thought about Sean and life in Dublin. Mentally, she built them a little apartment with a window overlooking the water. Being away from this world where she hid a part of herself and dealt with people constantly questioning her about Fiona would be perfect for her. A new start.

Stretching, Margaret pulled her hair into one long braid before throwing on an old robe that hung behind the door. She had today off to daydream and plan the perfect date with Sean tomorrow. Her stomach dipped a bit as she thought about Sean. She knew that her date with Sean tomorrow would change everything. Finally, she would step into womanhood.

Daydreaming, Margaret went into the kitchen to greet

Fiona, who stood at the counter, kneading dough for brown bread that Margaret knew would taste moist and perfect. Fiona's skills in the kitchen were almost as legendary as her healing remedies. Margaret supposed that they were one and the same, essentially just a mixing of ingredients.

"Good morning, love. Want some oatmeal?" Fiona asked with a smile.

"Sure, thanks," Margaret said and dropped down at the long table that dominated the main room of the cottage. Behind her, shelves lined the walls that were cluttered with hundreds of glass bottles and jars, all meticulously labeled. Margaret almost didn't see them anymore, being so accustomed to Fiona tinkering with ointments that she barely glanced at the wall.

Fiona stopped and sent a measured look at Margaret.

"So, you're in love then," Fiona said quietly.

Margaret's mouth dropped open and her spoon stilled on the way to her mouth. A fluttering of nervousness hit her stomach and she squirmed in her seat. It had always been like this. She could never hide anything from Fiona. If she had been bullied at school, Fiona knew. If she lied, Fiona called her out on it. If she was in love…well, Fiona could see it. Hating how different her little family was from the rest of the world, Margaret glared at Fiona.

"God, have you ever thought about giving my emotions some privacy? I don't have to share everything with you, you know," Margaret said sullenly, turning away so she didn't see the hurt in Fiona's eyes.

"I'm sorry. I suppose that you do have a right to your privacy," Fiona said stiffly and went back to the sink, carrying a plate with her. Margaret watched her mom's rigid shoulders and felt bad. Hoping to make amends, she sighed.

"What are you doing today? Do you need help?" Margaret asked, deliberately steering the conversation away from Sean.

"Yes, I need to collect some plants and moss from the cove. I'd love an extra set of hands," Fiona said.

"Sure, it's a nice day to go down there. Let me change," Margaret said quickly and, leaving her half-finished oatmeal on the table, she moved to her bedroom. She hummed softly to herself as she thought about tomorrow, pulling on a simple tank suit under a pair of shorts and a loose t-shirt. With no need for makeup, she grabbed a beach towel from the hook behind her door and went into the main room.

Fiona stood at the door with her customary foraging clothes on. Khaki shorts to her knees, a loose button-down shirt, and a wide-brimmed hat made for easy hiking clothes. She handed Margaret a burlap bag that Margaret knew would have smaller mesh bags, twine, and scissors in it. Margaret slipped the bag over her shoulder and both women pulled on ragged hiking boots.

Leaving the cottage, Margaret took a deep breath of the sea air that washed over her face on a wave of sunshine. Silently, the two women followed a well-worn path across green hills that ended abruptly at the edge of a steep cliff. Beyond the cliff, water as blue as the sky melted into the horizon. It was as picturesque Ireland as one could get, and Margaret often wondered why more people didn't set up vacation homes along this coast.

In short order, Margaret and Fiona reached the end of

the path that stopped at the top of the trail down into Grace's Cove. Margaret stood at the edge for a moment as Fiona gathered a handful of flowers nearby. Her mother always did this, Margaret thought. Some sort of weird gift ritual. Sighing, she turned her back on Fiona and gazed into the center of the cove.

The cove was a perfect half-circle of water surrounded by towering cliffs that guarded the long beach from sight. The cliffs protected a private, and singularly perfect, beach. The cove should have hundreds of people plastered on its shores, playing with their children in the shallows, and picnicking on the beach. Yet, the long stretch of sand remained empty. Margaret knew it was because of the rumors that the cove was cursed.

Remembering her mother's insistence that Grace O'Malley rested here, Margaret shivered as she felt the hum of power kiss her skin. It was always like this when she came to the cove. It was as if the air was thicker here. When Margaret was in the cove she felt sensitized, alive, and...*right*. Which was why she never came here alone. Margaret feared that she would answer its siren song and find herself swimming madly into the deep water.

"Ready?" Fiona asked behind her and Margaret jerked her eyes back to her mother.

"Yes."

Together, they navigated the path that switchbacked down the cliff walls before spilling out onto the beach. Margaret fought the wave of dizziness that always came over her as she wound her way down the rocky walls. It was as if all of her carefully crafted boundaries dropped away from her in the cove. She could literally feel everything, from the pulse of the water to the humming of the sun. It was almost hypnotic and Margaret always had to fight to keep a cool head here.

She stopped at the bottom of the path and bent to take her boots off as Fiona began her ritual.

Every time, without fail, Margaret thought as she watched her mother draw a circle in the sand with a stick she picked up along the way. Sighing, she stepped into the circle with her mother.

"We ask for your protection while we are in the cove today. We come here with purity of purpose and nothing but the utmost respect for those who rest here," Fiona said before throwing the flowers she held clutched in her hand into the air. Margaret watched as they separated in mid-air and scattered across the water. The waves seemed to rise up and swallow them and Margaret shivered.

"Good?" Margaret asked her mother sarcastically.

Fiona just raised an eyebrow at her daughter and nodded.

"You must always do this if you come here, Margaret. I know you think that it is silly, but people have died."

Margaret sighed. She knew that people had died here. But she suspected it was more from the wicked currents that ran along the outside of the cove than it was from some mystical power that sucked people underneath. Shrugging her shoulders, Margaret simply nodded at her mom before striding across the sand to the first tidal pool where her mom always collected seaweed.

They worked together, in rhythm, for almost an hour. Fiona chattered happily as she repeated, for the gazillionth time, the uses for the different plants they collected.

Margaret knew that Fiona hoped that one of these days she would take an interest in her practice. And Margaret also suspected that she would break Fiona's heart when she left for Dublin. A part of her already ached for Fiona. She loved her mother but they were just too different. Margaret wanted a normal, respectable life.

Daydreaming about her new career in real estate, Margaret dipped her toes in the water and watched as the waves pushed sand over her toes. Standing here, she felt so small, cupped by the cliffs, hidden from the world. If she admitted it to herself, she knew that she would leave a piece of herself behind in Grace's Cove. No matter what, this place would always call to her.

Almost fondly, she blew a soft kiss to the water and walked to where Fiona stood near the bottom of the path.

Impulsively, she threw an arm around Fiona's shoulders and kissed her cheek. There was no reason not to enjoy this time with her mother since she was leaving soon anyway. Fiona gave her a surprised look and then a bright smile. Together, they chatted over the local gossip that Margaret had picked up in the café as they climbed their way out of the cove, the sounds of the waves crashing against the rock walls of the cliffs slowly receding behind them.

Back at the house, Margaret could hear the phone ringing through the open windows of the cottage. Fiona broke into a jog and swung through the door of the main room, running to the corner where the phone sat.

"Hello?" Fiona said as she leaned against the arm of the rocking chair that stood next to the phone. Margaret eyed her as she pulled the strap of the burlap bag over her shoulder and deposited it on the table. Margaret listened to Fiona as she began to pull the small bags out and laid them on the smooth wood of the table. Fiona would later transfer them to her drying board.

"What's wrong? Pneumonia? In the summer? Why didn't you call me sooner?" Fiona said sternly as she peppered the caller with questions.

"Aye, we'll be there shortly," Fiona said and hung up.

Margaret jolted at the "we."

"We?"

"I'd like for you to come with me today. I think that you're ready to learn how I heal," Fiona said briskly as she moved to the shelves of bottles. Margaret's heartbeat sped up and she watched Fiona for a moment.

"Um, I know how you heal. With your ointments and whatnot. Do you really need me to go?" Margaret said, whining a little.

Fiona turned and met her eyes.

"It's time," she said simply and Margaret felt a cold wash of fear slice through her. Taking a deep breath, Margaret lectured herself. Her mother was asking for her help. Soon, she wouldn't be here to help her, so why not go now?

Coming to a decision, Margaret nodded. "Yes, I'll go with you. Just let me change out of my suit."

With a grateful smile, Fiona nodded and continued to pull bottles from the shelf.

"We'll leave in ten minutes."

CHAPTER 7

*M*OMENTS LATER, MARGARET got in the front seat of Fiona's dark green station wagon. She kept quiet as Fiona backed the car from the driveway and waited until they were on the curvy road that wound along the cliffs and into the harbor where the town of Grace's Cove nestled.

Staring out over the water, Margaret broke the silence. "Who is sick?"

"The Brady's child, Ainsley. She's but three years old and, apparently, is very sick. I only wish that they had called me sooner," Fiona said distractedly.

"Is it harder when it is a child?" Margaret wondered out loud.

"Aye, it is. Always harder. Children deserve a chance at life," Fiona said.

Margaret hoped that Fiona would remember those words when she left for Dublin. She was taking her chance.

"So, what do you do for pneumonia? How do you

know what to do?" Margaret asked.

Fiona looked at her in surprise. Margaret never expressed interest in Fiona's practice and she could see a wave of happiness ripple over her mother's beautiful face. A stab of guilt sliced through Margaret. Perhaps she shouldn't have been so selfish all this time and taken more interest in her mother's work.

"Well, I won't really know until I am there. I will have to feel it, sense what is going on," Fiona said and Margaret felt annoyance pass through her. She hated when Fiona referenced their gifts, though she suspected that Fiona had many more gifts than she did.

"So, how do you know what medicine to give?" Margaret said, deliberately steering the conversation away from their empathic powers.

"Ah, well, my book, you know. It has remedies that have been passed down for generations," Fiona said as her hands gripped the steering wheel tightly. Margaret knew that her cautious mother was trying to speed without endangering them.

"Yes. That book," Margaret hissed from between her teeth. Fiona was constantly buried in this old leather book that she carried with her everywhere. Aside from Margaret, it was the one thing that Fiona devoted much of her time to. Many nights, she would find Fiona scribbling in the book, the flames of the fire flickering over her face. Margaret wasn't sure if she resented or feared her mother's precious book. Either way, Fiona had never offered to share it with her.

"Margaret, you aren't a healer. The book isn't for you," Fiona said with a bite to her voice. Surprised at the steel behind Fiona's words, Margaret stiffened and lifted her chin, staring out of the window, away from her mother.

They drove the rest of the way to the outskirts of the village in silence. Just before they would enter into downtown Grace's Cove, Fiona took a sharp left turn and followed a narrow one-car-width road up a large hill before turning onto a gravel driveway. A few yards up sat a small three-room cottage. Stone walls rose to a thatched roof and the window shutters stood open to encourage the sea breezes.

A small woman opened the door and gestured for them to come in. Dirt streaked her face and her hair was pulled back in a bandana. Margaret got out of the car and hurried behind Fiona into the cottage. The woman pointed to the back room and Fiona went in without knocking. Looking around at the dark interior, Margaret followed Fiona into a small bedroom.

There, a single bed was tucked into the corner under the eaves of the thatched roof. A dingy window let in meager light above the bed. Margaret held back as two women who huddled over the still body of the child turned and rushed to Fiona.

"She's close, she can barely breathe. Please do something, anything," a large woman with brown curly hair and sad eyes begged Fiona. The other woman, a sister perhaps, pulled her back from Fiona.

Margaret was slammed with a wall of fear and sadness. It was so thick that she struggled to breathe under the weight of it. Taking a deep breath, she slowly built up her shields and pushed the emotions away from her.

Margaret stepped closer as Fiona glanced at her and

motioned her forward. Seeing that Fiona needed help, she reached out a hand to the sick child's mother.

"Hi, I'm Margaret. Can you tell me a little bit about what is going on?"

"My little Ainsley. She's been sick for a while. At first we thought it was just a cough. But it is so full of mucus that now she is close to being unable to breathe. We...we can't afford to take her to the hospital." The mother shuddered out her words and grasped Margaret's hands desperately.

"Okay, I understand how scared you must be. Let's just step back for a moment and allow Fiona to check Ainsley out," Margaret said and pulled the two women back from the bed.

Margaret wasn't sure what to expect. She never wanted to go with Fiona to a healing before. She heard enough whispers about Fiona's healing sessions to want to stay far away. Margaret fervently hoped that what she would see today would just be some of Fiona's fancy medicine at work.

Tension gripped her body and Margaret stood ramrod straight, unblinking, as she watched Fiona lean over the small girl. Ainsley's body was covered with a thin white sheet and the girl's face was pale, her dark braids stood out starkly against the whiteness of her skin. Margaret grimaced at the complete lack of expression on the little girl's face. She found herself rooting for Fiona's skills to work.

Fiona ran her hands over the small girl's body. Her eyes closed, she trailed her hands up the body until she landed on the girl's chest. Margaret held her breath as she heard her mother whispering softly to the girl. With a brief nod, Fiona took her hands from the girl and turned for her bag.

"I need hot water and a bowl," Fiona ordered and the two women ran from the room. Fiona turned to Margaret and motioned her closer. Pulling out her book, she paged through until she found what she was looking for.

"Pull out the seaweed we got from the cove today, mix it with the mustard seeds, garlic, and a touch of the moss from the cove as well." Fiona barked orders and Margaret jumped to do her bidding, keeping her questions to herself. She watched as Fiona pulled a small mortar and pestle from her bag and began grinding the ingredients into a pulp. Stopping, Fiona consulted her book again, and pulled a few more unrecognizable ingredients from jars in her bag. She whispered under her breath and continued to grind in a counterclockwise motion.

The women bustled back in with a steaming teapot and a small bowl. Fiona nodded her thanks to them. Putting it on a side table, she poured the steaming water into the bowl. Holding her mixture above the bowl, Fiona muttered over the water as she dropped her concoction into the hot water and stirred the water until it was muddy and brown. Fiona pulled a spoon from her bag and tasted the concoction. Nodding, she held the bowl to her lips and blew on the water, cooling it down.

"Ainsley, you must drink this," Fiona said softly to the girl. Margaret's heart clenched as the girl cracked her eyes open and slid them to look at Fiona. A barely perceptible nod came from the sick girl, and Fiona bent over her.

Ainsley sputtered out a cough as she tried to drink the

broth. Fiona laid a hand on her throat and whispered to her. Soon, Ainsley was able to swallow the entire broth without a cough.

Margaret tilted her head and squinted at Fiona. What had just happened there? How did Fiona stop Ainsley from coughing while swallowing the broth? Knowing that pneumonia made it almost impossible to swallow, Margaret was confused.

"Good job, Ainsley. Now, I want you to close your eyes and picture yourself running outside in the yard, playing your favorite game. Can you do that for me?"

Margaret felt tears prick her eyes as she stared down at the brave little girl. A small smile flitted across the girl's face as she looked trustingly at Fiona. Margaret found herself praying desperately that Fiona's broth would work.

Fiona kneeled by Ainsley's bed. Margaret watched in confusion as Fiona placed her hands directly on the small girl's chest. Bending her forehead to the mattress, Fiona looked the picture of supplication.

Margaret's heart hammered in her chest. She could barely breathe as she watched Fiona begin to murmur against the sheet. Over and over, Fiona repeated words that Margaret couldn't hear. Her eyes shot to Ainsley's face, but the girl's eyes remained closed.

Margaret jumped as a flash of…something blurred past her eyes and she heard a large crack from outside. The women sobbed and hugged each other, saying their Hail Marys.

Margaret was frozen, unable to tear her eyes away from Ainsley's face. Unable to breathe, unable to move, she watched, desperately searching for a sign of something. Ainsley's eyelashes fluttered across her cheeks. Margaret shuddered out a breath as the small girl sat up, the color returned to her cheeks.

"I'm hungry, Mum," Ainsley said in the sweetest little girl voice ever. The women ran to Ainsley and surrounded her on the bed, cooing and clucking over the girl.

Margaret stayed still as her fear and hatred of the abnormal washed through her. She didn't want this life. She didn't want to be different. Whatever had just happened here was beyond the realm of even her own abilities. Suddenly, these otherworldly gifts seemed like a penance.

Not meeting Fiona's eyes, she hurried to gather their supplies. Margaret bowed to the women and, barely able to stand, raced to the green station wagon. Margaret dumped her supplies in the backseat and moved around to sit on the edge of the bumper. She braced her arms on her knees and struggled to breathe.

What was that? What had just happened? Ainsley was near death. Margaret didn't care how much mud and seaweed Fiona shoved down the girl's throat: there was no way that she had cured Ainsley through her concoction alone.

Which left…Fiona's power. Margaret shook her head against a swell of nausea that hit her throat. Remembering the crack, she turned her head and peered around the edge of the car. A piece of lumber—a 2x4—lay splintered on the ground. Margaret gulped at the implications of that shattered board. Had Fiona done that?

Margaret began to shake as the potential for what just happened washed over her. A part of her—a very small part of her—was ecstatic that Fiona had saved Ainsley. It was amazing to see. And, yet. What happened in that bedroom defied explanation. Margaret couldn't imagine living her life with this kind of ability. No wonder people whispered about Fiona. It all made sense now.

"Margaret." Fiona's voice was shaky and Margaret merely turned her head to watch her mother.

Fiona looked older, her face tense with fatigue and something else. Margaret tested Fiona's emotions. Fear. Her mother was afraid, Margaret realized with surprise. She'd never known Fiona to be scared of anything before. Margaret looked down at her hands for a moment before responding.

"Let's get out of here," she whispered.

Fiona's face tensed but she said nothing and nodded. She held the keys up.

"I'll need you to drive. I'm too tired."

Margaret stared in surprise at her mother and realized that whatever she had just done had taken a lot out of her. Trembling, she took the keys from Fiona and walked around to the driver's-side door.

She stopped and looked at the small cottage, where a child's laughter now floated through the window. Moments ago the house had been shrouded in darkness and sadness and now, relief and happiness seemed to float around the home. Margaret shook her head and got into the car. How could this be a bad thing when the result was good? Confused and upset, she started the car and backed carefully down the driveway.

On the road home, she finally looked at Fiona.

"What are you?"

CHAPTER 8

*F*IONA SIGHED AND gave Margaret a disgusted look.

"I'm your mother first and foremost. Don't talk to me like that," Fiona ordered sternly. Margaret kept her eyes on the road, her mind trying to process everything.

"Are you a witch?" Margaret asked shakily.

Fiona sputtered out a laugh and Margaret felt a flush creep up her cheeks as her mother bent over in her seat and laughed from deep within her belly.

"Oh, I'm glad that you think this is so funny," Margaret hissed at Fiona. She sped up, wanting to be out of this car, away from Fiona, away from this crazy town.

"I'm no more a witch than you are," Fiona gasped out.

"I'm not a witch!" Margaret screamed and Fiona sat up straight, turning to put her hand on Margaret's arm. Margaret jerked her arm away, breathing heavily. "I'm normal. I want a normal life, I don't want any of this."

"You can't change who you are," Fiona said softly, "what you are."

Margaret pulled the car into their drive and got out right away. She felt the pain building in her heart; turning, she unleashed her fury on her mother.

"I don't want this—this life," Margaret said as she swooped her hands over the cottage and to the cove. "I don't want to know what other people are feeling. And I certainly don't want to watch my mother literally lift a sickness from someone with her bare hands. That—that is like beyond crazy. How am I supposed to live like this?" Margaret shouted, her chest heaving as she stared wildly at Fiona.

Fiona stood straight, her daughter's abuse falling on proud shoulders.

"I've told you that you are special. For years, I've tried to show you how your gift can help the world. I've chosen to use mine for good. I can no more change who or what I am than I can force you to accept yourself. But, until you do, you'll never be happy," Fiona said fiercely.

"Lies. All lies," Margaret hissed and paced in front of her mother. "My gift can't help anyone. And it's not a gift. It's a headache, an inconvenience. I don't need it."

Fiona watched Margaret pace but said nothing.

"I–I get that you did something great back there. You saved a life. Intellectually, I understand that what you did was of great service to that family. But, in my heart, I just can't accept it," Margaret whispered, and held her clenched fist to her heart. She saw the pain flash across Fiona's face and wished that she could do anything to feel differently, to be able to accept what was.

"Well, I suppose that is your problem then, not mine," Fiona said stiffly, walking past Margaret. Her hand on the door to the cottage, Fiona turned and looked Margaret up and down. "I only hope that someday you will stop running from yourself."

"I don't have to be what you want me to be!" Margaret shouted.

A small smile flitted across Fiona's face and she shook her head at Margaret, disappearing into the cottage. Margaret watched her go, feeling disconnected from this woman that she called mother. Who was this person? How was it possible that she could heal with her hands? It defied all laws of science.

Shaken to the core, Margaret looked down at her hands. They looked simple. Innocuous. How could something like that work? She watched as her hands shook with emotion. Tucking them in her pockets, she stumbled across the field leading to the cove, tears blinding her vision. Her breath hitched as she struggled to comprehend how her entire world had shifted in an instant.

Margaret came to a stop at the edge of the cliffs that lined the cove. Staring down at the peaceful water, she tried to regain the feeling of happiness she felt there earlier that morning. Instead, her angst and displeasure grew. Glaring at the cove, she raised her hands and shouted to the water.

"Why? Why me? I just want a normal life!"

Margaret dropped her hands down by her sides and glanced over her shoulder, realizing that she probably looked a little crazy. Margaret eyed the waters of the cove, looking for any change, any indication that the cove had heard.

"I'm done here. Understand? I will have no part of

this," Margaret threatened the cove. The waters continued to move gently, a contrast to the storm that raged inside of her. Margaret shook her head. What was she waiting for? Grace O'Malley to rise from the water and tell her that she'd be okay?

With a sigh, Margaret turned her back to the cove, vowing it would be for the last time. Tomorrow she would pack for Dublin. She could go ahead of Sean and get a job, find a place to live, and start a new life. Determination coursed through her, and Margaret moved toward the cottage, ready to throw off the bonds of the cove and what Fiona expected of her.

CHAPTER 9

*M*ARGARET DELIBERATELY STAYED in bed late the next morning, continuing to turn over and bury her head in the covers until she heard Fiona leave the cottage. Her resolve to flee had only strengthened after a night laced with dreams of magick and healing hands. Getting up, she leaned over her bed to peek out the window. Fiona's car was gone and Margaret breathed a sigh of relief. Her emotions were too mixed—too raw—for her to have a discussion with Fiona now. It was as though she had reached a crossroads and neither direction was clear for Margaret. She only knew that she needed to take the next major step in her life.

Grateful that she only had a short afternoon shift at the café, Margaret moved into the kitchen to pour herself a cup of tea. Finding fresh baked scones on the table, Margaret smiled. Somehow, Fiona always knew how to comfort her even when Fiona was the one she was mad at. Margaret snagged a scone and took it and her teacup back into her childhood room.

Standing in the small room, she turned and examined the years of her life accumulated in posters, drawings, pictures, and various knickknacks. Crossing the room, she stared at her favorite picture of her and Fiona. It was taken just as the sun was beginning to set, the light warming their laughing faces. They stood together, two peas in a pod laughing at a private joke with the ocean open behind them. Margaret felt a tug in her heart for Fiona and what she was leaving behind. Convinced that she was in the right, Margaret pulled the picture from the wall and laid it facedown on her dresser. She walked into her closet to begin the process of sorting her clothes.

She sighed as she examined the tumble of colors and fabrics that greeted her. She had always wanted what was in fashion, the newest and the best, but it was hard to come by the latest fashions in the small town of Grace's Cove. Humming, Margaret began to pick through her clothes, only keeping what she thought would look the best in big-city Dublin. She could only imagine all of the clothes shops that she could frequent once she established her new career. Daydreaming about her new life, Margaret almost forgot about her current job.

She gasped as she realized she would be late to work if she didn't hustle. After a quick shower, she pulled on a navy sundress with a skirt that hit just below her knees. Braiding her hair, she tucked it behind her ears and added dangling silver earrings. Margaret grabbed her bag and all but ran through the cottage to her car. She wasn't in Dublin yet, Margaret reminded herself. It wouldn't do to get in trouble at work now that she was so close to leaving. She would need every bit of money that she could make for her moving expenses.

Feeling unexpectedly light after such a heavy day yesterday, Margaret sang her heart out on the way into town. Snagging a parking spot right next to her work, she considered the day off to a good start. A small shiver of anticipation raced through her as she thought about seeing Sean tonight. She couldn't wait to tell him that she was ready to move *now*.

Margaret swung into the café and waved to a few regulars before ducking in back to take her purse off. Sarah stood at the counter, arranging scones on a platter.

"Those are for you," Sarah said, gesturing toward something in the back room.

Turning, Margaret found a vase full of white roses. Happiness lit through her and she raced to pluck the card from the milky-white petals. For a moment she stopped to caress the petals, loving the elegance of the white roses. Red roses were so cliché. But, white, well, it was as if Sean already knew her. Smiling, she opened the envelope.

"I've no fancy words for you. I haven't slept but for thinking about tonight. You light me up."

Margaret laughed and hugged the card to her chest, just for a moment.

"That's enough, lover girl. Get moving," Sarah said grumpily and nodded toward the customers who had just walked in. Margaret stuck her tongue out at Sarah when she turned her back and, tying on her apron, went to greet her customers.

The day raced by in a flurry of customers and

daydreams. Margaret knew that she had her head in the clouds after she'd messed up her fourth order. She apologized with a laugh and kept her eye on the clock. Closing was moments away. Ushering the last of her customers out, Margaret called to Sarah.

"You can go if you want. Sorry I've been off all day. I'll clean up," Margaret said generously.

Sarah stopped, surprised. She nodded at Margaret in thanks and, needing no further encouragement, left through the back door. Margaret shrugged and moved to the front door to lock it. This would give her time to change and do her makeup. She jumped as the door swung open, startling her.

"Sean!"

Margaret's hands fluttered in front of her in surprise and she was quite certain that her cheeks were on fire. She drank in the details of his face and the way his presence filled the room. Glancing around, Sean saw that the café was empty and moved straight for Margaret.

Without a word, he pulled Margaret into his arms, sliding his lips over hers in the most gentle of kisses. Margaret sighed into his mouth, allowing her body to melt into the heat and hardness of his body. It was as if everything from yesterday fell away and only this mattered. She stumbled a bit as Sean broke the kiss and stepped back.

"Can you leave from here? I have a surprise for you," Sean asked, his brown eyes eager.

"But, sure, I just need to change."

"No, you look perfect. Stunning. Don't change, I like this dress," Sean said, admiration lacing his voice as he looked her up and down.

Margaret smoothed the dress over her body and smiled up at him. "But I worked in it. I must look a mess."

"Nope. Beautiful. Come with?"

"Okay, I just need to do a few things," Margaret said, eyeing the dishes.

"I'll help. What can I do?"

"Um, the dishes. I'll count the money," Margaret said and smiled as Sean immediately moved to the kitchen. He looked at home there, scrubbing the dishes that had piled up during the day. But it seemed like Sean looked confident wherever he was, Margaret thought. She smiled at him and raced through her closing duties.

"All done," Sean called from the kitchen.

"Me too," Margaret said breathlessly and turned to find Sean standing behind her. She swore that she could feel his lust and she shivered at the promise in his eyes. Sean grabbed her hand and ran his thumb over her palm, sending tingles up her arm.

"Let's go," he said and led her out the back door. He waited patiently while she locked the café and then pulled her around the corner to where his beat-up pick-up truck was parked.

"I know it's not the fanciest, but it's reliable," Sean said, shrugging his shoulders sheepishly as he helped her into the truck.

"It's perfect," Margaret said happily. Sean could have picked her up in a horse and buggy and she wouldn't have cared.

"Well, I don't know about that, but it's been good to me," Sean said as he patted the dashboard. Margaret noted that it was painstakingly neat and admired that he took care of what he owned.

"So, uh, how have you been? How was work?" Sean asked as he started the truck and pulled out onto the main road that led away from the village.

Thinking about her day yesterday, Margaret wished that she could tell Sean about how things had really been in her life. Knowing that it would probably send him screaming for the hills, she smiled at him instead.

"Oh, you know, work was work," she said lightly. "A mysterious vase of flowers made it much better though."

Sean's cheeks burned pink and Margaret laughed at him.

"Thank you, they were perfect."

"They reminded me of you, elegant, perfect, untouched," Sean said gruffly and Margaret glanced at him. Did he know that she was a virgin? It almost left her lips to tell him but she decided to wait and see how their date went before discussing serious matters.

"Well, I loved them. I'll have to get them when you take me back for my car later," Margaret said. She eyed the road they were traveling. It was the same route she used to get to her house.

"Where are we going?"

Sean only smiled and ran a finger over her lips. "You'll see."

Margaret shivered at his touch and the huskiness in his voice. She smiled at him, trying to appear relaxed. Letting down her defenses, she allowed his feelings to wash over her. Lust, love, and a healthy male interest all intertwined to make Margaret feel like she was burning from within. She had never been as certain of a person as she was of Sean. It didn't matter where he took her; if he loved her as she felt he did, she'd go anywhere with him.

CHAPTER 10

"*The* cove?" Margaret squeaked out as panic laced her chest. Sean had driven to a small gravel road a half mile down the lane from her house. The road dead-ended on one side of the cliffs that led to the cove.

"Cool, right? I've heard so many crazy stories about it but haven't been yet. I thought it would be a great place for a picnic," Sean said eagerly, the light of adventure in his eyes. Margaret stared at him, her heart lost as she tried to come up with a good excuse for not going back to the very place she had sworn out of her life the night before. She stayed in her seat and turned her head to look out at the water.

"What have you heard?" Margaret said carefully, keeping her eyes trained on the soft line of the horizon where sky and water blurred into one.

"I've heard that the beach is stunning but that people won't go there because they think it is cursed. Which is ridiculous." Sean scoffed at the thought.

"Is it?" Margaret said and turned her head to search his face.

Confusion flitted across Sean's face and he squinted his eyes at her. "You don't believe that the cove could actually be cursed, do you? That's crazy."

Margaret shrugged her shoulder. "Sometimes there are things that defy explanation."

"No way. I was raised a good Catholic. Curses do not exist," Sean said staunchly. Suddenly hesitant, he reached out to run a hand down her arm. "Hey, we don't have to go there if you are scared."

Margaret closed her eyes for a moment and took a deep breath. She didn't want to live her life in fear anymore—fear of being different, fear of never being accepted. Today, she wanted to step into her new life.

"No, it's fine. I can't wait to see what you have planned." Margaret smiled up at him while her heart pounded in her chest. A relieved look passed over Sean's face and he leapt from the truck, running around to open her door and help her out. He chattered about the nice weather as he went around to the bed of the truck. Pulling out a picnic basket and a plaid blanket, he gestured for her to come with him. Together, they made their way across the field before they reached the entrance to the path at the top of the cliffs.

"Wow, just wow. This is amazing," Sean whispered. Margaret nodded, trying to appreciate it from his viewpoint.

"How is this beach not packed? I can't believe that people don't come here," Sean exclaimed as his eyes took in the long sand beach tucked between the cliffs.

"Ah, well, you know. Small-town people are superstitious," Margaret said softly.

"I hadn't realized this was such a climb. Will you be able to do it?"

Margaret bit back her initial response, which was to tell him that she had been climbing these cliffs since she was a child. Instead, she smiled at him and his consideration. "I'll be fine. Good thing I wore my flats today."

Sean glanced sheepishly at her shoes. "Yeah, I should have thought of that. I guess I hadn't realized it was such a climb down."

"I'm okay. Really," Margaret said gently.

They began the hike down, Sean leading the way and warning her of any upcoming turn or bump in the path. Margaret could have walked the path blind, she knew it so well, but not wanting to ruin his excitement, she kept her mouth shut. Her mind worked furiously as she tried to figure out a way to do Fiona's protection circle before they stepped into the cove. If she believed Fiona about anything, it was not to enter the cove without providing something as an offering. Mindful of this, Margaret collected flowers on the way down to the beach. Just as they reached the bottom, she reached out and snagged Sean's hand before he could step onto the sand.

"So, uh, the locals sort of have this thing that they do… before they say that they can spend time on this beach," Margaret said carefully.

Sean raised an eyebrow at her. "Oh yeah? Some sort of voodoo dance?"

"Something like that. Let's do it just in case, okay?"

Margaret smiled her brightest smile at him, hoping to pull him under with her charm.

"Anything you want," Sean said carefully, lost in her eyes.

Margaret blew out a breath and nodded.

"Okay, so it goes kind of like this," she said, slipping off her shoes and stepping onto the sand. Quickly, she drew a large circle with her big toe while Sean watched her with his eyebrow raised. She motioned for him to step inside of the circle and he did so without saying anything.

Though she knew the blessing by heart, Margaret played stupid.

"So, I think it goes something like this. Um, hey there, cove, we aren't here to cause harm or to do anything bad. We just want to have fun. Here are some flowers for you. Because, we, uh, respect you." Margaret grinned at Sean and rolled her eyes before tossing the flowers into the water.

Sean let out a long peal of laughter. "That's the most ridiculous thing that I have ever seen."

"I know, right?" Margaret scoffed with him, though she kept an eye on the water of the cove. Sensing no change in the waves, she motioned for Sean to step from the circle.

"Let's eat, I'm famished," Margaret said, quickly changing the subject.

"Let's find the perfect spot," Sean said eagerly, and carrying the basket in one hand, he took her hand in his other. Margaret smiled up at him as they walked the length of the beach, listening as Sean exclaimed at the beauty of the empty beach and the stark magnificence of the surrounding cliff walls. Margaret tried to block out the power that she felt here and focused only on Sean's happiness.

Sean spread the plaid blanket on a high patch of sand that was sheltered by an outcropping of rocks. The setting sun had warmed the sand and the breeze was light. She laughed as Sean pulled out several mini tiki torches and placed them around the blanket, taking his time with lighting them in the breeze.

"Here, let me help," Margaret insisted and held her hands around the match as he lit each torch.

"I was worried that we would lose the light. Maybe later we can build a bonfire...though it doesn't look like there is a lot of driftwood down here to light a fire."

An image of a burning funeral pyre floating in the water of the cove flashed into Margaret's mind and she gasped and whipped her head around.

"What? Did you hear something?"

"No, um, sorry, a bug hit my face," Margaret laughed at him. Sean cupped her face in his hand and examined her face.

"No, still perfect," he said softly and brushed his lips across hers. A thrill of happiness washed through Margaret and she pushed the thoughts of Grace O'Malley's last night at the cove from her head.

"So, what did you make for me, oh mighty chef?" Margaret teased him and kneeled on the blanket by the basket.

"Peanut butter and jelly sandwiches, of course," Sean laughed at her as he pulled sandwiches from a small cooler, along with a hunk of cheese, and a plate of fruit. Reaching in, he pulled out a bottle of red wine and brandished it proudly for her. "Red wine, since you didn't get any the other night."

Margaret's heart melted a little bit. "Thank you, this looks lovely." She watched Sean as he patiently worked the cork from the bottle. She wanted his hands on her, not on the bottle. A blush crept up her cheeks as she thought about how her body had responded to him the other day. As if sensing her thoughts, he sliced a glance at her, his eyes heavy with lust. Margaret gulped. Whoo, boy, she thought.

Sean was wicked and pulled two plastic cups from the hamper. Pouring a generous cupful for each of them, he handed her a cup across the blanket. Settling back next to her, he touched the brim of his cup to hers.

"To us," Sean whispered.

"To us," Margaret said, love in her eyes. She took a sip of the wine, allowing the liquid to warm against her tongue. Sean watched her and groaned.

"Food, we need to eat," Sean said, tearing his eyes away from her lips. Margaret smiled to herself as Sean prepared plates of food for the both of them. She felt powerful in this relationship, and confidence crept through her at this newfound ability to seduce. Margaret eyed him as she slipped a grape between her lips and Sean groaned.

"Now you're torturing me," Sean protested.

Margaret found herself laughing freely and she threw her arms around Sean's neck before giving him a quick peck.

"This is fun, thank you for bringing me," Margaret breathed against his mouth.

"Pleasure. Mine. Ah, my pleasure, that is," Sean said

gruffly and Margaret leaned back to look out at the water and to savor this moment. The before. She'd never be here again, she thought.

"I want to talk to you about something," Margaret said.

"Oh, you sound serious. Okay, what?" Sean said, his eyes trained on her face.

"I want to talk about Dublin. Were you serious?" Margaret pushed her big toe into the sand, praying that Sean would still want to do what they had talked about.

"I'm totally serious. I have a few more months on my apprenticeship and then I'll be all set," Sean said, and took another bite of his sandwich. Margaret nodded and looked down at the furrow that her toe was digging in the sand.

"How do you feel about me going sooner? Like within a week or so?" Margaret asked.

"You want to leave me?" Sean gaped at her.

"No, I want to leave here. I've lived here my whole life. I'm done. It's time for me to grow. I've been researching real-estate firms in Dublin and there is this great one that my cousin in Boston knows about that has an apprenticeship program, too. I can waitress in any café while I work towards getting my license," Margaret said all in a rush and then waited, holding her breath.

"Wow, you really want to get out of here, huh?"

"I do. I really, really do."

"Can't you wait a few more months?"

"I don't think that I can, at that. I really feel like it is time for me to go. I don't know why, but I keep dreaming about me packing and leaving. It's like I have to go." Margaret shrugged, feeling silly. Sean reached out and touched her arm.

"No, I feel you. It was kind of how I felt about taking this apprenticeship. I just needed to go." Sean nodded at her.

"Exactly. We can see each other on weekends, I'm sure. I could...you know...look for a place or something," Margaret said shyly.

"Oh? Are you asking me to live with you, Margaret O'Brien?" Sean raised an eyebrow at her as he moved the hamper from between them. Margaret giggled as he took the plate from her hand and threw it onto the sand. Sean crept forward until he kneeled between her outstretched legs, his hands braced on her sides. Margaret leaned back on her elbows and looked up at Sean's face, love and laughter shining from her face.

"Well, I suppose that I am," Margaret said cheekily and laughed up at Sean.

"Well, if I must," Sean said and lowered himself onto Margaret until she was pressed back against the blanket, the sand soft beneath her. Margaret squirmed at the feel of Sean's body between her legs, and already lost, she arched into his chest, wrapping her arms around his muscular shoulders.

Sean stopped, his lips a hairsbreadth from hers. "I know this is crazy, but I've wanted you since the moment I set eyes on you. It's taken me months to finally talk to you."

Margaret all but melted into him. "Me too. I couldn't stop looking at you. You were so different than the other boys that I've met."

"Don't talk about them," Sean urged and Margaret stopped his kiss. Pulling back, she looked at him.

"There hasn't been anyone," Margaret said softly and Sean's eyes widened.

"Even better. Mine, all mine," Sean whispered reverently and Margaret's heart swelled.

"Do you mean that? Do you really mean that?" Margaret whispered against his lips.

"I do. Mine. We'll build a new life together in Dublin. Us against the world, sweet Maggie," Sean murmured to her.

"I want you, Sean. All of you, okay?" Margaret said. "Don't stop. I want to be a woman with you."

Sean shuddered in her arms and nodded his face against the nape of her neck.

"I'm honored. Let me love you, Margaret," Sean said as he kissed his way up her neck until he found her lips. Lost in his kiss, Margaret moaned into his mouth as he rubbed his lips over hers. Teasing her, he nipped and nibbled at her bottom lip. She moaned when he sucked gently at her lip before slipping his tongue between her lips. Entranced, Margaret felt heat rush through her as they played with each other, teasing, lingering.

Margaret gasped as Sean nudged her legs wider. Her skirt rode up to her hips and she tried not to blush. Sean broke away from her lips and knelt between her legs. Tugging on the hem of her dress, he raised an eyebrow at her in question.

"Yes," Margaret said breathlessly.

She leaned up as Sean pulled the dress over her head and the cool sea air brushed over her skin. The last of the light from the setting sun washed over her and the tiki torches glowed around her head. Margaret shivered as she lay before Sean in her bra and underwear and watched him appraise her body.

"Sweet Jesus," Sean whispered and Margaret found herself laughing.

"You like?" She laughed at him, though she wished that she had worn a prettier pair of underwear. Her simple cotton bikini bottoms and white bra weren't that exciting, though she knew that she filled her bra out nicely.

"I never want to leave," Sean breathed and bent to kiss her neck, trailing his mouth down to her breast. Margaret laughed and pushed him back.

"Um, you too, sir," Margaret said as she pointed to his clothes.

"Huh? Oh, sure," Sean said. Haste made him clumsy and Margaret laughed as he tripped over his pants, struggling to pull them off his legs. His shirt sailed after them and soon, he stood before her naked. Margaret drew in a deep breath. She'd never seen a fully naked man in real life before and the sight was intoxicating. She wanted to trace her hands over his muscles and kiss her way down his chest. It was very apparent that he was just as excited as she was. Margaret nibbled her lip as she wondered how someone so large would fit with her body.

"God, don't nibble your lips. You're driving me crazy," Sean breathed and knelt back between her legs.

Margaret gasped as he ran his hands up along her sides before reaching behind her to unclip her bra. Suddenly feeling very wanton, Margaret slipped the bra from her shoulders and tossed it away from her. Sliding her legs up, she whipped her underwear off and tossed them aside. Sean's tongue nearly fell out of his mouth at her movements and she found herself laughing helplessly again.

Oh, how she wanted this. Love, and laughter, and normalcy. Lying back, she held her arms up to Sean, beckoning him closer.

Sean needed no invitation. Bracing himself over her, he kissed his way down her breasts, paying careful attention to spots where she let out helpless moans. Margaret shivered as he traced his lips over her stomach before finding the sweet spot in the V between her legs. Shocked, she leaned back against the sand and stared up at the stars that were peering back through the darkening sky. Her body felt liquid and loose, and Sean's mouth on her was a dream. Her shields down, Margaret could no longer define where her feelings stopped and Sean's started. A wave of love and lust seemed to envelop them and in a matter of moments, Margaret felt herself shuddering against Sean's mouth as he pushed her over the edge.

Rearing up, Sean braced himself over her.

"Margaret, I need you, I can't even think, I want you so badly," Sean whispered, and kissed her deeply. Pulling back, he met her eyes.

"Yes, Sean, now," Margaret commanded.

Sean groaned against her mouth and kissing her softly, he murmured words of love as he took her across the threshold into womanhood. Margaret jerked against him at the intrusion, but soon fell into the sweep of lust that moved through her. Unable to think, only to feel, she wrapped her arms around Sean as he brought her to completion, finding his own shortly thereafter.

Sean buried his face in her neck and Margaret held him

there, never wanting him to leave her. He felt so right, as though he was a part of her. Margaret was so glad that she had waited for this. It couldn't have been more perfect and tears pricked her eyes at the beauty of the gift that she had just been given. Unable to stop herself, she trembled against Sean and he drew back to look in her eyes.

"Hey, why are you crying? Did I hurt you?" Sean said, worry in his eyes.

"No, God, no. It was perfect. It's just all of this was so great. So right. Thank you," Margaret said against his lips.

"You and me, sweet Maggie, you and me," Sean whispered.

Maggie closed her eyes and brought her forehead to Sean's. A light seemed to pulse through her eyelids and she blinked her eyes open, thinking it was the flame of the tiki torch. She gasped as a glowing blue light fell over them.

"What?" Sean said, looking down at her. And then seeing the same light as her, hurriedly sat back on his knees.

"What the...?" Sean said and turned to look at the water.

A brilliant blue light shot from the depths of the water, illuminating the cliff walls that hugged the cove and stretching out into the night sky. Margaret's mouth fell open as she stared at the water. She'd never seen nor heard of this before.

"What the hell, Margaret?" Sean said furiously, looking back at her. Margaret realized that he thought she knew what was happening.

"I...I don't know. I don't know. Oh, God, what's happening?" Margaret shouted and leapt up, looking for her clothes in the sand. Leaving her underwear, she pulled her dress over her head and watched as Sean tugged his pants on. Grabbing his shoes, he left the hamper behind and Margaret had to race to keep up with him. Terrified of the water, of the light, of what was happening, Margaret ran for her life.

They panted up the path, not saying a word. As they neared the top, Margaret began to grow cold inside. She could feel Sean's anger, his confusion, and his hurt. She could tell that he thought that she knew about what was happening in the cove. Hanging her head in shame, she walked the last few steps to the top where he stood, looking down at the glowing water. The further they had gotten from it, the more the light had dimmed.

"You think this is funny?" Sean hissed, his chest heaving with his struggle to breathe.

Margaret shook her head and reached out to him but he stepped back, evading her hand. "That little circle thing you did at the bottom. That's what witches do, right? This is all part of that, isn't it? I thought it was crazy rumors. But it's not. It's all true. You lied to me."

"No, Sean, please. I didn't lie. I told you that I'd heard weird stuff about the cove. I'm just as scared as you. I have no idea what this is," Margaret pleaded for Sean to understand. He stood back and ran his hands through his dark hair, his face looking murderous in the pale light of the moon.

"I can't. I just can't deal with this. It's too messed up. I'm sorry...I have to go," Sean said and turned and ran from her.

Margaret stared after him in shock, her heart cracking

open and shattering inside of her. The man who had just professed to love her and wanted to start a new life with her had just run...*run* from her. Margaret collapsed to her knees as a keening sound reached her ears. Realizing that it came from her, she covered her mouth as sobs racked her body. Turning to look at the cove in accusation, Margaret wanted to scream.

The light was gone.

CHAPTER 11

MOMENTS, MINUTES, HOURS later...Margaret pulled herself up and trudged toward her house. She'd grabbed her purse when she ran for the trail but cared little about the rest of her clothing that lay on the beach. The gravel stung her feet with each step and, knowing the way home by heart, Margaret crossed into the softer grass and cut across the hill where her house shone its light warmly into the night.

Margaret tried to contain her sobs but there was little she could do. Her heart was left behind in the cove.

Weakly, she pushed the door to the cottage open, not bothering to clean herself up or to put on a happy face for her mother. There was no way that Fiona wouldn't know what had just happened.

"Margaret!" Fiona exclaimed and jumped up from her rocking chair in the alcove where she was writing in her book.

That damn book, Margaret thought. She raised a hand to stop Fiona in her tracks.

"Don't," Margaret said.

"But...are you okay? Oh, honey, let me help you," Fiona whispered.

Margaret vehemently shook her head though a part of her wanted to run to Fiona and curl up with her head in Fiona's lap.

"This is your fault. Yours. Grace's. And every other freak like me," Margaret shouted, her wrath pouring over Fiona. Fiona recoiled as if Margaret had slapped her and Margaret stormed past her, slamming the door to her bedroom behind her.

She looked blindly around at the piles of clothes, remnants of her happy dreams earlier in the day. Laughing bitterly at herself, Margaret kicked at a pile of clothes before going into the bathroom. Pulling the shower curtain open, she pulled the handle down and stepped directly into the cold stream, dress and all. As the cold water washed over her, Margaret swallowed her sobs, struggling to build her walls back up. Over and over, she tried to contain her hurt, but sobs continued to break through her resolve. Leaning against the wall, she allowed the spray to cover her.

Pulling her soggy dress over her head, Margaret grabbed the soap and, suddenly wanting to wash the pain away, scrubbed her skin vigorously. Her hand stopped as she touched between her legs and felt a sensitivity there that she had never felt before. Remembering the perfectness of that moment, Margaret sobbed even harder. Her dreams had been ripped from her in a matter of moments.

Shutting off the water, Margaret wrapped her hair in a towel before stuffing her arms into her bathrobe. She trudged into her bedroom and stopped at the plate of scones and hot tea that stood by her bed. A note sat propped against the teapot.

This, too, shall pass.

Suddenly furious, Margaret reached down and ripped the card up.

Turning off the light, Margaret crawled into bed, and stared blankly at the rafters above her.

One day, she'd get out of here. *One day soon*, she thought before exhaustion claimed her with a dreamless sleep.

CHAPTER 12

*T*HE FOLLOWING DAYS passed in a blur of gray. Margaret all but refused to talk to Fiona, restricting their conversations to the briefest of words. Several times she caught Fiona looking at her worriedly.

Margaret found herself closing up, more than ever. Her usually sunny demeanor with her customers was replaced with sullen, brief sentences. Even Sarah began to look at her with worry in her eyes.

"Is everything okay, Margaret?" Sarah finally asked one day.

"Fine," Margaret said and brushed past Sarah to fill the tray of salt shakers.

"Well, it just seems like you are upset," Sarah ventured and Margaret turned to meet her eyes.

"I said that I am fine," Margaret said stonily and Sarah shrugged her shoulders and left her alone.

Alone. That was all she wanted, to be alone. She didn't need Fiona's prying questions or her customers' questioning glances. Margaret knew that she was a wreck. But, so what if she didn't always want to put a happy face on? For once in her life, Margaret settled in for a good long sulk.

Her entire life had shifted in a matter of days, Margaret shouted in her head. She wished that she could confide in someone. Anyone. But what would she say?

Oh, hey, my mom can heal with her hands and I lost my virginity by an enchanted water that lit up…scaring the crap out of myself and what I thought was my future husband. It's cool though, no biggie, Margaret thought.

What I need is to get out…

Her mind strayed to the letter that she had placed in the mail two days ago. It was addressed to her older cousin who lived in Boston. Maybe, just maybe, there was a chance for her to start over there.

"I'm leaving. Do you need help?" Sarah asked timidly and Margaret waved her away. She didn't want help, only privacy.

Craning her neck, she waited until she saw Sarah walk past the front window. Walking into the back room, Margaret plopped into the chair by the desk and reached for the phone. She pulled a sheet of paper from her pocket and dialed the number on it.

"Shannon Airport, how may I direct your call?"

"Um, I'd like to see how much a flight to Boston is. Oh, and what the schedule is," Margaret said meekly.

"That's reservations. Hold, please," the tinny voice echoed back at her.

Margaret held the phone impatiently, her pencil poised on the paper.

"Reservations."

"Yes, how much is the flight to Boston from Shannon?"

"Round-trip or one way?"

"One way," Margaret whispered.

"What was that? I'm sorry, I couldn't hear you," the voice at the other end said.

"I'm sorry. One way, please." Margaret spoke briskly.

"We have an eleven a.m. flight that leaves every other day from Shannon to Boston. Flight will be 360 pounds."

Margaret gulped. That was almost the exact amount that she had saved for moving to Dublin.

"Ah, thank you. Can I buy a ticket the day of or do I need to reserve now?" Margaret asked, unsure of how it worked.

"You can buy a ticket day of, love. These flights are rarely full."

"Thank you," Margaret said softly and placed the phone back in the receiver.

She stared blindly at the paper, clutched in her trembling hand. Could she do this? Pick up and leave for Boston? A part of her cried yes. And…a very sad part of her that she tried to tamp down wanted to stay here. Every time the door opened at the café she looked up, hope flinging its way through her for a brief millisecond.

Sean hadn't called. He hadn't stopped by the café or her house. She'd even gone to the pub, hoping to run into him. Instead, the happy voices only caused her more heartache and she quickly retreated to her car.

Which is where she was spending most of her time. Camped out in her car on the side of the road, reading books on real estate that she checked out from the town library. It was the only thing that she could process right now. Everything else hurt too much. Margaret even found herself avoiding driving past the harbor, scared that she would see Sean flirting with another girl.

As Margaret stared at the piece of paper in her hand, she promised herself that if her cousin got back to her and Sean hadn't come to see her by then, she would leave. Her pride wouldn't allow her to wait for a man to come around any longer than that. On a nod, she shoved the paper in her pocket and pulled her real-estate book from her bag, flipping it open to the chapter she had last been reading. In a matter of moments, Margaret was engrossed in the chapters and making notes on a small pad of paper. Her future hung suspended around her. Waiting.

CHAPTER 13

*T*HREE AND A HALF weeks later, Margaret dragged herself from her bed. She felt like she was tired all the time lately. *And weepy*, Margaret thought. *Oh-so-weepy*. Nothing had panned out as she had expected. No word from her cousin and no word from Sean. She'd only glimpsed him once and had ducked behind the corner of a building so that he didn't see her.

She was barely eating and Margaret knew that Fiona was desperately worried about her. She expected an intervention from her some day soon.

Pulling on a long sleeve shirt over her t-shirt and pajama pants, Margaret wandered into the kitchen and stopped short. Fiona sat at the table, a pot of tea with two cups in front of her and a paper bag on the table.

"Sit," Fiona ordered.

Groaning, Margaret sat. There was no use arguing with that tone. Or with the fact that this was a long time coming. Margaret assumed this was going to be her intervention. *Buck up and move on, my child*, Margaret mimicked her mom in her head.

"I'm worried about you," Fiona said softly.

Margaret shrugged, even though her mother's soft words brought an unexpected sheen of tears to her eyes.

"It's fine," Margaret said grumpily and poured herself a cup of tea.

"It's hard for me to sit here and watch you starve yourself. It isn't good for you. Or..." Fiona cut herself off. Margaret tilted her head and looked at her mother for the first time in weeks. Really looked at her. Fiona wasn't just worried, Margaret thought. She was scared.

"Or...what?" Margaret asked. Knowing Fiona's ability to sense illness, Margaret's heart seized up.

"Am I sick? Like really sick? Not just heartsick?" Margaret demanded, slapping her cup on the table.

Fiona blew out a breath and Margaret watched as Fiona raised her eyes to the ceiling and said a small prayer. Scared now, she waited for her mother to speak.

"Ah, so this is a delicate matter. When was the last time you had your menses?" Fiona asked softly.

"My menses? You mean my period? I just..." Margaret trailed off as the realization hit her. She'd had her period about a week or so before that night with Sean. And they hadn't used protection. She counted back the days and felt the blood drain from her face as she realized that she was late. Her mouth gaped open as she met Fiona's eyes.

Fiona smiled gently at her, "It only takes once, honey."

"No, no, no," Margaret pushed back from the table as panic raced through her. Sweat beaded across her back and she punched her fist into her other hand repeatedly.

Fiona observed her daughter for a moment before sighing and opening the bag. She pushed a white and black box across the table at Margaret as Margaret looked at her in horror.

"What is that?"

"It's a home pregnancy test. They are said to be fairly accurate," Fiona said.

"No. No, this can not be happening," Margaret said, backing away from the box.

"Why don't you just see first before you jump to any conclusions?" Fiona asked.

Margaret turned and glared at her. "But you know, don't you? You can see it?" Margaret couldn't bring herself to call it a baby. A baby! Her head swam at the thought.

Fiona nodded. "Aye, I can. But you'll never believe me unless you see for yourself. So, go on, test," Fiona gestured to the box.

Margaret stared at it, her future in Boston dwindling away from her at a disastrous speed.

"Fine," Margaret said and grabbed the box, slamming her bedroom door behind her. Her hand shook as she moved into the bathroom and put the box on the counter. Opening the box, she read the instructions, the paper shaking in front of her face. On an oath, she sat to perform the test.

Minutes ticked by as she waited. Pacing the room, Margaret felt panic swell up in her, threatening to close off her airway. The door cracked open and she whirled to see Fiona standing there.

"I haven't checked yet," Margaret said angrily.

Fiona nodded and gestured for her to do so.

Her back straight, Margaret marched stiffly to the bathroom and looked at the test.

Positive.

Her heart dropped to her stomach and she slipped into a ball on the floor. Wrapping her arms around her legs, she pressed her face to her pajama pants and let the tears flood her. She jerked slightly as her mother's arms came around her.

"Shh, it'll be okay. This is probably just the hormones. We'll take care of it. You'll be fine."

"Having a baby out of wedlock is not exactly accepted in this country, you know," Margaret gasped against her legs. God, if she thought she would be shunned for her gift, she could only imagine for her pregnancy.

Pregnancy. She was pregnant.

"You'll have to tell him, of course," Fiona said matter-of-factly. Margaret whirled on her in horror.

"I will do no such thing! He left me," Margaret said.

"Aye, and now you've a babe to think of. He'll know one way or the other," Fiona said and stood. She held her hands down to her daughter and Margaret allowed her to pull her up.

"Let me get you some medicine for your stomach. I don't want you to upset the babe with your histrionics," Fiona said and left the room.

Margaret paced the room. A baby. How had this even happened? She shook her head with a soft laugh. She knew how it happened. In the best and the worst moment of her life.

Placing a hand on her belly, she wondered if she could

feel her baby. Could she know that a baby was there? Letting down her shields, she reached inward.

Margaret gasped, as a little glow of love and light reached out to her from within.

Her baby.

A profound sense of joy filled her. Unable to move, unable to speak, Margaret gaped down at her stomach.

Her baby. Nobody else's.

The wheels turning, Margaret straightened her shoulders and went to take Fiona's medicine.

A thought occurred to her as her hand reached for the door.

Conceived in the cove.

All daughters of Grace would be touched with a gift. *Something*.

Horror filled Margaret at the thought of her daughter growing up subjected to the same abnormal lifestyle she had. Margaret rushed into the main room of the cottage.

"Can you tell if it is a girl?" Margaret all but shouted at Fiona.

Fiona's hands stilled on the cup of medicine that she was mixing in a bowl. Turning, she met Margaret's eyes.

"Why?"

"Why? Why! Because, then she'd be different. A freak!" Margaret shrieked at her mother and Fiona's face fell.

"We are not freaks. We are special," Fiona said.

"I have a right to my own opinion," Margaret said defiantly.

"Aye, that you do. Yes, it's a girl," Fiona said stonily and slammed the cup of medicine on the table in front of her daughter. Turning, she walked out of the cottage and Margaret's gaze trailed after her.

A girl.

"Oh no, oh, I'm sorry," Margaret whispered to the small ball of light in her stomach. "I'll protect you. I'll take you away from all of this."

Margaret drank her medicine and began to plan.

CHAPTER 14

THE NEXT DAY, a knock startled Margaret as she was sorting through a pile of clothes. She wondered what would still fit her in just a matter of weeks. Fiona had left earlier that day, presumably to collect herbs for her remedies, Margaret thought as she walked to the front door.

Opening the door, she saw the post office truck outside and her heart did a little skip.

"International letter for you, Margaret," the mailman said and handed her a paper to sign. Margaret's hand trembled as she signed the receipt and grabbed the letter. Without a backward glance, she closed the door and hurried to Fiona's rocking chair.

Sitting down, she slit the letter open and pulled the sheet of paper out.

HI MARGARET,
Yes, please come! I'd love to have family here. I live in

South Boston and we have an extra room for you. There are plenty of real estate companies that are hiring too. Come over, I need to hear more Irish voices around me! Here is my phone number and my schedule.

The words blurred in front of Margaret's eyes as the tears came, fast and furious. Her out. She finally had an out.

"I'm taking you away from this all, little one. We'll start a new life away from this weirdness. And you'll have nothing but the best," Margaret vowed.

Standing, Margaret rushed into her room and threw the rest of her clothes into a suitcase. Turning, she scanned the room for anything else that she would need. Seeing nothing, she moved into the main room and sat at the long table with a pen and paper. She owed Fiona a letter.

CHAPTER 15

Fiona stopped as she stepped through the door later that night. She'd driven to the next town over that day and was excited to show Margaret the things she purchased for the baby. She knew with a little prodding, her stubborn daughter would come around and eventually be happy about her pregnancy.

Fiona's eyes tracked over the house. Something was different. She could feel it.

Her eyes landed on her book laying outside of its usual spot on the middle of the table. It was open to a page. A letter with her name on it lay on top.

Fiona's hands began to shake as she walked toward the book. Lifting the letter she looked to where the book was open. She sighed and, without having to read the letter, knew that Margaret was gone. The page Margaret had picked held an ancient Celtic ritual to encourage forgiveness in others. In her own way, Margaret was asking her mother to forgive her.

Fiona dropped the sacks of clothes and toys she had purchased and moved to sit in her rocking chair.

The warm wood enveloped her and she relaxed back into its familiar grooves before slitting the envelope open and pulling the sheet of paper out.

I'm sorry.

I'll just start with that. I'm sorry that I said all those nasty things to you. I'm sorry that I was never the daughter that you wanted. But, I just can't understand this life. It's too much for me. Maybe I'm too sensitive, maybe it's my ability. This is too hard for me to accept. And, I can't live here, knowing that my daughter will be exposed to all of this. What if she is something worse? What weird gift will the cove bring out in her? I need to get her as far away as possible from all of this. I have to give her a chance. A fighting chance at a normal life.

And, I suppose that I need to give myself a chance. I want something more. More than this town has to offer me. I'm going to try my hand at selling real estate. I've been studying for weeks now and I know that I'll be good at it. I need to go. To take this chance. For the both of us.

Just so you don't worry, I've gone to Boston to stay with Cousin Mary. She's going to help me get on my feet. I'm leaving my car at the Shannon airport with the key tucked under the bumper. I'm sorry that you'll have to send someone to get it.

I don't hate you. I really don't. But, I can't understand you. I'm not like you. Please understand that.

I love you and I promise to write. Don't worry about me, I'll take care of myself and my daughter. She'll have the best life that I can give her.

If Sean ever comes for me, tell him to start a new life without me. I'll raise my daughter on my own. I don't want him near me.

Love,

Margaret

Tears dripped down Fiona's face and plopped onto the paper. Although she sensed this day was coming soon, Margaret had surprised her. Fiona had never expected her to leave the country. A wave of sadness washed through her. A sadness for what was. What could have been.

A knock at the door startled her. Wiping her eyes quickly, Fiona glanced at the clock on the mantle. It was 9:00 in the evening. Who could be knocking at her door now?

Straightening her back, she went to the door and cracked it open.

Her heart dropped.

Sean stood there, his hat in his hands.

"Ma'am," Sean said, bobbing his head respectfully at her.

"Oh no," Fiona said, shaking her head back and forth.

"What? Oh, please, I know Margaret hates me, but I've come to apologize to her. Is she around?" Sean looked over Fiona's head eagerly.

"Sean. Come in," Fiona said and turned, heading straight for the cabinet that housed her whiskey.

"Thanks, is she here?" Sean said, anxiously turning his cap in his hands.

"Sit," Fiona ordered.

Sean took a seat next to the pile of baby clothes which had fallen from the bags Fiona dropped. He glanced at the clothes and looked away. Fiona sighed as she thought about how she would have to handle this.

"Sean, Margaret's gone," Fiona said, deciding on brevity.

"Okay, when will she be back? I can wait," Sean said.

"No. Gone, packed her bags, left town," Fiona said. She watched as Sean's face dropped.

"She went to Dublin without me, didn't she. I knew that I should have come to see her sooner," Sean said morosely.

Fiona poured him a small glass of whiskey.

"She's not in Dublin."

"Where is she?" Sean asked, confusion crossing his handsome face.

"Why don't you tell me what happened first?" Fiona asked and watched Sean's face poker up. She sighed.

"I'm well aware that you had sex with my daughter. Tell me why you left."

Sean gaped at her for a moment before picking up the glass and downing the whiskey in one gulp.

"Um, it wasn't her. I never really wanted to leave her. I love her. But, it was something that happened."

Fiona gestured with her own glass of whiskey for Sean to continue.

"The water. It just glowed. I know this sounds crazy. But one moment it was normal and the next it was shining this brilliant blue light. We ran for our lives. I…I turned on Margaret. Blamed her for it. I left her there to walk home alone," Sean said sheepishly.

Fiona reached out and poured Sean another glass of whiskey. She swallowed a lump in her throat, knowing now that her daughter flew away from her one true love. The cove had been trying to send them both a message.

"What made you come back?" Fiona inquired, bypassing the reason for the cove glowing blue.

"Well, I kind of asked around town about…Seems like it might just be this phenomenon that happens there. But, it wasn't Margaret, I'm sure of that now." Sean said.

Fiona closed her eyes as she thought about the pain her daughter had been in. Sean running from her had only confirmed Margaret's belief that she was a freak. It was the perfect storm.

Knowing that she was about to rock this boy's world forever, Fiona drained her glass of whiskey.

"She's on a plane to Boston. For good," Fiona said and watched as the color drained from Sean's cheeks.

"No," Sean said, shaking his head in disbelief and denial.

"She left." Fiona said.

"Then I'll go get her." Sean said, determination ringing in his voice. Fiona sighed.

"Sean, what do you see sitting next to you?"

"Baby clothes. So?" Sean shrugged and played with his glass. His hands stilled as realization washed over him.

"Yes, Sean. Baby clothes. Do you think that I'm pregnant?" Fiona inquired of him.

"Baby…Margaret. Margaret's pregnant? And, she left? Just like that?" Sean slammed his fist onto the table and got up to pace. "I have rights as a father, you know. She can't just leave!"

"Well, I'm sorry, Sean, but she did. She didn't believe in you. Frankly, neither did I."

"I'm going after her," Sean declared.

"No," Fiona said forcefully. Sighing, she handed him Margaret's letter and watched as his heart broke in front of her.

Sighing, Fiona pulled him into her arms as he sobbed. Together, they both cried for a love lost, a life lost, and for an unknown future.

CHAPTER 16

*M*ARGARET STARED OUT the window as the plane approached Boston. She stayed awake the entire flight, questioning her choice. Every time, she came to the conclusion that she'd had none.

This was her new life.

Smiling, she patted her stomach and watched Boston's downtown come into view. It was a whole new world for her and her baby. Together, they'd make it.

CHAPTER 17

TWENTY-EIGHT YEARS LATER

MARGARET TOOK A sip of her wine, watching Keelin dance her first dance as a married woman. How had she grown up so fast?

And somehow, Keelin had ended up back in Grace's Cove. The one place Margaret had sworn she'd never go back to. Margaret bit back the old feeling of bitterness that swelled in her throat.

"Long time no see," Sean drawled from behind her and Margaret's back stiffened. Taking a deep breath, she turned to measure Sean with her eyes.

Damn, the man was as handsome as ever. The well-cut tux showcased his broad shoulders. Though a few grays peppered his hair, his presence still radiated strength and virility. She'd done her best to steer clear of him since she'd arrived in Grace's Cove the night before, but it looked like their confrontation had arrived. Bracing her shoulders, and lifting her chin, Margaret eyed him.

"Sean," Margaret said coolly.

"Come on, Maggie, that's the best you can do?" Sean asked, raising his eyebrow at her.

"It might be," she said, sticking her nose in the air at her nickname.

"I don't like that answer," Sean said, stepping closer and forcing her to look up at him. Margaret hadn't expected the punch of him. Heat licked low in her stomach.

"Well, you can't always get what you want," Margaret said flippantly.

"Yeah, so I've learned," Sean said bitterly. "But this time, I plan to."

Margaret's heart leapt into her throat as he pulled the wine glass from her hand and stepped closer, forcing her to step backwards into the darkness.

"What are you doing?"

"What I've been meaning to do for a long time," Sean said.

"Excuse me?" Margaret asked, steel lacing her voice.

And found the air all but knocked out of her as Sean reached down and hoisted her so that her body hung over his shoulder, her face staring at a very attractive bottom clad in tuxedo pants.

"You're crazy," Margaret hissed, turning and smacking Sean lightly on the head. "Put me down this instant. This is unbecoming."

"I'll show you unbecoming," Sean muttered, continuing to stalk into the darkness. Margaret had a sinking suspicion of just where Sean was headed.

The site of their last showdown.

Of course Keelin had to go and have the wedding on

the cliffs overlooking the most pivotal moment in her life, Margaret grumbled to herself, praying that none of the guests dancing in the tent had seen Sean carry her off.

"Hello, Shane," Sean called and Margaret whipped her head around to see the dim outline of Shane, a local realtor she'd met the night before, stalking away from the cove.

"Sean!" Margaret gasped, feeling heat creep into her cheeks. She'd never found herself in such a compromising position before.

Oh wait, just that one time. With this same man.

And wasn't this just *why* she had stayed away from Grace's Cove?

CHAPTER 18

"PUT ME DOWN," Margaret hissed again, as dizziness began to overtake her from swinging upside down from Sean's shoulder. The darkness had enveloped them and the lights of the tent looked like dainty fairy lights, twinkling on the hillside just above the cliffs that Sean now stood on.

The sound of waves crashing far below made Margaret's blood begin to hum, and she knew the cove was calling to her, welcoming her home.

Too bad she never wanted any part of this home, Margaret thought on a shiver.

"Hey!" She gasped when Sean reached up to cup her bottom, pulling her over his shoulder and sliding her down the front of his body, heat trailing between.

This time when Margaret shivered, it was for a different reason.

"Sean," Margaret began, moving to distance herself from his body, surprised that she felt so nervous. It wasn't often that Margaret was caught off guard, but five minutes back in Sean's presence and she couldn't find her ground.

"Save it," Sean bit out, before pulling Margaret to him and sliding his lips over hers, dragging her down into a storm of emotions that threatened to overwhelm her.

For a moment – just a moment – Margaret allowed herself to be pulled under by the promise of Sean, years of buried feelings coming to a head in her heart. Realizing that she needed to be the adult here, Margaret tore her lips away from his and put her hand on Sean's chest, pushing back from him.

"Enough," she said firmly, doing her best to regulate her breathing and not show just how much the kiss had affected her.

Or to acknowledge the press of his feelings, which she desperately tried to batter away from her mind. Margaret was surprised that her gift – one she kept strongly sheltered – had kicked up so strongly since she'd been home.

"It will never be enough, Margaret O'Brien," Sean swore and stepped away from her. He let out a stream of curses that made her glance nervously around to see if any wedding guests had wandered close to them.

"Could you please not curse at my daughter's wedding?" Margaret asked primly, smoothing her silk dress.

Sean swung back around and advanced until their noses were almost touching. Margaret could feel her heart beating wildly in her chest, and did her best to level her gaze at Sean.

"*Our* daughter. Ours," Sean spat out.

"Yes, I suppose that's true," Margaret said, delicately shrugging her shoulders.

"I could throttle you," Sean said, bringing his hands to her shoulders to squeeze her tightly. The sound of the waves kicked up below and Margaret felt a flutter of panic as she wondered what the magic from the cove would do if Sean tried to hurt her.

"Oh, knock it off," Sean turned and shouted down into the cove. Margaret's mouth dropped open in surprise.

"Sure and you haven't gone off the deep end, have you now?" Margaret asked, genuine concern lacing her voice.

"You think that I haven't learned all about the little tricks the cove will pull? My daughter's one of Grace's. Both of my daughters," Sean spit out, stepping back to pace. Margaret watched him warily, unsure of where this conversation was going.

"Maggie, I'm so damn angry with you," Sean finally said; Margaret couldn't help but feel her heart crack a bit for the love they'd once had – two foolish lovers thinking they could take on the world together.

"You left me," Margaret said, running her hands up and down her arms against a sudden chill.

"You damn well know that you should have told me about the baby," Sean shouted again, his eyes hard in the dim light.

"You left me!" Margaret shrieked, surprised to find herself going toe-to-toe with Sean. "You knew that I didn't want to be in this town. And I certainly wasn't going to raise my daughter around this," she waved at the cove.

"You should have told me," Sean insisted.

"You left me. For over a month. You never came back

for me. As far as I knew, you were done with us," Margaret's voice cracked, and she was surprised to feel the old resentment bubbling up.

"Aw, shite, Maggie. You've never heard of an Irish temper before? You know we hold our anger for a while."

"You could have come to Boston!" Margaret shouted, surprised at herself.

Sean shook his head wearily. "Aye, Maggie. I was lost when you were gone. Torn up. I'd gone on a drinking binge. The thought of you with our baby..." His voice broke and he ran a hand through his hair. "I couldn't handle not being able to see you. And, I'm not proud of myself, but I hated being alone. I...I just fell into the first safe woman I could find. It was a mistake," Sean said softly, meeting her eyes.

Margaret couldn't believe what she was hearing. All those years she'd lain awake at night, wondering why Sean hadn't come for her – why he hadn't called her bluff. When she'd heard wind that he'd married, she'd closed the door on him forever.

And yet here they stood.

"I'm sorry your marriage didn't work out," Margaret said stiffly.

"I'm grateful for Aislinn and Colin, that I won't ever regret. I shouldn't have rushed so blindly into my relationship. And I should have come for you. I can't believe I took your stupid letter at face value," Sean swore again.

"Stupid?" Margaret felt her blood heat, remembering the sheer terror that had coursed through her when she'd written the note. Her chin went up. "Well, you waited too long and lost out on a lifetime. If you don't mind, I'd like to go," Margaret said stiffly, moving to step past Sean.

He blocked her path easily, looking down at her. Margaret stared at his tuxedo coat, refusing to meet his eyes until Sean brought a hand to her chin and lifted her face to his.

"If you think this is over, you aren't the woman that I once knew," Sean whispered, before tracing his lips gently over hers once more.

"You barely knew me then. And you *certainly* don't know me now," Margaret spat out.

This time when Margaret shoved past him, Sean let her go.

CHAPTER 19

"GOOD MORNING, LOVE." Fiona's voice carried from the bedroom door. Margaret pushed her hair from her face and rolled over.

"Eww!" Margaret squealed when Ronan, Fiona's Irish setter, swiped his tongue across her face in greeting.

"Ronan, come here," Fiona chuckled. "I've got breakfast on. Keelin will be by in a bit to collect some of her gifts."

Margaret struggled to a sitting position, feeling desperately awkward in the room that she had grown up in and had vowed to leave forever.

Her relationship with Fiona had evolved over the years – from awkwardness to quiet acceptance, then to the sort of resignation that comes from living in two different worlds, countries apart. It had been a comfortable distance for Margaret, but being back home was bringing up a slew of unwanted emotions. Most notably was that Margaret was realizing just how much she had missed her mother.

"Thank you, I'll be out shortly," Margaret said, offering a smile. She rose and stretched, moving across the simple room with white stucco walls, dark wood beams lining the ceiling, and a hand-stitched quilt that overlay the queen-sized bed. Margaret slid the door open to the tiny en suite bathroom and shook her head at the dark circles that mirrored her eyes.

"And how was I supposed to get any sleep anyway," Margaret huffed, brushing her teeth quickly before ducking her head under the warm spray of water from the tiny shower nozzle.

Snapshots of Sean – along with images of the cove glowing – had haunted her dreams, causing her to toss and turn and have a few come-to-Jesus moments about the choices that she had made in her life.

Margaret wasn't entirely sure where she stood as of yet, but there were only so many battles she could tackle at once.

"One at a time," she said to herself as she toweled off, leaving her blonde bob to dry naturally, and pulled on slim-cut jeans and a rose-colored t-shirt.

Making her way out into the main room, Margaret smiled at the spread that Fiona had laid out on the large farm table that dominated the living area of the house. Fiona's cottage was larger than it seemed from the outside, with grey stone walls, a cheerful red door, and flowers on the windowsills. Inside, the main room housed the kitchen, eating, and sitting area, all in one expanse. Shelves lined the wall over the table, holding hundreds of bottles and jars with tiny labels affixed to them. Margaret did her best not to look at the bottles, reminding her as they did of her natural aversion to her mother's healing abilities.

"This looks amazing," Margaret said, surveying the contents of the table. Rashers of bacon, scrambled eggs, cooked tomatoes, toast, scones, and jars of marmalade and jam sat on platters with linen place mats below them.

"Tea?" Fiona asked from where she stood by the stove.

"It wouldn't be a proper Irish without it," Margaret said with a smile, grabbing a plate and using a pair of tongs to pile food on. With all the nerves of Keelin's wedding day yesterday, she'd barely been able to eat.

"What a beautiful wedding," Fiona said on a sigh, settling onto the seat across from Margaret and placing a pot of tea between them.

"It really was. I'm glad she decided to not go with a traditional wedding. And she really seems happy. I know that I had some reservations about this, but Flynn really is a stand-up guy," Margaret said as she slathered strawberry jelly on her scone.

"He's like a son to me," Fiona said, gesturing with her cup of tea. "I can't count how many times he's helped me out in a bind."

Margaret knew Fiona didn't mean to sound accusatory, but it didn't stop the sting nonetheless.

"Yes, and if I hadn't left you alone, I'd have been here to help. I get it," Margaret said on a sniff, burying her nose in her tea.

"That is not what I said," Fiona said, raising an eyebrow at her.

"Yes, well, I can certainly read between the lines. Let's not fight," Margaret said, meeting her mother's eyes.

"I'm not the one fighting," Fiona said, tilting her head as she looked at Margaret.

Damn the woman for always being right, Margaret thought as she sipped her tea and studied Fiona. At forty-seven years old, she still couldn't shake the sting of being scolded by her mother.

And at forty-seven years old, don't you think that you're adult enough to apologize? Her conscience scolded her and Margaret blew out a sigh. She supposed it was now or never.

"Mom, I'm…I'm really sorry for leaving like I did. I shouldn't have left you here on your own. It wasn't right of me," Margaret said softly, searching the weathered lines of her mother's face, hoping for acceptance of her apology.

Fiona sniffed and waited a beat before responding.

"I wasn't the one raising a child on my own. Why would you put yourself in such a position?"

"I don't want to talk about it," Margaret insisted, refusing to get drawn into a conversation about the power that lay buried deep inside her.

"It's a valid question. But if you want to skirt the issue, that's on you," Fiona said, shaking her head at Margaret. "However, if you would like me to accept your apology, I do. I've missed you – and have never stopped loving you for a moment."

Margaret felt tears blink into her eyes as she reached across the table for her mother's hand.

"I've always loved you. You have to know that."

"I know that. You hurt me, Margaret. You really hurt me. It wasn't easy for me to let you go. I can only hope that you'll find it in your heart to start fresh with our relationship," Fiona said steadily, her words like arrows to Margaret's heart.

"I know that I hurt you. I don't think I realized how much until Keelin took off for Ireland and never came home. There is an emptiness that comes with that. I never understood – not fully," Margaret said, shrugging and picking up her tea again.

"It's a horrible feeling to be a world apart from your only daughter. But to have one who left angry? And uncommunicative for a while? Well, that was awful. So many times I almost flew there to track you down and knock some sense into you."

"Why didn't you?" Margaret had always wondered why Fiona hadn't come to visit her in Boston.

"We all have our own lessons to learn," Fiona said softly.

"I would have welcomed you," Margaret argued.

"You never invited me. The stop sign was loud and clear with every phone conversation that we had," Fiona argued right back. Margaret couldn't help but smile. She absolutely knew where her stubborn streak came from.

"So where does that leave us now?"

"I suppose we have a lot of years to make up for," Fiona said.

"I suppose you're right," Margaret murmured.

Fiona reached across the table and patted her hand.

"We'll go for a walk later today and talk about breaking down walls. For now, I hear Ronan barking, which means Keelin is here."

Margaret groaned internally, knowing that the walk later in the day would be unpleasant. Hadn't she gone to therapy and broken down enough walls? Knowing that she was about to be put on the chopping block made her shoulders stiffen. Pasting on a smile, she turned towards the door.

"Keelin!"

CHAPTER 20

MARGARET JUMPED UP and crossed the room to crush her daughter in a hug. Leaning back, she took Keelin's shoulders and surveyed her face.

"You're positively glowing," Margaret said.

"I'm happy," Keelin said simply.

"Then I'm happy," Margaret said, stepping back to let Keelin inside. Fiona moved around the table to hug Keelin, and Margaret smiled as Flynn's tall frame filled the doorway.

"Fiona has a breakfast for you both," Margaret said.

"Great, I'm starving," Flynn said, dropping a kiss on Margaret's cheek before moving to the table. Margaret's chin went up as another shadow fell across the doorframe.

"Sean," she said stiffly.

"Maggie," Sean said, deliberately using his nickname for her. Before she could stop him, he bent and brushed a kiss over her lips, then sauntered to the table to crush Fiona in a hug.

Margaret felt like swatting him across the back of his

head, but, tamping down on her anger, she turned and smoothed her hands over her pants, praying that everybody's backs had been turned.

And came up short to see both Fiona and Keelin grinning madly at her.

"Nothing out of you both," Margaret hissed as she breezed past them to refill her teacup, studiously ignoring Sean.

He looked good today, his dark hair still wet from the shower and curling slightly at the ends, a plaid button-down shirt rolled on his forearms. A workingman, Margaret thought with another sniff, far from the cultured elite she was used to dating in Boston. She turned to talk to Keelin.

"Keelin, what a wonderful wedding. Everything was perfect," Margaret said and saw Keelin's smile cross her face.

"It really was, wasn't it?" Keelin gushed, reaching for a scone.

"When do you leave for the Aran Islands?"

"Right after breakfast. We'll head up the coast and take a small plane over. I've got a nice surprise waiting," Flynn said with a smile. He laughed when Keelin turned and poked her finger into his side.

"No more surprises! You've already done enough."

"Never enough for you, my love," Flynn beamed down at Keelin. Their banter made Margaret's heart happy. She had worried when Keelin first told her about Flynn, but after many conversations over the months and finally meeting him in person, Margaret had lost her reservations.

"Sean, when do you go back to Dublin?" Fiona asked.

Margaret turned to take her plate to the kitchen counter, signaling that she wasn't listening.

Not that she cared when he left.

"After breakfast as well. I've got some business to get in order before the week starts," Sean said. Margaret rolled her eyes as she washed her plate, looking out the window above the sink. The rolling meadow fell away into sky and ocean, and Margaret could only imagine what price this view would command back in Boston. She couldn't help herself from thinking in real estate terms even when she wasn't working.

"How's business?" Flynn asked. Sean and Flynn each ran similar fishing enterprises at different ends of Ireland. Both men were successful – from what Margaret had heard – and often worked together when larger orders came up.

"Good, I certainly can't complain. Though I think we'll need to be upgrading some of our business systems soon. New software, new website, that kind of stuff," Sean shrugged and shook his head.

"Ah, yes. Tough to keep up with that side of things, it seems," Flynn agreed.

"It's certainly been a shift," Sean agreed. "Everyone wants to arrange stuff online and over emails these days. Not easy being attached to a computer and out on a boat all day."

Margaret rolled her eyes. Had the man never heard of a smartphone before?

"Maybe I can come help?" Keelin asked. Margaret turned to watch how Sean responded to Keelin. From her conversations with Keelin, Margaret knew they had been slowly working on their relationship over the course of the past year.

Sean reached out and ran a tender hand over Keelin's hair, causing Margaret's heart to clench. For a moment she could imagine that this happy family image was real, that she and Sean had raised Keelin together. Clamping down on her emotions, she pursed her lips and didn't say anything as Keelin smiled up at Sean.

"You just enjoy being a newlywed. I'll hire someone to help," Sean said. Turning, he caught Margaret's eye. "I'd like to speak with you outside, Margaret."

It was more of a demand than a request, and Margaret raised her eyebrow as she stared him down.

"Or we can do this right here," Sean said sweetly.

Margaret's typically polite demeanor almost slipped as a string of Gaelic curses stopped short on her lips. Nodding curtly, she breezed past Sean, her head held high.

Stepping outside into the sunshine, Margaret stomped around the side of the house to where a table and chairs sat, overlooking the gently rolling green meadow. Ronan followed her, a stick in his mouth.

"Sure, I'll throw that for you," Margaret said, leaning down to tug the stick from Ronan's mouth and launched it into the air. She sat down and watched, smiling, as Ronan tumbled over himself to race across the fields in pursuit of the stick.

A shadow crossed over her and Margaret kept her eyes on the thin line where the water met the sky, suddenly feeling irrepressibly small and uncertain of where she stood in this world.

"Come to Dublin."

Margaret's head jerked up; she shielded her eyes from the sun as she looked up to meet Sean's eyes.

"Excuse me?" Margaret asked, her mouth dropping open.

"Come with me to Dublin. I know your flight leaves from there," Sean insisted.

Margaret just shook her head at him, overwhelmed by indecision and the inability to process her thoughts. For so long she had led a neat and orderly life, one in which she had total control; now she didn't know what to do with this messy rush of feelings that clawed at her stomach.

"Damn it, Maggie," Sean swore and paced in front of her. "You owe me. I deserve a chance."

"I owe you?" Margaret's words sounded shrill, even to herself. A warm rush of anger flooded through her.

"Yes. *You owe me.* You took my daughter from me…" Sean began and Margaret jumped up, going toe-to-toe with Sean, her body shaking with rage.

"I owe you nothing! You left. I raised her on my own. Without your support. Without *any* support. If anything, *you* owe *me*," she spat out, her fists clenched at her side.

"Fine, I owe you. I'll make it up to you if you come to Dublin with me," Sean said softly, warmth infusing his words. His eyes dilated as he looked at her, sheer need etched across his face.

Well, she'd just walked right into that one, hadn't she, Margaret chided herself as Sean's emotions pounded at her, making her breath hitch in her chest.

"I don't know if I can," she whispered, stepping back.

Sean watched her for a moment before he wiped his face clear of emotion. Nodding, he dipped his hand into his back pocket and pulled out his wallet, reaching inside for a business card.

"Door's always open," Sean said curtly, handing her the card. He leaned down to brush a soft kiss over her cheek before stepping past her to walk around the corner of the house.

Margaret instinctively turned, wanting to call out after him, wanting to say something to soothe the hurt she'd heard in his words.

But her voice came up empty.

Defeated, she slumped into the chair, bending over to rub Ronan's soft ears as he shoved his head between her knees with the stick.

Perhaps it was best to leave the past in the past after all.

CHAPTER 21

"YOU OKAY?"

Margaret jumped as Keelin wandered around the side of the cottage to where Margaret had been staring listlessly at the ocean, dangerously close to feeling very sorry for herself.

"Of course, sweetie, I'm fine," Margaret said automatically, patting the bench next to her. Keelin slid onto the bench and Margaret opened her arm, pulling Keelin in so her head rested on her mother's shoulder. It wasn't a customary embrace for them, but in this moment it felt natural.

"Why don't you go after him?" Keelin asked. Margaret pulled back to look down at her daughter.

"You heard that?"

"Kitchen window was open."

Margaret groaned and rolled her eyes, imagining the group inside hanging on every word.

"It's complicated, Keelin."

"So make it uncomplicated."

Margaret laughed, shaking her head at her daughter. "Ah the innocence of youth," she said, smiling at Keelin.

"I'm not that young, may I remind you? And I'm certainly not innocent. Go after him, Mom. Don't you want to take a risk?" Keelin asked.

Margaret turned and looked out towards the water again, considering her daughter's words.

"I don't know if I can take *that* risk," she said softly.

"This from the woman who left her country and started fresh on her own? Building up a real estate empire from nothing?" Keelin raised an eyebrow at Margaret.

"That's a different type of risk," Margaret said, patting her daughter's leg.

"What are you afraid of?" Keelin asked, shaking her head.

"I…I've worked really hard for what I have, Keelin," Margaret said, surprised to find her voice cracking.

"And you think that you'll lose that?"

"What's the point of going back through all this? There's a lot of hurt. Years of resentment. And even if we move past it…I have a life in Boston and he has a life here. There's no point," Margaret said.

"I'm surprised at you," Keelin said. "I've never thought you were someone who gave up so easily."

Margaret knew her daughter well enough to know that she was being goaded, so she just shrugged her shoulders. "I'm sorry you feel that way, Keelin."

"Oh Mom, I just want you to be happy," Keelin said, leaning over to pull her mother into a hug.

"Honey, don't worry about me. Go on your honeymoon. These are the best days of your life. Go…enjoy, relax. I'm fine. Trust me," Margaret insisted, squeezing her daughter.

"But you never got those best days. Don't you think its time?" Keelin said as she stood to join Flynn, who was waiting by his truck.

"Everything has its time, dear. Don't try to force it," Margaret said, stepping smoothly back into her role as mother. "Now call me when you get to the islands. Have a wonderful time."

"I love you," Keelin said, dropping a kiss on Margaret's cheek and all but bouncing her way over to Flynn. Margaret shook her head at Keelin's exuberance, but felt a lightness lift her heart at her daughter's obvious joy.

It was all a mother could ask for.

"Aye. It is. So what are we going to do about *your* joy?"

CHAPTER 22

MARGARET WHIPPED HER head around to look at Fiona.

"Stay out of my mind," she said, only half-joking, uncomfortable with the brush of power she felt emanating from Fiona.

Fiona came forward, a walking stick in each hand. Khaki pants, a button-down linen shirt and a wide-brimmed hat completed her hiking-in-the hills outfit, and Margaret knew they were going to the cove.

"Stick?" Fiona asked, breezing past Margaret's comment.

"Sure," Margaret said, standing up and taking one of the well-oiled walking sticks Fiona held. Together, they set out across the meadow, though they moved more slowly than Margaret remembered from her youth. With a jolt, Margaret realized that Fiona was slowing down.

"Beautiful day," Fiona commented as they made their way over the gently sloping hill along a well-worn path in the grass that led directly to the cove. Ronan raced ahead of them through the field, his ears streaming behind him.

"It is," Margaret agreed, glad they were keeping the conversation light. And it was a beautiful day. There's nothing quite like a sunny day in Ireland, Margaret thought, when the clouds have cleared, the threat of rain isn't imminent, and a breeze gently blows the grasses. She took a deep breath, the scent of seawater and damp earth filling her nose.

It smelled like home.

Continuing on in silence, they reached the edge of the cliffs where the trail ended its easy path and began a switchback down the side of the cliffs. Margaret paused, allowing herself to soak in the sight of the cove, the very place she had sworn never to come back to.

Fiona stopped, seeming to sense that Margaret needed a moment.

Margaret stared down into the crystalline blue waters, lapping gently at a perfect half moon of a golden sand beach, the high cliff walls lovingly cupping the water in an almost perfect circle. Directly across from where they stood, a small entrance allowed the tide to flow in and out from the ocean. At sunset, the light would pierce the opening and illuminate the cliff walls in a fiery display of arrogance.

Margaret waited for the old anger to rise up inside of her. She'd hated coming here as a child, hated knowing that something about her – and about the cove – was *different*.

Instead, she found herself being soothed by the gentle

crash of the waves against the beach far below her, the cry of a gull swooping through the air making her smile.

Where had her fear and anger of this place gone?

"Ready?" Fiona asked.

"I am," Margaret said, meaning it. She slowly followed Fiona down the ancient path, keeping close to the rock wall, an eye on her mother's pace in front of her. Though Fiona was slower than she had been in Margaret's youth, her step was strong and she navigated the path with a confidence borne from years of walking the hills.

Margaret watched as Fiona gathered flowers and stones along the way, gathering her offering to the cove. Margaret was surprised to find she didn't seem to mind that some things hadn't changed.

And wondered if maybe she was the one who had changed.

Margaret watched as Fiona drew a wide circle in the sand with her walking stick, motioning for Margaret to step inside with her.

Fiona opened her mouth to speak, facing the waters of the cove, her hands held high, full of their offerings.

"Let me," Margaret blurted out, interrupting Fiona and surprising herself.

Fiona cast a look at her but didn't say anything, simply nodding.

Margaret cleared her throat and stared at the gentle blue waters in front of her.

"I know it's been a long time since I've been here. I…I was really angry. About a lot of things that happened here. I'm still not sure that I'm ready to accept everything about the powers that lie within your waters. Or that lie within me as well. But I will say that I'm sorry that I've turned my back on this world," Margaret didn't know if she was apologizing to the cove, Fiona, or herself. Perhaps all three. "I think I was too young to understand any of this. So, while I may never accept certain aspects of who I am. I no longer hate those who do claim their powers. So, I guess what I am trying to say is...we come in peace."

Margaret was surprised to feel tears surge into her eyes. She blinked them quickly away, watching as Fiona tossed her gifts into the water. Turning, the older woman reached out to squeeze Margaret's hand, the press of her leathery skin warm against Margaret's palm.

"Thank you. I wasn't sure if I would ever hear that from you. I'm glad you don't hate us," Fiona said, referring to herself and the others touched with something special.

They walked along the beach as Margaret tried to sort through the tumbled thoughts rushing through her head. On one end of the beach, the emotions from nearly three decades ago seemed to pulse gently at her, reminding her of where she had given up her innocence.

Of everything she'd given up since that time.

It all seemed to twist and convolute in her mind, and she needed a moment to sort through her feelings.

Finally, she blew out a breath and turned to Fiona.

"I was just a kid," Margaret said and Fiona nodded, encouraging her to continue.

"I was just a kid," Margaret repeated, "And I was so angry. I wanted to be normal. I never wanted to be something different. Although I could see the good you did with your healing, I couldn't see the benefits of being *different*.

I literally just couldn't handle what I saw that night. And I was selfish because it was all about *me*. Who would accept me if I was the freak? How would I start my life if I had this extra power? I would never be able to tell anyone."

Margaret stopped as she found her chest beginning to heave with emotion. Fiona reached out and ran a hand down her arm, sending a cooling, calming force through her.

Margaret ventured a smile. "Thank you. So I ran. I ran because Sean saw the cove glow that night. And he ran from me. He ran away and left me. It confirmed everything I had thought about who we were and what the cove meant to me and my future. And so I ran, as far away as I could," Margaret said softly, turning to meet Fiona's eyes.

"I know why you ran. You never told me about the cove glowing, though," Fiona said, musing over those words.

"Well, it lit up like a million Christmas trees and Sean hightailed it for his car," Margaret said bitterly.

A snort broke her reverie and Margaret's head shot up.

"Are you laughing at me?"

Fiona gasped, smothering her mouth with her hand, her shoulders shaking.

"I'm sorry. Just the picture of him running across the field from the light. I can't..." Fiona laughed even harder and to her surprise, Margaret found herself joining in, feeling a lightness pervade the sadness of her memory.

"Mom, it was so awful. But so dramatic and ridiculous," Margaret said finally, wiping her eyes again.

"It's even funnier that he ended up with not one, but two daughters with Grace O'Malley's bloodline."

"Yes, so he said. Seems like he's all fine and dandy with the cove these days," Margaret said, swooping her arm out dramatically.

"Ah, yes. The angst of youth. You love strongly and rage fiercely. The true test of love, though, is if it can find its way through time," Fiona said, turning to look at Margaret. Margaret stopped, feeling a flutter of nerves in her stomach.

"Ah well, I think that ship has sailed," Margaret said, digging her toe into the sand.

"Do you know why the cove glows?"

"Um, no, actually I don't. To scare boyfriends away?" Margaret asked, raising an eyebrow and surprising another chuckle from Fiona.

"Not quite. It glows in the presence of love. Real love. Familial love. Lasting love. And at its best? For true, strong, pure romantic love."

Margaret's mouth went dry.

"You mean Sean's my...my true love?"

"The cove seems to think so," Fiona said softly.

Margaret turned and stared at the waters, anger beginning to course through her. "Then why'd you have to go and scare him away?" she screeched at the water.

Fiona reached out to wrap an arm around Margaret. "There's a time for everything," she murmured, echoing Margaret's earlier words to Keelin.

"Shitty timing," Margaret cursed, feeling frustrated.

"You know that our souls are here to learn lessons. Maybe you had a few lessons to learn first. Maybe you still have a few more to go," Fiona said.

"The easy thing would be just to go home," Margaret said, bitterness lacing her words.

"Aye, you're used to running," Fiona agreed, and Margaret felt her back stiffen.

"That's not fair," Margaret said.

"Isn't it?" Fiona wondered and Margaret sighed, finding it hard to argue with the truth. She'd been running for years now.

"Why does it have to be so hard?" Margaret asked, furious that everything in her life seemed to be a battle.

"If it were easy, it wouldn't be worth it," Fiona murmured against her ear as they watched a wave roll in and swallow the circle they had drawn in the sand.

CHAPTER 23

*S*EAN STARED AT the road ahead of him, mindlessly driving the route from Grace's Cove to Dublin, just as he had done hundreds of times before.

And yet this time felt so very different.

Seeing Margaret again had almost swiped his knees out from under him. He'd been certain that he was over her – that she would just be a faded memory in his mind. He hadn't been prepared for the feelings that washed over him.

He'd damn near wanted to rip David McCormick's head off when David had taken Margaret for a spin on the dance floor. Sean's possessiveness had surprised him at first.

But he was a successful businessman now and used to making decisions quickly. One look at the vulnerability in Margaret's eyes at the rehearsal dinner had brought it all back to him.

She'd hovered near the door, unsure of her welcome, looking lovely in her pastel pencil skirt and silk blouse, pearls at her throat. All buttoned up and prim, just waiting for him to rediscover what was under her shirt.

Sean groaned and slammed his fist onto the steering wheel.

Their past was such a mess.

At least he'd been willing to try again, Sean thought and punched the steering wheel again. He was angry at Margaret for not falling into his arms, angry at himself for leaving her again.

Certain that he'd screwed up, Sean continued on towards Dublin, forcing himself to let go of a dream unrealized.

It was just too late for all that, he thought.

CHAPTER 24

MARGARET STOOD AT her bed, her suitcase open, as she folded a blouse, her hands trembling with indecision.

"You're going to go to him, aren't you?" Fiona said from the door.

"I think that I have to," Margaret admitted.

"Good, 'bout time you showed some backbone," Fiona sniffed.

Margaret turned and raised an eyebrow at her mother.

"Yes, because starting a business while raising my child on my own in another country clearly showed little backbone," she said dryly.

Fiona chuckled, caught. "Fair enough."

"I'm sorry if this cuts our visit short," Margaret said suddenly, realizing that she was ditching out on the few days that she and Fiona had planned to spend together.

"You'll be back," Fiona said simply – and Margaret realized she was right.

Even leaving Sean out of the picture, there was no way

Margaret wouldn't be coming back to see Keelin and Fiona.

"It's an easy flight from Boston," Margaret agreed, zipping her suitcase up and dropping it to the floor.

"Maybe I can come see it someday," Fiona said gently, and Margaret realized she had never truly invited her mother to come visit her.

"Yes, I'd love that. In fact why don't we start planning it? I'll buy you a ticket when I get home."

"I'd love that," Fiona said, stepping forward with her arms out.

Margaret bent and wrapped her arms around Fiona, pulling her close, and allowed her shields to drop so that the full force of her mother's love pulsed through her.

Maybe she needed to feel that, truly *feel* that, with all of her gift, in order to finally let go of the past, Margaret thought as she stepped back.

"I love you very much," Margaret said, pressing her hand to her mother's cheek.

"You too. Oh, and Margaret," Fiona said as Margaret stepped past her, pulling her suitcase behind her.

"Yes?"

"Don't fall into your old patterns."

Margaret bit off the automatically sarcastic response and studied Fiona.

"I'll do my best not to."

CHAPTER 25

"Left side, left side," Margaret repeated to herself, forcing her rental car back from the right side of the road. It appeared she'd been living in Boston without a car long enough to forget how precarious driving in Ireland could be.

It would be at least two more hours before Margaret reached Dublin, and the time in the car had allowed her to think about what she was going to do.

Trying to rekindle a romance with someone she'd known for a few months, twenty-eight years ago? Who was she kidding?

Margaret laughed at herself, shaking her head. She didn't even identify with that person anymore, couldn't even remember half of the things she had thought about or said during that period in her life. Time had done its job, blurring the memory of the girl she once was, leaving only a vague emotional imprint of that time in her life.

Sean's the love of your life.

Fiona's words echoed in her head.

How could you love someone when you barely knew them? Sure, at nineteen she had been all caught up in hormones and dreams of a new life, but now? Margaret highly doubted that love could persist like that.

Yeah, maybe I am a little jaded, she thought with a sniff.

It hadn't been easy being a single mother in Boston twenty-eight years ago, Margaret thought, remembering the difficulties of traversing a new country, raising Keelin, and forcing her way into the fairly male-dominated real estate industry.

Love life? She laughed to herself. It hadn't been until Keelin was in her teens that Margaret had even come up for air from the demands of her job to consider dating. Then, she'd thrown herself into the dating scene with relish, choosing only the best and most esteemed men she could find in the city, men who were sophisticated and suave.

Everything that was worlds away from the men she would find in Grace's Cove.

From Sean, if she was being honest with herself.

And since this trip seemed to be about being honest with herself, Margaret shrugged and admitted that yes, she definitely had dated the most successful men she could find, hoping desperately to feel that pull of attraction she had only found with one scruffy boy on a beach in Ireland.

It hadn't happened – not for lack of Margaret's trying. After a few years of dating, she let that part of her life go and focused on her business and Keelin.

What else did she really need?

A life, Margaret thought. Maybe it was time to step

outside of her whirlwind life in Boston and really live her life. She'd built up one of the most respected real estate agencies in Boston, had more money than she knew what to do with, yet she realized now – she was bored.

The thrill of finding her clients their perfect home was gone for her; most of the time she was too busy dealing with the administrative and managerial tasks of running her business to be able to work directly with clients. And there were only so many charitable dinners that she could attend alone anymore.

If she was being truly honest with herself – she was lonely, and more than a little bored. With Keelin no longer living in Boston, Margaret had little to focus on other than her business.

Margaret sighed and stared at the farmland rolling past her window. She couldn't deny the charm of Ireland, that was for sure.

Her thoughts drifted to Sean and to what she was doing. Nerves kicked up in her stomach as she thought about knocking on his door.

Fiona had called her a runner.

Well, maybe this time she would run *towards* love.

CHAPTER 26

*E*VEN THOUGH SHE'D spent the entire drive building up her courage, Margaret couldn't quite bring herself to step out of the rental car. She'd parked in front of a gated driveway at a house located just outside Dublin City Centre. Scanning the neighborhood, Margaret approved of the elegant gates and neatly kept houses that lined the street. It was clear to her that Sean's business was doing just fine if the house behind the gate was any indication.

A brick house with two carriage lights and tidy flower boxes sporting happy purple flowers was situated back from the street, a neat lawn in front. Margaret wondered who took care of the flowers; she just couldn't imagine Sean standing outside watering his plants. She wondered if he had a housekeeper – or perhaps even a long time girlfriend that she didn't know about. What was she even doing here? She should probably just go and get a hotel downtown. Nodding to herself, Margaret put her hand to the key.

"You going to sit outside all day or were you planning on coming in?"

"Eek!" Margaret jumped, and then was slammed back against her seat, her seatbelt all but choking her as it caught. Putting her hand to where her heart slammed against her chest, she turned to glare out the window at Sean.

"Sure and you didn't need to be sneaking up on me now," Margaret said, her Irish accent growing thicker with her anger.

"I've been walking up the street for five minutes now. It wasn't exactly stealth. If you'd glanced in your mirrors you'd have seen me," Sean said reasonably, rocking back on his heels, a leash in his hands. Margaret followed the line of the leash to where a scruffy small dog in shades of brown, black, and white sat patiently staring up at her, his tongue lolling from his mouth.

"What is that?" Margaret asked, strangely fascinated by the odd little creature.

"That is a dog," Sean said patiently.

"I'm aware it's a dog, Sean. What kind?" Margaret said impatiently.

"It's a mutt. Baron was the oldest dog at the shelter. Nobody wanted him. I suppose I identified with that," Sean shrugged, a pink stain spreading up his cheeks. "So I took him home with me for company. We're pals now."

Margaret felt her heart clench a bit at his words, seeing a new side of Sean for the first time. Not only his loneliness, but his kindness in taking in the ugly dog that nobody else wanted.

"That's quite a regal name," Margaret said, finding

herself smiling down at the little mutt. Baron was beginning to grow on her.

"I thought he needed something to boost his self-esteem," Sean agreed, turning his gaze on her again. "So, were you planning on sitting in your car or did you want to come in?"

"I haven't decided yet," Margaret admitted, turning to stare back at the road.

"Baron thinks you should come throw the ball for him," Sean said.

"Is that so?" Margaret shifted her gaze down to where Baron's body vibrated on the ground, clearly wanting her to get out of the car.

"That's what he told me," Sean said.

"I suppose that I can't disappoint him," Margaret agreed, fighting to keep a smile off of her face.

Sean reached over and pulled her car door open and Margaret unbuckled her seat belt, turning to swing her feet onto the ground. Baron immediately jumped into her lap, turning to give her face a thorough swipe with his tongue.

"See? He likes you," Sean said.

"Yes, I'm sure that's a trick you pull with all the ladies," Margaret grumbled, but she couldn't help but run her hands over Baron's shaggy fur. "You're quite the mismatched pup, aren't you, Baron?"

Baron swiped his tongue over her hand and Margaret smiled again.

"He is really charming," she said finally, looking up to Sean's eyes.

"Us old guys still have some charm left, you know," Sean said.

"I've yet to see it," Margaret said and then pressed her lips together to keep from laughing out loud at the look on Sean's face.

"If it's charm you want, it's charm you'll get," Sean said, tugging lightly on the leash to encourage Baron to jump down from Margaret's lap. Holding his hand out to Margaret, he waited until she tentatively placed her palm in his, then pulled her gently from the car.

"Your bags, madam?" Sean said drolly and Margaret found herself stifling a giggle.

"The trunk," Margaret said, though she wasn't entirely sure that she wanted Sean to take her bag from the trunk. That would imply she was staying with him. Margaret didn't want to send any mixed messages.

And what kind of message was she giving him by driving from Grace's Cove to sit in front of his house, she wondered.

"Maybe we leave the bag," Margaret suggested but Sean was already pulling it out.

"Harder for you to escape this way," Sean said lightly, stopping to push the gate to his driveway open and letting Baron off the leash. The dog bounced across the yard, showing a surprising agility for his old age. Margaret tried to push down the nervousness that Sean's words raised in her as she moved into the yard, jolting at the clang of the gate closing behind her.

"Cute," Margaret said, then looked down at Baron when he bounded back to her with a slimy green ball in his mouth.

"He doesn't think I'm actually going to pick that up, does he?"

In response, Baron spit the ball out onto her foot and wagged his stump of a tail at Margaret. She couldn't resist the hopeful look in his eyes and, bending over, she gingerly picked up the soggy ball with her fingertips. She tossed it across the yard, helpless not to laugh as Baron went scrambling after it.

Margaret looked down at her slimy hand.

"Got a towel?"

"Sure, come on in," Sean said, moving towards his front door and unlocking it. Margaret walked past him as he ushered her into the house, unsure of what to expect.

A slate-tiled entryway led into an open living room that fed into a large kitchen area on one end. The design itself was a departure from the typical Irish house where the sitting room, dining room, and kitchen were all walled off. Tall windows ranged one side of the living room letting in the sunlight that shone onto a lone couch and table that sat across from a television. The walls were bare and the kitchen counter had nothing on it.

"I'm just going to put your bag in your room," Sean called cheerfully, and Margaret felt her shoulders stiffen.

"You most certainly will not," she ordered, steel lacing her voice.

"I won't?" Sean asked, slowly taking his hand off of her bag and crossing his arms over his chest.

"I don't even know what I'm doing here. It's a bit presumptuous to assume that I'll be spending the night," Margaret sniffed and lifted her chin at him.

"Well, I think we both know what you're doing here," Sean said evenly.

"Is that so?" Margaret said, her heart pounding against her chest.

"You missed me and couldn't stay away from me," Sean said, striding across the room until just inches separated them. Margaret was forced to look up from his chest to meet his eyes. Her mouth went dry for a second as her brain scrambled for thought.

"Still full of yourself, I see," Margaret said lightly, and a devastatingly sexy smile cracked Sean's face.

"Still stubborn, I see," Sean said, leaning in until his lips hovered close to hers.

A swarm of emotions battered at Margaret's mind, from lust to laughter to deeply buried bitterness. The force of it almost swallowed her and she knew that it was the combination of both their feelings. Putting a hand to his chest, she pushed back from him, taking a deep breath when he let her go.

The room spun a bit and she closed her eyes, breathing through her nose to steady herself.

"Are you okay?" Sean said, all playfulness gone as he reached up a hand to stroke her arm.

"Can I have a glass of water?" Margaret asked, needing a moment to compose herself.

"Sure," Sean said as he hurried across the room.

Margaret dropped to the couch, leaning back on the cushions and automatically reaching out to pet Baron when he jumped up next to her to snuggle at her side.

Sure, it was fun to banter with Sean a bit. But in all reality they had a tough history; Margaret was fooling herself if she thought they'd get past it.

"Here," Sean said, coming to stand by her side with a cobalt blue glass in his hands.

"Thank you," Margaret said, taking a sip of the cool liquid before leaning over to put the glass on the table in front of her. Sean sat down on the couch and leaned back into the cushions, his eyes shuttered.

"Sean," Margaret began and stopped when he raised his hand.

"Don't, Maggie. I don't think that I can take it," Sean said softly, and Margaret felt sadness wash through her.

She hesitated.

"I just think there's too much anger. Too much history. How would we get past that?" Margaret asked, pleading with Sean to understand her.

"You just *do*. We all have choices, Maggie. You can hold on to years of anger over something that you can no longer change, or you can choose to be free from the chains of it," Sean said, meeting her eyes, his words ringing with a truth that she couldn't deny.

Margaret took in a deep breath and leaned back against the cushions, staring out at the garden in his back yard. Could it be so simple? Could she just let it go and start fresh?

"I don't know if I'm the type of person who can just let something like that go," Margaret admitted, "Being angry with you – hating our familial gift – it's so deep-rooted in me that it became the foundation of what I'd built my new life upon."

Margaret shuddered out a breath as she realized what she spoke was the truth. Her new life in Boston had been fueled by pure rage and fear – and a determination to never return to Ireland again. What would happen to her if that foundation crumbled?

"And how's that worked out for you?"

Sean probably didn't mean to sound sarcastic, but it came across as such, causing Margaret to bristle a bit.

"I don't know, Sean, does running the most successful woman-owned real estate company in Boston seem like it worked out okay?" Margaret asked, raising an eyebrow.

"I don't doubt you would have been able to accomplish that either way," Sean said soothingly, and his words had a ring of truth to them.

"I don't know," Margaret said, tugging at a crease in her pants. "I may have needed that anger to fuel my determination."

"No, you always had it. Don't you remember how you were sneaking real estate books into your bed at night? That's someone who is determined. Anger or not."

Margaret tried to look back at her nineteen-year-old self with clearer eyes.

"I suppose I *was* determined. But, Sean, there's just so much anger and unhappiness from that time in my life. How am I supposed to just forget that and jump into bed with you?"

Sean choked and coughed, covering his mouth with his hand before shaking his head ruefully at her.

"Why don't we start with dinner?"

"Dinner?" Margaret asked, tilting her head at him in question.

"Yes, Maggie. Dinner. Let me take you out to dinner. Why don't we start there? Nobody is saying you have to jump into bed with me – though I sure wouldn't turn you away if you offered. But," he raised his hand to shush her, "why don't we take it a step at a time."

"But –" Margaret said, confusion swirling in her mind.

"When does your plane leave?"

"Two days. Tuesday around noon."

"Well, okay. That's not a lot of time. But I can do my best to make you think twice about stepping on that plane."

Margaret felt heat rush over her at his words, and she looked down at her hands, clenched tightly in her lap. Would it be so bad to loosen up and have a little fun for once?

Remember what happened the last time you loosened up with this man, her conscience scolded her. Margaret fought an internal debate before taking a deep breath and turning to meet Sean's eyes.

"Friends. Let's do this as friends," she said.

"Aw, Maggie, we've always been friends," he said, reaching out to squeeze her hand.

"Have we? Because I feel like we were lovers and then you were my ex-boyfriend non-existent father of my child," Margaret said icily – and was surprised to see Sean laugh again.

"See? There you go. Let it all out," he said soothingly.

"Don't placate me!" Margaret said, surprised to find her temper revving from zero to sixty again.

"I'm not placating you. Listen, let's lay it on the table. Again," Sean said and Margaret slammed back into the cushions, crossing her arms over her chest as her foot kicked in circles.

"One, I was a total fool for allowing the cove to freak

me out. I never should have run," Sean said, holding up his hand to stop Margaret when she began to agree with him. "Two, I should have never taken your word for it that you didn't want me to come to Boston. I should have come after you."

Margaret was surprised to feel tears building up and she swallowed quickly, trying to blink them from her eyes. She had honestly never thought she'd hear those words from Sean.

"Three, you should have had the decency to tell me to my face about Keelin," Sean said and Margaret's mouth dropped open.

He was right.

She shouldn't have run off without telling Sean about her situation, about their baby. No matter what the situation was, she didn't have the right to take that from him.

"I..." Margaret almost stomped her foot when he silenced her again.

"Four, I shouldn't have blindly tumbled into the next relationship without coming for you. I didn't handle being alone well. I'm better at it now," Sean said evenly.

Margaret nodded vehemently at that one. Damn right he shouldn't have married the next trollop that came along, she thought to herself.

"Five, you should have had faith in us that we would have figured it out," Sean said, and at that Margaret turned and almost spat at him.

"*I* should have?" she all but shrieked.

"We should have," Sean amended, his gaze steady.

Margaret looked at Sean – really looked at him – for the first time since she had arrived in Ireland. His eyes held pain but an undercurrent of hope ran through them too; she could read it from a mile away.

"You're right," Margaret found herself saying, unsure why she was so drawn to this man. "We should have."

"So let's try this again. Margaret O'Brien, can I take you to dinner?" Sean said, standing up and holding out his hand.

"I…I'd like that," Margaret said shyly, slipping her palm into his.

She felt like she was nineteen years old all over again.

CHAPTER 27

MARGARET CHANGED IN the spare bedroom, where she had ended up allowing Sean to take her suitcase after all. It wasn't like anything had to happen between them. They were both adults and the past they shared was eons away.

Fiddling with her hair in the mirror, Margaret tried to tamp down on the nerves that raced through her stomach. It seemed like all she'd done since she'd come to Ireland was feel waves of emotion wash through her. It was as though she'd been living in black and white in Boston and all she could do was see in color here. Margaret knew that it had a lot to do with her gift, the gift she so furiously controlled at home seemingly coming to life now that she was back in Ireland.

It made her nervous. She was struggling more with keeping her shields up and in doing so, her old resentment about her gift was beginning to burn in her chest.

"Ready?" Sean called and Margaret smoothed her hands over the red silk blouse she wore tucked into a white pencil skirt. Clasping a statement necklace around her neck – one of Aislinn's that Keelin had given her – Margaret took one last look in the mirror and straightened her shoulders.

"Yes," she said, opening the door from the sparsely furnished spare bedroom to walk down the plain white hallway to where Sean stood in the entryway, Baron sitting at his feet.

Lord, the man was still gorgeous, Margaret thought as she took in his crisp khaki pants, white button down, and plaid driving cap on his dark hair. He looked elegant, at ease with himself, and more handsome than he'd been all those years ago. Margaret swallowed against the sudden lump at her throat and found herself giggling when he let out a low whistle when she walked towards him.

"Sure and my eyes must be deceiving me…the prettiest woman in Dublin as my date? How did I get so lucky?" Sean asked, directing his question down to Baron who wiggled at his feet eagerly.

"Oh, stop," Margaret said, blushing.

"Sure and you're a sight for sore eyes, Maggie," Sean said, offering her his arm.

"Thank you. You look very nice yourself," she said primly as she slid her arm into his and stepped out the front door.

"No parties while we're gone," Sean ordered Baron, causing Margaret to chuckle again.

When was the last time she had laughed so freely? Margaret loved her life in Boston, but she hadn't realized just how uptight she had been. She was always so focused on putting out the next fire at her business that she never really took much down time to relax or have fun.

And wouldn't having fun be a nice change of pace?

"Where are we going?" Margaret asked as they walked to the garage – then gasped when the door opened up to reveal a spiffy red two-seater convertible. "Sean!"

"Aye, a man has to have some toys, doesn't he?" Sean said with a wink, coming around to open the door for Margaret. She laughed as she slid onto the soft leather seats, admiring the contrast of cream-colored leather with the red of the car's exterior.

"Why, you match!" Sean exclaimed, laughing as he slid into the driver's seat.

"I guess it was meant to be," Margaret said flippantly, then found herself biting her tongue.

"I think we've always known that," Sean said, keeping his eyes on the rearview mirror as he reversed from the garage. Margaret found herself shivering at his words.

"Whoa," Margaret laughed as they zoomed away from his driveway, Sean obviously speeding a bit to show off. Smiling at her, he slowed down to a more sedate speed as they cruised through his neighborhood.

"Want to take a drive out along the water before dinner?" Sean asked and Margaret nodded.

"That'd be nice."

They lapsed into comfortable silence as the wind whipped through her hair and Sean steered the car away from the city centre. Sean flicked on the radio as they cruised along the water's edge, the sun's light warm on their shoulders, the lilting Irish accent of the radio announcer soothing Margaret.

Maybe she could do this.

"I hope you like Mediterranean," Sean said over the wind as he left the shore drive and turned the snappy little convertible back towards the city.

"I do," Margaret said, surprised that he had picked one of her favorite choices.

"Good," Sean said, a smile flashing across his face.

"I have to admit. I love this car," Margaret said, laughing over at him. There was something so freeing about driving around with the top down, zipping past people. It was fun. She really needed to have more fun in her life.

They pulled up at a funky little restaurant with lively music playing from speakers outside and windows left open to catch the breeze. Sean got out and tossed the keys to the valet, who smiled graciously at him, then came around to open Margaret's door for her.

"Madam," the valet said with a smile, and Margaret smiled automatically.

Madam.

Didn't that just put her right back in her place? Margaret shook her head as she rounded the car to meet Sean. She was almost fifty years old, for Christ's sake. What was she doing tooling around in a convertible and giggling like a schoolgirl? Reminding herself to keep it in check, she smiled politely as the hostess led them to a wide leather booth tucked in a private alcove. The scents from the kitchen already had her mouth watering.

"Sean, this place is great," Margaret said, turning to scan the restaurant. It was sleek and modern, with a lot of metal and white wood, but somehow it still gave off a cozy charm.

"Yes, Dublin's really come into its own over the past twenty years or so. The art scene is really lovely, more musical acts, and the restaurants are great."

"You go to art galleries?" Margaret asked, raising an eyebrow at him while smiling at the waiter who approached their table.

"Well, Margaret, you know that Aislinn is a famous artist. I'm sure I'm not as classy as you are, but I can still appreciate art," Sean said stiffly before turning to address the waiter. Margaret shot a puzzled glance at him before berating herself for being a snob. The Sean she had known years ago couldn't afford art galleries. It was clear that a lot had changed since then.

Margaret waited until they ordered drinks before reaching out to put her hand on Sean's arm.

"I'm sorry. That came across as snobby," she said quietly, meeting his eyes.

"I suppose that we have a lot to learn about each other," Sean said.

"I suppose we do," Margaret said softly, smiling when the waiter re-appeared at their table and poured two glasses of red wine.

"Tell me about your business," Sean said, smoothly moving on; Margaret was grateful that he hadn't stayed angry.

"You really want to know?" Margaret asked, taking a sip of her wine and watching Sean carefully. The men she dated back in Boston usually spent most of the evening talking about their own businesses and just how successful they were. It was a refreshing change to be asked about her business.

"Of course I do. I want to know everything about you," Sean said, his words seeming to caress her body with their meaning. Margaret felt a shiver whisper through her and she took another sip of her wine to wet her suddenly dry mouth.

"Well, it's real estate, as you know," Margaret said.

"I know. I'm so glad that you didn't give up on that dream," Sean said, smiling at her.

"Thank you, I am as well," Margaret said, smiling back at him. The conversation lulled as they put their food order in.

"Go on," Sean said after the waiter had left. He handed her the bread basket and Margaret found herself dipping a crusty piece of warm bread in oil, eating it without giving any thought to calories or her waistline, something she never overlooked back in Boston.

"I started off with just one client at a time. My cousin let me stay for a while with Keelin and she was a great help. I'll forever be indebted to her."

"I should've been there to help," Sean said softly, regret passing across his handsome features.

Margaret waved the bread in her hand at him.

"I think that I needed to do it on my own. Though my heart was broken at the time, I needed to see what I was made of. And one client turned into five and slowly expanded until now I have fifty agents working under me. I barely have time to even show houses anymore, I'm so busy running the business," Margaret laughed.

"Your heart was broken?" Sean asked, zeroing in on the admission Margaret had made.

Margaret felt her cheeks warm and she turned away for a moment, taking another sip of her wine.

"It was. At least for the feelings I had for you at that time. I don't know if it was love or if it was just the raw emotion of youth, but I pined for you for a long time. I won't lie," Margaret said on a shrug, taking another sip of her wine and watching Sean's expression from under lowered eyelids.

"I was heartbroken when you left as well. I was all but blinded by my depression. I lost myself in my drink, barely surfacing but to get out on the boat, returning directly to the pub after work each day. Fiona was the one who pulled me out of it," Sean admitted.

"You drank too much?" Margaret asked, tilting her head.

"Aye, it was my only outlet. Until Fiona basically said I needed to get busy living or just finish myself off. It was a right kick to the head that I needed," Sean said.

"And so you met your wife," Margaret said, encouraging the conversation, though she was surprised to find the thought of him taking a wife still stung.

"I did. It...it was foolish of me. We were never a good match. She's a good woman and she put up with me far longer than she should have. But she knew that my heart wasn't in it. I suppose we both thought we could make a go of it. And when the twins came...well. What else was there to do?" Sean asked, shrugging his shoulders.

"I can understand that," Margaret said and Sean looked at her in relief.

"Really?"

"Yes, really. Children change everything. I can see where you would just try to hold on and give them a good life," Margaret said. As a parent, she truly did understand where Sean was coming from.

"Well, it still didn't last all that long. We ended up separating when they were teenagers," Sean said, running his fingers over a crease in the tablecloth.

"That had to have been tough," Margaret said.

"It was. Aislinn wanted little to do with me. It's taken a while to get back into her good graces. Colin was a little more understanding. Now I've got another daughter to work on a relationship with. Seems like parenting never ends, does it?"

"No, it doesn't. Keelin seems to be pretty responsive to the two of you having a relationship," Margaret said carefully, not wanting to reveal any of Keelin's private views of Sean.

"She does. And, I'm grateful at that. We're figuring it out. I'm glad that she and Aislinn have become friends. I think that has really helped Keelin and me to strengthen our relationship as well," Sean smiled as the waiter brought them a steaming platter of meats, accompanied by two more platters of olives, cheese, hummus, and fruits. Margaret laughed at all the food.

"I think there's enough here to feed ten people," Margaret gushed.

"You'll love it," Sean guaranteed.

And love it she did. The whole night, in fact. After a few stumbling blocks where they touched on the awkward areas in their past, Margaret was surprised to find that they had a lot in common – from owning their own businesses to a shared love of Bruce Springsteen – and by the time they pulled up to his house, Margaret was relaxed and laughing.

"I can't believe you ordered dessert," Margaret laughed and put her hand across her stomach where she was certain her tummy strained against her skirt.

"It was worth it, wasn't it?" Sean said, smiling at her as he jumped out of the car and rounded the convertible to hold her door open. Margaret got out and brushed past him, feeling his nearness like a palpable wave across her body.

"It certainly was decadent," Margaret agreed, waiting as he unlocked the front door and immediately bent to pet an excited Baron.

"I've just got to get him his dinner," Sean explained and Margaret followed him to the kitchen, pulling herself onto one of the stools at the counter. She watched as he went through what was clearly a dinner ritual of sit, stay, roll over with Baron.

"That's cute," Margaret observed.

"Ah, just a little thing we do," Sean said, his cheeks a bit pink at her appraisal.

"Baron must be good company," Margaret observed, turning slightly to scan the empty walls. "No girlfriends to keep you company?" she asked, not meeting his eyes but really wanting to know the answer.

"Ah, there have been some. Nobody special though," Sean said and Margaret felt a little wave of relief go through her.

"I can tell you're single," she said, gesturing to the

blank walls. Confusion crossed Sean's face before he realized what she meant.

"Aye, I keep meaning to put pictures up but always forget to. Business keeps me pretty busy," he admitted, coming around to where Margaret sat and standing by her stool.

"You work tomorrow?" Margaret asked, barely daring to breathe; his closeness put her on edge.

"I do. Would you like to come out on the boat with me?" Sean asked.

Margaret glanced up at him in surprise. "Fishing?"

"No, one of the tour boats. Unless you've an interest in fishing?" Sean said, laughing down at her.

"A tour would be nice," Margaret said and then felt herself stiffening when Sean reached out and touched the back of her chair, turning the stool until her legs caught on his and he stood between them. Margaret blushed at the intimacy, unsure if she was ready for this, surprised at how quickly her body seemed to respond to him.

"Ah, Maggie," Sean said, bringing his forehead to hers before brushing his lips softly against hers, his hands running up her arms.

Margaret didn't know why his touch made her want to weep. There was so much history with him, she wasn't sure they could go back. Pressing back, Margaret allowed herself to be taken under in the kiss, moaning softly in protest when he broke the kiss. Gathering herself, she pulled back to meet the question in his eyes.

And came to a resolution.

"Thank you for dinner. I really am tired, it was a late night last night with Keelin's wedding," Margaret said, withdrawing from his touch and putting her emotional boundaries back up. Disappointment flashed through his eyes before he nodded and stepped back.

"Do you need anything? There are towels in the bathroom. A glass of water?"

"Water would be nice, thank you," Margaret said, staying quiet as he filled a glass and carried it back to where she stood.

"We could be really great – if you let us," Sean said softly, looking down at Margaret. She felt her heart squeeze as she gently took the glass of water from him, his skin brushing against hers shaking her resolve.

"I'm not the person that I used to be. I don't make rash decisions anymore," Margaret said, shrugging one shoulder, but refusing to change her position.

"I guess I can understand that. Sweet dreams, pretty Margaret," Sean said, reaching up to run a finger down her cheek before whistling to Baron as he stepped to the back door. "Wake me if you need anything."

Margaret swallowed against a lump in her throat as she made her way down the hallway. Was she making a mistake? Her heart screamed at her to go back and jump the man, but her backbone – one which she'd honed to steel – forced her to continue her march to the bedroom.

She'd already had one life-changing moment with this man. Margaret wasn't sure her heart could handle another.

CHAPTER 28

"Tea's on," Sean called, knocking softly at her door and Margaret pulled the pillow from over her head and groaned.

"What time is it?" she grumbled.

"Half six," Sean called cheerfully through the door and Margaret groaned again. Half six meant it was around 12:30 in the morning back in Boston. She sighed and swung her legs from the bed, moving to use the en suite bathroom.

What was she complaining about anyway? It wasn't like she'd gotten much sleep. If Margaret thought her dreams about Sean the night before had been vivid, last night's dreams stole the show. Knowing that he was just feet from where she tried to sleep had heightened the experience and Margaret had woken more than once on a cry of pleasure, imagining his hands on her. She shook her head as she stepped into the shower, praying that her voice had been quiet enough so as not to waken Sean. Margaret wasn't sure she would be able to face him today if he had heard her.

After a peek out the window, Margaret decided on jeans and a deep blue lightweight sweater over a white silk t-shirt. Knowing how the winds could shift on the water, she wanted to be prepared. Taking one spin in the mirror, Margaret had to agree with Keelin.

Jeans did make her butt look good.

Margaret opened the door to find Baron waiting for her. The small dog wiggled in joy and rolled over on his back, immediately charming her.

"Well, aren't you just the sweetest thing," Margaret cooed, bending to scratch Baron's belly. The mismatched little mutt was really starting to grow on her and she wondered if she could manage to care for a dog and run a business.

"Sure and he gets all the love this morning? Where are my belly scratches?" Sean asked, raising an eyebrow at her as he cooked eggs at the stove.

Margaret was surprised to find herself laughing at him again and on impulse, she rounded the corner and brushed her lips over his cheek.

"Sure now you kiss me when I've got me hands full of eggs and a hot pan," Sean growled and Margaret laughed again, moving past him to sit at the counter and pour a cup of breakfast tea from the cheerful red pot that sat on the counter.

"Just keeping you on your toes," she said lightly, adding cream and sugar to her tea and stirring with a spoon. Taking a small sip, Margaret watched Sean work in the kitchen. He moved with ease, transferring the eggs, buttering the toast, pulling out a jar of jam. Margaret was startled to realize she had never had a man cook for her before. It was a surprisingly nice experience.

"Ah, I'd jump through hoops for you all day, Maggie girl," Sean said smoothly, turning to slide a heaping plate of eggs and toast across the counter to her. Margaret laughed down at it and then up at him.

"I usually just have tea and fruit for breakfast. This is a lot of food," she explained.

"Oh. I have fruit. Do you want fruit? Let me get it," Sean said, and Margaret rushed to stop him as he bustled around the kitchen to look in the fridge for his fruit.

"No, really, this is great. Thank you," Margaret said shyly, finding his eagerness endearing. Scooping up a bite of eggs, she began to work her way through the mound of food on her plate.

"We've got two tours today, but I'll only be heading up the morning one. Then I'll need to spend some time in the office so you can either hang out or – maybe you feel like walking around Dublin? Doing some shopping? Then I figured we'd catch dinner again, or I could cook something here," Sean said, excitement ringing through his voice as he offered up all his options to her on a platter.

He's really lonely, Margaret realized with a sudden twist in her gut. She could feel it emanating from him in thick waves.

"Sure, I'd like that. No need for shopping, I can just hang around," Margaret said. Boston had some of the best shops in the world lining Newbury Street so she wasn't too concerned with adding more to her closet.

"Alright, let me just get Baron ready to go," Sean said,

pushing away from the counter and putting his dish in the sink.

"Baron goes with you?"

"Of course," Sean said, shaking his head at her.

"Of course," Margaret echoed, rising from her chair. "I'll get the dishes then."

"Thanks, I'd appreciate that," Sean sounded relieved as he stepped away from the sink. Margaret just shook her head.

Men would do anything to get out of doing the dishes.

Margaret sighed when she opened the cupboard and realized that the two plates she had just washed were his only plates. Curious she opened another cupboard door to find a mismatched array of glasses lining the shelves. Shooting a glance over her shoulder to see if Sean was looking at her, she ducked her head into a few more cabinets and came up, surprised at the complete lack of kitchenware.

"Looking for something?" Sean asked from across the room where he had a little bag packed and a leash in one hand.

"Just trying to figure out where your pan goes," Margaret said with a smile, holding up the pan in her hand. "Though it seems like it can go anywhere, there's not much in your cabinets. Did you just move in or something?"

"No, I've been here about six years now?" Sean said, scrunching up his face as he thought about her question.

"Six years and you only own two plates? Don't you ever entertain?" Margaret was genuinely curious. It was positively un-Irish not to invite people to your home.

"Sure, I entertain at restaurants and pubs. Rarely do I have people over," Sean said, shrugging and moving to the front hallway. "Ready?"

"I'll just get my purse," Margaret said, realizing the conversation was over.

And wondered just why his house seemed so unlived in.

CHAPTER 29

*R*IDING IN THE large black pickup truck to Sean's business proved to be a far different experience than in his natty little convertible, Margaret thought as they rode further out of the city and towards the docks.

Not that she minded. It was kind of nice to sit higher up in a truck. At home, Margaret didn't even own a car. She either took the T, walked, or used a car service for longer drives. The cost and inconvenience of owning a car while living on Beacon Hill just didn't make sense to Margaret.

The morning radio show discouraged conversation, and Margaret found herself biting back a smile as Sean cursed about a score in last night's hurling match. She'd forgotten how incensed the Irish could become when their local team lost out at the nation's favorite sport.

Sean pulled up to a large warehouse by the docks, a chain link fence surrounding the lot. He waved at the guard and the gate slid open so he could motor past.

Margaret felt her jaw dropping open at the sheer expanse of the enterprise laid out before her. The warehouse was easily a football field large, with a large parking lot of semi-trucks where workers were bustling about with dollies and boxes. To the right, a long line of docks housed impressive fishing boats, some of which were already motoring away from the dock while others looked like they were in the process of being serviced. Margaret knew enough about commercial real estate to know that this space along the water had to have cost a small fortune.

"Moved up in the world, have we?" Margaret asked, raising an eyebrow at Sean. He barked out a laugh and shook his head, but Margaret could see the pleasure on his face.

"Told you I was going to build a big enterprise," Sean said, shrugging her words away. Yet there was something there. Margaret felt a low press of anger wash over her, along with self-satisfaction. She wondered if Sean thought she had ever doubted that he would be successful.

"I always knew you would," Margaret said lightly as they pulled into the parking spot marked "Owner."

"Did you?" Sean said, matching her tone, then hopping from the truck. This time he didn't come around to open the door for Margaret and she wondered just what sort of landmine she'd stepped on now.

Slamming the door, Margaret straightened her shoulders and waited for Sean to direct her.

"Come on over to the main office, I've got to check in," Sean said easily, the anger in his voice having now been replaced with a polite tone. Margaret knew that sometimes silence was the best answer to sticky situations, so she nodded and followed Sean quietly as he walked through a large garage type door that was pulled open to welcome the sea breezes.

Again, Margaret was astounded at the sheer magnitude of people working for Sean. It seemed that everywhere she looked people were bustling about, packing boxes with dry ice, walking in and out of coolers, shouting orders across the room. From her estimation, Sean's business looked like a tightly run ship.

She wrinkled her nose against the fishy smell that emanated from the warehouse, wondering how they worked around the scent every day. Margaret supposed they stopped noticing it after a while. Trying her best to just breathe through her mouth, Margaret followed Sean across the warehouse to where glassed-in offices lined one wall.

Sean stopped at a door and waited for Margaret, smiling politely before he swung the door open for her, ushering her into a waiting room of sorts. Margaret automatically smiled at the woman who sat at the desk, assuming she was the receptionist.

"Adeline, this is...an old friend of mine, Margaret O'Brien," Sean said, pausing for a second as he stumbled over how to introduce her. Margaret didn't blame him – who wanted to introduce their non-existent child's parent?

Margaret's eyebrows shot up as Adeline surveyed her. The woman was compact, but curvy in all the right places, her figure showcased in a snug grey knit sweater, black leather pants, and high heels that made Margaret cringe just to think about wearing. Flowing red hair – not an Irish red but from a bottle, Margaret noted with a sniff – topped an attractive face, with entirely too much makeup for this time of the morning. Margaret estimated her to be close to their age. Margaret's back stiffened as she was met with a wave of disapproval from Adeline that belied the smile on her face.

So it's like that, Margaret thought, holding out her hand and pasting a polite smile on her face.

"Sure and it's nice to meet you. We just love having friends come visit us, don't we, Sean?" Adeline said, standing next to Sean and patting his arm briefly. It would take a blind man to miss the look of adoration she shot Sean, and Margaret was surprised to feel her Irish beginning to kick up.

"Um, that we do," Sean said, clearing his throat. "I thought I'd take Maggie on the boat tour this morning and show her around."

"Well, I'm just sure that...*Maggie*...will love that," Adeline purred, moving around the desk to pick up a folder. "Here's your passenger list today. If you need me to spend any time showing Maggie around, I'd be happy to."

Sweet as peaches and cream aren't you? Margaret rolled her eyes behind Adeline's back.

"That'd be great," Sean said, at the same time Margaret said, "I'll be fine on my own, thanks."

"Um," Sean said, turning his head between the two women.

"I would hate to take her away from her receptionist duties," Margaret explained lightly and was rewarded when Adeline narrowed her eyes at her.

"I'm the manager, not the receptionist," Adeline said, flipping her hair back and placing her hands on her hips.

"Oops," Margaret said, shrugging her shoulders.

"You two can chat more later," Sean said, pulling his nose out of the folder he was reading, oblivious to the tension in the room, "We've got to get down to the boat."

"Have a good tour," Adeline said, running her hand down Sean's arm again. He barely nodded at her as he continued to peruse the folder, walking out of the office.

"Bye, Maggie," Adeline called sweetly. The way she was using Margaret's nickname – that only Sean called her – really grated on Margaret's nerves. Swiveling on her heels at the door, she shot a look at Adeline.

"Bye, Addie."

The woman's eyes flashed again and Margaret considered her job done as she hurried to catch up with Sean.

And wondered just exactly what she'd gotten herself back into.

CHAPTER 30

"She seems nice," Margaret said sweetly, wondering if Sean would pick up on the sarcasm in her voice.

"Who? Oh, Adeline? Yeah, she's fairly new. Been here about six months or so. Our last manager quit suddenly and we were in a bind," Sean said, tucking the folder under his arm and holding out his hand to help Margaret step over some rope onto the dock.

"Why'd your manager quit?" Margaret asked, matching Sean's step as they passed several docks, most of them empty, as they wound their way towards a cheerful tour boat docked at the end. Margaret could already see a line of passengers waiting to board.

"Said he wasn't compensated fairly for what he put up with," Sean scoffed. "I don't even know what he means – we've got a great crew of people working for us."

Margaret's alarm bells went off at that comment but they reached the boat before she could react.

"Hi folks! I'm just going to run through my safety

check and we'll get you boarded quickly," Sean called, motioning for Margaret to step past the line of people to where the little plank for boarding the boat lay.

Margaret skipped, holding onto Sean's hand to board the boat, and hopped lightly onto the deck of the party-boat style vessel. It was a large rectangular boat with benches lining all sides of it, with a cheerful blue and white canopy for shade above. The Captain's chair was situated at the back with a large microphone and speakers attached. One of Sean's men went around the boat, ticking off the number of life vests tucked under the benches, while Sean moved to the Captain's chair.

"Here, you can sit next to me," Sean said, motioning to where part of the bench was tucked behind the Captain's chair. She'd still have great views but wouldn't need to be squished in next to the rest of the people. Margaret smiled in gratitude at Sean and sat down, leaning back to cross her arms and watch Sean's operation in motion. Margaret wondered why he even bothered to run tours when it was clear his fishing business was doing so well.

"All aboard!" Sean shouted into the microphone like a train conductor, startling Margaret from her relaxed position on the bench. Sean went over and stood by the plank to the boat, shaking everyone's hand as they came aboard, helping those who needed it. Laughing, cracking jokes, and telling stories already, Margaret could see that Sean was in his element.

Her mind flitted back to his sparsely decorated home. She wondered if the reason he still ran tours was because he craved companionship. Margaret would be the first to admit that getting older on her own certainly had its lonely moments. In mere moments, Margaret found herself laughing along with Sean as he teased a pie-eyed child about sharks in the water.

"Nah, I'm just pulling your leg," Sean said, crouching down to cuff the little girl's chin and Margaret felt her heart tug. Was this what it would have been like to raise Keelin with Sean? What if she had stayed to find out instead of running? Pressing her lips into a tight line, she turned to stare out over the harbor, refusing to let regrets creep into her carefully planned past. What's done is done, she thought.

Sean got behind the wheel and, signaling to his first mate, waited while the lines were untied from the dock before reversing into the water. The tourists let up a cheer as Sean clanged the bell at his side, causing Margaret to jump and laugh again. Flicking a switch to play traditional Irish music from the speakers, Sean let his guests take in the view as they puttered away from the dock, giving them a different view of Ireland. As they pulled further out and began to move down the coast, Margaret found herself relaxing into her seat, transfixed by Sean's animated face as he detailed great battles that had once been fought along the shore.

Margaret's heart clenched a bit as she studied his face, his mannerisms, the way he stood. She could see Keelin in him – or perhaps it was the other way around, and Keelin shared many of *his* traits. Guilt crept up her spine as she thought about how little she had told Keelin about her father over the years. Even though Sean had never come for her or tried to initiate contact, Margaret could still have given Keelin more of an idea of the man she came from.

Chalk it up as one more thing she could regret about her past, Margaret thought on a sigh and turned to look out over the coastline, wondering not for the first time what she was doing here.

With him.

As people laughed at his patter, Margaret tuned back in to listen to Sean, pushing her morose thoughts aside to study him again. She'd be lying to herself if she said that she and Sean didn't still have chemistry. Margaret just wasn't sure if it was anything more than that.

And one lesson she'd learned long ago was that leading with her heart would only get her into trouble.

"Having fun?" Sean asked, breaking into her thoughts. Margaret looked up at him with a smile.

"Of course, this is a great tour," she gushed.

"Glad you like it. You probably wonder why I still run them," Sean said sheepishly, covering the microphone with his hand.

"No, I think I see why you do it," Margaret said.

"You do?"

"You love it. You love Ireland, the history, the stories…and you love entertaining people. It's clear that this is a great joy for you," Margaret said.

Sean beamed down at her, pleased that she understood. He shrugged a shoulder sheepishly, "I know it isn't a huge moneymaker and probably not the best use of my time."

"Sometimes business doesn't have to be only about money. Especially when you already have a business that is working for you," Margaret said gently and then sat back again to consider her words.

If it wasn't about the money, then what was she doing

spending all her time running her business and not doing what she loved? The problem was that Margaret couldn't really figure out what it was she loved. Sure, helping people find their dream home was great, but Margaret also missed the days back when her business was just a start-up. Problem-solving came naturally to her and she'd loved digging her hands in, figuring out all the ins and outs of running her business. Problem was, her business was so well-run now that they'd all but urged her to go on vacation, promising they wouldn't miss her in the slightest.

And wasn't that the truth? Her phone hadn't beeped with a single email in the days since she'd left. Which should make her proud, Margaret thought on a sniff. Not annoyed.

Margaret laughed when the tourists booed at Sean's turning the boat around, but he was so cheerful about the tour coming to an end that they had nothing to do but smile and shake Sean's hand back at the dock. Margaret waited for him to say goodbye to everyone before she drifted over to where he stood.

"Nice job, Captain," Margaret said, leaning up to brush a kiss over his cheek.

"I'm happy to take you for a ride any time," Sean said eagerly, then blushed furiously when he realized what he had said.

Margaret couldn't help but bend over and howl with laughter.

Sometimes there were no words.

CHAPTER 31

"Penny for your thoughts, pretty Maggie?" Sean asked as they sat at a picnic table down by the water, eating a lunch of fish and chips that Sean had picked up from the best take-out restaurant in town. Supplied with his fish, naturally.

"I was thinking that you were right, this is the best fish and chips I've ever had," Margaret said, even though that hadn't been what she'd been thinking about.

A sense of melancholy had washed over her after the boat tour, while she'd waited for Sean to pick up lunch. Luckily, she'd been spared a run-in with Adeline by sitting out on the harbor. The minutes spent staring out at the water and contemplating her life's direction had left her moody and quiet when Sean had returned with their food.

"Aye, it is," Sean agreed, leveling his gaze on her. He waited patiently, which caused Margaret to be even more annoyed.

"I'm just in a mood," she finally said, exasperated that he was making her talk.

"About?" Sean said cheerfully, and she wanted to smack him.

"This week hasn't exactly been easy for me," Margaret said stiffly, hoping that would end the conversation.

"Aye, it's got to be hard to watch your daughter get married," Sean agreed.

"I thought it was *'our'* daughter," Margaret said snippily.

"'Tis. But she's more your daughter than mine. I can imagine that brings a lot of bittersweet emotions with it," Sean said easily, brushing her comment away.

"It does. Though I feel pretty good about Flynn. I know he loves our daughter," Margaret said stiffly, her mind flashing to her gift, wondering if she and Sean would ever discuss her abilities. He'd yet to bring it up – which was fine with her.

"Flynn's a good man. I've worked with him for years. He'll be a good husband," Sean said.

"I can see that. Feel that. I'm really happy for them. It's just…been a lot," Margaret shrugged, not sure she wanted to get into everything right now.

"First time back in Ireland since you went tearing off in a tizzy. I can see where that would be hard," Sean said agreeably, leaning back against the table to stretch his legs out in front of him.

"A tizzy?" Margaret's voice squeaked and she felt her blood begin to boil.

"Well, you know, a snit," Sean said.

"A *snit*? Sean, you left me on the side of the cove after taking my virginity and I didn't hear from you for like five weeks!" Margaret shot back, her heart beginning to race. A tizzy? Was this man *insane*?

Realizing that the temperature of their conversation had just passed the boiling point, Sean sat up quickly and reached out to put an arm around her. Margaret pulled back, not wanting him to touch her right now.

"Okay, tizzy isn't the right word, I'm sorry," Sean said, trying to placate her. Margaret just shook her head at him.

"Don't ever try to downplay what was the most pivotal and difficult decision that I have ever had to make in my life. It wasn't in a tizzy. It was to start a new life. Without the person who had broken my heart," Margaret said, standing up to take her trash to a nearby rubbish can. Her heart pounded in her chest. It didn't seem they would ever get past this endless circle of blame and hurt.

And maybe that's just what she needed to know. Margaret could go back to Boston with a clear answer as to what would have happened if she and Sean had ever gotten together.

Maybe she'd finally be able to move on.

Turning, Margaret pasted a smile across her face.

"Let's just move on, okay?" she said sweetly, not wanting to get into it, especially when she saw Adeline marching across the grass towards them.

"But..." Sean said, confusion crossing his face. He turned when Adeline called his name.

"Sean, call from New York," Adeline said and Sean popped up, turning to apologize to Margaret.

"I've got to take this. A big deal in the works. Adeline, can you keep Margaret company?" Sean asked, already breezing past the two women and heading for his office.

"Anything for you, Sean," Adeline called sweetly over her shoulder, turning to stare daggers at Margaret.

Lovely, just lovely, Margaret thought as she slammed the rest of the trash in the bin. Her last day in Ireland was shaping up to be a real beauty.

CHAPTER 32

"You'll have to sit in my office, I'm busy this afternoon," Adeline said curtly, swinging her red hair behind her shoulder as she stalked off towards the warehouse. Casting a resigned look back at the park bench, Margaret almost declined to go with Adeline.

Except her curiosity was just too great.

"Have you worked for Sean long?" Margaret said, striding next to Adeline, looking down at the woman's leather leggings and wondering how they passed for suitable attire for a manager of a large fishing corporation. Deciding to bite her tongue, she kept her eyes trained straight ahead.

"Six months or so," Adeline said, offering no more.

"What'd you do before then?" Margaret asked and was surprised when the woman whipped around to get in her face.

"My prior work experience is none of your business," Adeline hissed and Margaret's eyebrows shot to the top of her forehead.

"My apologies," Margaret said, holding up her hands and wondering what particular brand of crazy Sean had gotten himself into with this one.

"Sit there," Adeline ordered, pointing to a chair across from her desk and Margaret slid silently into the chair, wondering just exactly why she was listening to this woman's orders. Probably because Margaret was fascinated by how Adeline had become a manager and just what she and Sean were to each other. Biting her tongue, she sat back to observe.

An hour later, Margaret's tongue was almost bloody from the number of times she had been forced to stop herself from speaking.

Sean's business was in trouble and Adeline was a mess. Margaret found it surprising that Sean hadn't noticed how horribly his company was currently being run. She cringed as Adeline put another call on hold to search a file cabinet full of over-stuffed folders to look for a purchase order.

If this had been her company, she'd have modernized everything by now and purchase orders would be tracked in the computer. Margaret watched in fascination as Adeline pulled out file after file, stuffing them back in no particular order, before finally finding the file she was looking for. On a little crow of satisfaction she returned to the desk.

"Hello? I've got the..." her voice trailed off as she looked in confusion at the phone. "Hmm, must've gotten cut off."

Or they realize that time is money, and messing around

with a company that takes ten minutes to locate a purchase order means they won't be a return customer.

"Can I ask a question?" Margaret asked and Adeline turned to glare at her.

"What?"

"Why aren't the purchase orders in the computer?"

"Because we don't have a system to manage that?" Adeline spoke slowly, as though she was talking to someone with the intelligence of a fourth-grader.

"Wouldn't your job be to find a software that does?" Margaret said, raising an eyebrow at her.

"What the hell do you even know about running a company?" Adeline seethed, tossing her hair over her shoulder again.

"Oh, I don't know, I only run one of the most successful real estate companies in Boston. You know… annual revenue in the millions," Margaret said easily, studying her nails as Adeline fumed at her desk.

"This isn't real estate. This is a large fishing corporation. You have no idea what you are talking about," Adeline bit out and then narrowed her eyes at Margaret. "What do you want with Sean, then? If you're not after his money?"

Margaret's mouth dropped open.

"Excuse me?"

"You heard me. Why are you sniffing around him if you don't need his money?"

"Is that really an appropriate question to be asking about your boss?" Margaret said, pulling out her "I mean business" look, which usually quieted even the most unruly of her employees.

"He's not just my boss," Adeline seethed, coming around to lean against the desk, her arms crossed against her chest, her gaze focused on Margaret.

"Is that so?" Margaret asked, feeling her heart clench and the beginnings of an "I told you so" from her subconscious trickling through her mind.

"We're dating. So I'd appreciate it if you'd back off," Adeline said.

"Dating? You're dating your boss? Isn't that unethical?" Margaret knew she should just drop it, but it infuriated her to think Sean had led her on.

"Listen, honey, I didn't come to this job for the title. I came for the man. Sean's one of the most eligible bachelors in the city. And I'm his perfect catch," Adeline said, running her eyes over Margaret, who suddenly felt frumpy in what, just this morning, she had thought were her cute jeans. Not used to direct competition from women over a man, Margaret decided to play it easy.

"Well, it's obvious you're not here for the job," she said sweetly.

"What's that supposed to mean?" Adeline said, straightening up from the desk.

Margaret swooped her arm around to the messy desk and overflowing file cabinets.

"It's a hot mess in here," she said.

"Well, I should be taken care of, not forced to work. Sean will see that soon enough," Adeline said, sniffing as she checked her nails.

"Ah, well, it looks like you've got it all figured out then," Margaret said, biting back the bitterness that welled up in her throat. She'd known it had been a risk to come to

Dublin to see Sean. She'd been stupid to think he wouldn't be involved with someone at this point in his life.

Even if that someone was a tramp like Adeline, Margaret thought on a sniff as she stood.

"Well, now that you've made yourself clear, you can tell Sean I'll be by the water when he's ready to take me to dinner."

"What do you mean, he's taking you to dinner?" Adeline blurted, worry crossing her face.

"Oh, didn't he tell you? I'm staying with him," Margaret said sweetly, slamming the office door on Adeline's curses.

Maybe it was small of her, but she couldn't help the smile that crossed her face as she strolled away from the office to the water.

Yeah, that had felt good.

CHAPTER 33

An hour later, Margaret found herself uselessly obsessing about Sean and Adeline. She wondered why she even cared – the whole point of her coming here was to prove that she and Sean didn't have a connection anymore. Or was that just what she was telling herself now that Sean had let her down?

Again.

Sighing, Margaret stood up as she saw Sean leave his building and wave to her. Pasting a smile on her face, she sauntered over to where he stood.

"I'm cutting out early so we can have a nice dinner," Sean explained, smiling as she approached.

Not wanting to bring anything up when she was sure that Adeline would be watching their interaction from her office window, Margaret smiled up at him.

"That'd be great. Where are we going? I'll probably need to change," she said, looking ruefully down at her jeans.

"Nah, you're fine. Just have to make one stop on the

way," Sean said with a smile, this time opening the door of his truck for her. Margaret wondered if he had forgotten about his earlier hint of anger or if he had just tamped it down for now.

Staring out the window as they pulled out of the lot, Margaret felt a rush of sadness go through her about all of the anger and past hurts they had caused each other. For such a short relationship, they'd certainly managed to explode a karmic boom into each other's lives. Margaret thought back to his use of the word 'tizzy' earlier and how it had enraged her. It seemed like they were just destined to circle each other and continue to cause hurt feelings. And now with another woman in the picture?

She'd been right all along to stay in Boston.

Margaret took a deep breath and began building her walls up again, knowing that she had been silly to drop them for a moment and think that she and Sean might have had a chance. Maybe she could just begin to look at him as an old friend instead.

Looking over at him fondly, she reached out and patted his thigh.

"Thanks for today. It was nice to see what you've built up," Margaret said, holding back her thoughts on Adeline and just what she thought that woman was doing to the business. It wasn't her place, after all. If Sean couldn't see the problems in his business, who was she to do anything about it? Margaret knew that she had a tendency to be controlling – as Keelin liked to point out often – and the last thing Sean needed after so proudly showing her his business was for her to tell him all the things wrong with it.

"I'm glad you came up. It was nice having you here," Sean said as he pulled into the parking lot of a small market. "Back in a moment."

Margaret watched as he jumped out and ran into the grocer, and wondered if he was picking up some wine or dog food for Baron. The market was charming, with fruit loaded into its front windows and a striped awning above. Quaint groceries were something that she often missed, living in Boston where goliath supermarkets ran the show.

Sean exited the market carrying a box in his arms, his face split wide in a smile. Margaret couldn't help but smile back at him, though she reminded herself it was just because he was a good friend.

That's all he really could be. Their lives were just too far apart.

"Baron sure eats a lot," Margaret commented when they were back on the road.

"Why do you say that?"

"Box of food?" Margaret asked, pointing her thumb at the back seat.

"Ah, sure," Sean said, grinning as he hit the remote for the gate to his house. Margaret glanced at the street to make sure her rental car was still intact and did a mental calculation of the amount of time she would need before her flight to Boston in the morning. She'd need to be in bed by ten at the latest if she wanted any semblance of good sleep.

Following Sean into the house, Margaret smiled as Baron trailed after him to the kitchen, his tail wagging, obviously ready for whatever was in the box.

"What should I wear for dinner?" Margaret called,

waiting in the hallway. Sean glanced up, his eyes trailing over her body, igniting heat low in Margaret's stomach.

"What you've got on is fine. Though I'd prefer less," Sean winked, and Margaret's eyebrow shot up.

"The restaurant is okay with jeans?" she asked, breezing past Sean's suggestive comment.

"Seeing as how I'm the chef, I can say that I approve of the jeans," Sean said, digging into the box and pulling out two bottles of wine.

"You're cooking?" Margaret said, surprise lacing her voice.

"Sure and you don't think I can't cook for you, do you?"

Margaret didn't want to offend Sean, but it was clear from the lack of cooking utensils in his kitchen that he didn't have much cooking experience.

"I'm sure it will be lovely," Margaret said tactfully, causing Sean to chuckle.

"Have no fear. I've got two shepherd's pies ready to heat. Ma O'Sullivan makes the best in the city. I'd be offending her if I tried to make it on my own," Sean said as he pulled two covered dishes from the box.

Margaret felt relief wash through her, then found herself laughing at Sean again when he looked up at her.

"You don't have to look so relieved."

"Well, I *was* going to point out your serious lack of anything to cook with in this kitchen, but I decided against it," she said as she slid onto a stool across from him.

"Right kind of you, then," Sean said, popping the cork on a bottle of red and dashing some of the liquid into a glass for Margaret. Sliding it across the counter, he waited while she sampled.

"Yum, this is a nice full-bodied wine. What is it?" Margaret asked, turning to peer at the label.

"A Grenache. One of my new favorites," Sean said.

"You're a wine guy? I always figured you as a Guinness man," Margaret mused, taking another sip of the wine.

"Sure and nothing can get between me and my pint, but a nice bottle of wine with a pretty lady isn't beneath me now and then," Sean said, sticking his nose in the air and pretending his pint was classier than the wine. Margaret laughed again, though she was unhappy to feel a little stab of jealousy shoot through her at the thought of Sean wining and dining other women.

Margaret really needed to stop. Sean was a friend. She'd certainly dated in the past twenty-eight years, and it wasn't like he was supposed to be celibate either.

"What's wrong?" Sean asked, having turned from setting the stove to heat.

"Hm? Nothing," Margaret waved it away.

"If you're sure?"

"I just need to get a few things organized before my flight tomorrow, is all," Margaret shrugged.

"Why don't you go do that now? We've got time. I'll get some cheese and fruit out for a snack with the wine."

"That'd be nice," Margaret said, sliding off her stool, taking the wine glass with her.

Baron followed her down the hallway and Margaret couldn't help but feel a rush of love for the little mutt.

He'd grown on her in such a short time and Margaret could understand why Sean kept a dog in the house.

Margaret took her time laying out her outfit for travel, checking her flight times, pulling out her passport. Debating briefly whether she should call Fiona, she found herself standing in front of the mirror in the guest room bathroom.

And wondering if she was really ready to leave.

CHAPTER 34

SEAN PULLED A few hunks of cheese, wrapped in brown wax paper, from the box and let his thoughts drift to where Margaret was packing in the guest room. It felt nice to have company in his house, even nicer that it was Margaret. He hadn't known what to expect from seeing her again.

Which certainly hadn't stopped him from getting a haircut and buying a brand new suit, he reminded himself.

And if he was being totally honest, once he'd seen the writing on the wall with Keelin and Flynn, Sean had started a weight loss program to get in better shape for Margaret's eventual visit. He'd known that there was no way she'd stay away from Keelin for long.

He hadn't been prepared for just how much of an impact she'd have on him when he saw her again. All of a sudden – she was just *there*. All beauty and light and buttoned up. Sean had wanted to walk across the rehearsal dinner and rip her primly buttoned blouse open to see if she was just as soft and warm as he remembered.

Having her show up at his door had been a blessing in disguise, and if Sean had anything do with it? She wouldn't be leaving either.

"Baron. What do you think about sharing your house, hey boy?" Sean asked down to the little dog that had wandered back to the kitchen when he'd heard food being prepared.

Baron wagged his tail, which Sean took for a yes.

Now he just needed to convince Margaret to stay.

CHAPTER 35

"*All set?*" Sean asked when Margaret came down the hallway a few moments later. She'd changed her top, a silky maroon blouse that clung to her curves.

And her underwear too. But Sean didn't need to know that.

"Yes, all packed and ready to go," Margaret said, holding up her empty wine glass.

"Ah, I'll get that," Sean said, smiling at her as he filled her glass.

"I've got us set up outside if you'd like to sit out there," Sean said, gesturing to his patio where a small table and two chairs sat. A fat candle sputtered in the middle next to a vase of flowers and Margaret found herself charmed.

"Flowers, huh?"

"Flowers for a pretty girl," Sean said, holding the door open with one hand and a tray of cheese in the other hand. Though the comment had been simple, Margaret found herself blushing like a schoolgirl.

"This is lovely," Margaret decided, as she sat on the chair and surveyed Sean's yard. Fairy lights were strung up along the fence, and Baron sauntered over to a rose bush standing in the corner and promptly lifted his leg, causing Margaret to snort out a giggle.

"Ah, yes, his favorite spot," Sean sighed, shaking his head as he sat across from Margaret, placing the board of food between them. "Try some."

Margaret took a sliver of cheese on a small cracker and groaned as it melted in her mouth.

"This is excellent."

"I let Ma O'Sullivan do all the pairings. She's excellent."

"So do you order dinner like this often?"

"Well, perhaps not this grandiose, but a few times a week I pick up meals from there."

Margaret sipped her wine and nodded. It wasn't far off from her life.

"A few nights a week I go to my favorite sushi place. Half the time I'm eating over my desk anyway," she said.

"Don't I know that," Sean agreed, clinking his glass lightly against hers.

"We're workaholics," Margaret said.

"We just might be at that."

"Do you ever see yourself hanging it up?" Margaret was genuinely curious. She wondered if Sean ever ached to travel. She certainly did.

"Sure, at some point. Colin's working on his MBA and he's expressed an interest in running the business. I'll most likely start grooming him to step into a role beneath me over the next few years," Sean shrugged and reached down to pick up a small ball at his feet. Margaret watched as Baron went on full alert, his eyes trained on the ball.

"Get it," Sean crowed, laughing as Baron scrambled across the yard to chase the little ball.

"That will be nice. To have family working for you," Margaret said lightly. She'd always hoped that Keelin would be interested in real estate but it had been the furthest thing from her marine biology-loving daughter's mind. Cooped up in an office all day? Definitely not Keelin's style.

"It will. And if Colin is closer then I can spend more time with Finn," Sean said, Margaret arched an eyebrow at him.

"I keep forgetting that you're a grandfather. God, we sound so old," Margaret said on a sigh, drinking more wine down.

"Age is in the heart, my love," Sean said as he stood, whisking inside to answer the beep of the oven timer.

And left Margaret stumbling over the word "love." Would it really be so easy to fall back into love with him? Margaret wondered how he could so casually throw that word out to a woman he barely knew. He must use it often, as a casual term of endearment, she decided as she bent over to pick up the soggy ball Baron had deposited at her feet. Gingerly holding it between her fingers, she tossed it lightly away from her and was rewarded when Baron barked joyously and sprung after it.

"Can you grab the door?"

"Oh, of course," Margaret said, jumping up and pulling the door open so that Sean could step outside, two steaming dishes of shepherd's pie in his hands. Margaret's eyes widened at the sheer mass of mashed potatoes on top of each dish.

"There's no way I can finish all that," Margaret said in alarm.

"That's okay. It heats up well as leftovers," Sean said easily and then stilled.

"You can take it to work with you then. I'll just eat out of one half of the dish," Margaret said quickly, guessing he had remembered she wouldn't be around to eat the second half of her dish in the morning.

"Sure, I'll do that," Sean said softly as he eased the dish in front of her, then took his seat. Leaning over the table, he raised his glass and held it in the air until Margaret picked her glass up and touched it to his.

"To new beginnings."

Margaret could only nod and sip, the wine burning a trail down her throat, as she wondered what she was walking away from.

CHAPTER 36

An hour later and almost a bottle and a half of wine gone, Margaret found herself snuggled up on the couch, laughing hysterically at Sean as he ridiculed her.

"And there you are in this prim blouse – all but threatening the world with the expression on your face," Sean said, talking about when she had walked into the rehearsal dinner the other night.

"I was not!" Margaret said, leaning over and smacking his arm as she laughed at him.

"Oh, you were. I think the entire room gave a collective gasp, wondering who the wicked witch was," Sean said, smiling as he tugged her arm down until she leaned against him.

"I can't help that my style is polished," Margaret sniffed.

"You can help that bitchy look on your face," Sean said and Margaret's mouth dropped open as she looked up at Sean, ready to argue.

And was silenced with a kiss.

Oh, but she'd been craving his hands on her ever since he'd thrown her over his shoulder the night of Keelin's wedding. That longing was all Margaret could think of as his lips slid over hers, kicking up lust low in her belly. Margaret found herself leaning into the kiss, all but crawling up his chest as they settled deeper into the couch. She'd be lying to herself if she said she didn't want this.

She'd changed her underwear, hadn't she?

Margaret moaned as Sean slid his tongue past her lips to dance against hers, dragging her further down into his heat, the press of his body heavy on hers. A feeling of rightness settled inside of her, shaking her more than the kisses he rained upon her face.

Maybe Fiona was right after all.

Sean could possibly be the one for her. Margaret's body certainly thought so, as she arched against his hard length, pressed to her very core, the beginnings of pleasure simmering below the surface. Margaret moaned as Sean tore his lips away from hers to pop the buttons on her blouse, exposing her nude lace bra. She shivered as his breath ran hot over her skin, trailing down her neck until he nudged the lace away to capture one very sensitive nipple in his mouth. Sensations pounded Margaret, threatening to overwhelm her as he brought her close to the edge with only his mouth, beginning to move gently between her legs in an even rhythm.

Margaret couldn't even think of the last time she'd tussled with a partner on a couch. So much of her love life had been dignified dating; now the wantonness of Sean's need tore at her, threatening to overwhelm her as her shields went down and his emotions poured over her.

Oh, she'd craved this. For so long. That true, honest connection of loving someone heart to heart. Margaret could feel it pulse from Sean, in a manner that almost scared her, only to be matched by her own desperate emotions. They touched each other like lovers lost, never knowing if they would have another minute together.

She supposed it was the only type of love they'd ever known.

A shrill ring from the coffee table distracted her and Margaret broke away to try and peek over Sean's shoulder.

"Ignore it," Sean ordered, continuing to unbutton her shirt.

"I can't ignore it. What if it's important?" Margaret asked. As a business owner, she knew that phone calls late at night were rarely good news.

"It's not. This is important," Sean said, looking down at her body like he wanted to worship every inch of it. Margaret shivered at his gaze. Pointing to the table, she nodded at him.

"Just answer it."

"Fine. Don't move," Sean cursed and pulled himself from her, leaning forward to answer his phone without looking at the caller. Margaret felt a strange sort of emptiness when he pulled away from her, but she took a deep breath, pulling her blouse closed a bit. It would be good not to get too carried away, she reminded herself.

She didn't even have any birth control, for god's sake, Margaret thought, almost slapping her head. Sure it hadn't really been an issue for the past few years, but she'd yet to hit menopause, and knowing her and Sean's history – well, it was best that she make sure they were covered, Margaret thought.

"Sean here," Sean barked out, his chest rising with his heavy breath. "Adeline, what's wrong?"

Margaret's hands stilled at the button of her blouse, her heart jumping into her throat.

"Is that really a discussion we need to have right now?" Sean said, lowering his voice, though it was useless to try to hide what he was saying when Margaret was a foot away from him. Margaret felt her newly vulnerable heart begin to shatter; she quickly finished buttoning her shirt as she cursed long and steady in her mind.

And began to build her wall back up.

"This isn't appropriate," Sean said, risking a glance at Margaret, his brows furrowing as he saw her sitting up, her arms crossed across her chest.

"Adeline, I can't answer that for you right now. I have to go," Sean said, not waiting to hear what she had to say before clicking the phone off. Turning to face Margaret, he raised an eyebrow at her buttoned-up appearance.

"It's not what you think," he began.

"Oh, it's exactly what I think," Margaret hissed, her blood beginning a slow boil as she worked herself towards mad.

"It's not. I swear. She can get a little…exuberant sometimes."

Margaret could feel the lie coming from him, her gift giving her the ability to read him like a book. It hurt – knowing what she had just been about to do with him –it hurt more than she had words for. She stood from the couch, needing to put distance between herself and him.

"You're lying," Margaret said from the other side of the coffee table, her arms crossed against her chest as she paced.

"I'm not," Sean said, lying again.

Margaret whipped her head around to glare at him, biting down on her lips as she forced herself to filter the words she wanted to say.

"Sean, do you remember when we first made love?" Margaret asked, turning to pin him with her gaze.

"I could never forget. One of the best moments of my life," Sean said, and Margaret knew it was the truth.

"What about after?" Margaret prompted him.

"Well, that was a little intense. But I'm okay with it now," Sean said, watching her carefully.

"Did you ever think about *why* the cove glowed with that light? About the touch of magic that runs in my family? In Aislinn's family as well?"

Sean looked uncomfortable as he shrugged a shoulder and nodded, "Well, sure. I've kind of had to come to terms with it, seeing as both of my daughters have...extra abilities."

"And did it ever occur to you that my daughter only has abilities because I do as well?" Margaret asked softly.

The silence stretched between them as Sean worked that out in his head, realization dawning across his face.

"I suppose I hadn't. I never thought too deeply into how it all worked, to be honest," Sean said.

"Well, let me clue you in on my lovely little gift. I'm an empath. Which means I can feel other's people's feelings and I can sure as hell tell when I am being lied to. And that load of crap you just served me was an out-and-out lie," Margaret seethed, reaching down for her glass, wanting to throw something.

And saw Baron under the table, cowering from her shouts.

Easing the glass back down on the table, Margaret stood silently across from Sean, her body trembling with anger.

"Listen, it's not what you think," Sean began and Margaret held a finger up to stop him.

"Did you sleep with her?"

"No, gosh, never, she's an employee," Sean said, stuttering through his words.

"Are you dating her?" Margaret asked, her eyes trained on his.

"I…I, well, yes, we've gone out to dinner a few times. Nothing major," Sean shrugged again.

"Did you kiss?" Margaret asked and wanted to scream as Sean blushed, nodding, this time his eyes on the floor in front of him.

"Just once. She threw herself at me after a couple glasses of wine. That's all it was, I swear."

"Well, she certainly seems to think differently," Margaret said.

"Maggie, I swear to you I don't have feelings for her. I only want to be with you," Sean pleaded.

"Do you? You say that, but you don't even know me! You didn't even think about the fact that I have an extra ability! Do you still 'love' me now?" Margaret shouted, her chest heaving. "Do you? Can you live with me knowing that I'll know every time you'll tell me a lie? Knowing that our daughter can heal people with her hands? That the cove will glow when we are near it? Are you telling me you're okay with that?"

Sean's face looked battered as he nodded at her.

"I think I'll be able to work through that. If I have you to work through it with me," he said quietly.

"I don't buy it. You left me before. Now you aren't really mine. This is just like last time," Margaret fumed and Sean threw his hands up in the air.

"Just like last time how?"

"You can't be alone. I'm surprised you aren't married again! It didn't take you long to stumble into a marriage the last time. And here I finally am and you're involved with another woman!"

"Well excuse me, princess!" Sean stood as he shouted, causing Margaret to draw back from where she leaned over the table. "I'm sorry that I can't just turn my life on and off whenever you decide to waltz into it. Maybe it's not all about you all the time."

"Excuse me? Nobody asked you to stop living."

"And yet I'm in trouble because I got married or I went on dates. Please. I've never once asked you about your sexual history. Have I?! I understand that you're an adult and need companionship. Hell, I've even wanted you to be happy. But you've no right to come back and yell at me because I've gone on some dates. Who do you think you are?"

Margaret's mouth moved, but nothing would come out. Anger pulsed at her from Sean, from herself, from everywhere.

She'd been stupid to come here. There was just too much history. Taking a deep breath, Margaret lifted her chin.

"Thank you for the hospitality. I'll just see myself out," she said stiffly.

"Oh sure, here we go," Sean shouted after her as Margaret hurried down the hall, desperately surprised to find tears blinding her vision. Shoving her travel outfit into her bag, she scooped up her toiletries from the bathroom, refusing to look at herself in the mirror. With one last glance around, Margaret grabbed her bag and her purse and left the guest room, heading straight for the hallway.

She stood for a moment, looking at Sean, shaking her head at him.

"This could have been great."

Turning, she opened the door and stalked outside, refusing to say goodbye to Baron because she knew that the tears would flow furiously if she did.

"There you go. Running away again. Just like you do every time," Sean's words carried to her just as the door slammed shut and it was all Margaret could do not to turn around to argue with him.

She wasn't running. He'd misled her. He should have been honest about his relationship with Adeline all along. Margaret comforted herself with those thoughts as she drove her car to a hotel near the airport, knowing she wouldn't get a wink of sleep anyway.

And wondered if she was running from herself or Sean.

CHAPTER 37

Sean threw a pillow from the couch at the door, furious with himself, furious with Margaret for running out on him again. He went to stand at the front window, hoping that she wouldn't get in the rental car.

Pressing his forehead to the glass, his heart clenched as he watched the taillights of her car wink over the horizon, disappearing from his life.

Sean wondered if it would be forever.

Baron whined nervously at his feet and Sean bent to pick him up, pressing his face into the dog's soft fur for a second.

"Sorry, buddy," Sean said, as he carried Baron back to the couch. Baron turned in his arms and looked toward the front door.

"I know. I didn't want her to go either."

Sean leaned back against the cushions and ran through everything that had just happened – from when he'd been about to lose his mind with lust, right up to when Margaret had slammed the door on his shout.

At least this time he'd gotten the last word, Sean thought, then sat up straight as an idea came to him.

Just because Margaret was repeating her old patterns didn't mean that he had to, Sean thought as he moved to the kitchen to find a notepad.

It appeared as though he had a woman to romance.

CHAPTER 38

SIX MONTHS LATER

MARGARET STUDIED THE large package that leaned against the wall across from her desk at her real estate office in downtown Boston. The worn brown paper was at odds with the sleek lines of her office, and she suspected she knew just who this package was from.

Margaret sighed and turned her chair to stare out of her window overlooking the Charles River. Though the rent was steep in this building, the views alone were worth it. Plus, Margaret knew keeping up appearances meant everything in this business – when new clients walked into the waiting room and were greeted with floor-to-ceiling views of the Charles, they were sold on using her real estate agency.

Margaret's hands clenched in her lap as she forced herself not to run across her office and tear the paper off of the package.

It had been months since she'd left Ireland. Months since she'd brushed against the potential for full-blown love with Sean. Every morning she told herself that she was lucky for having escaped what was destined for certain catastrophe. And every night she lay awake wondering what she'd missed out on.

It certainly didn't help that Sean had unleashed a campaign to woo her, Margaret sniffed. She'd come home to Boston determined to leave the past in Ireland, and had been surprised when a pot of daisies had shown up on her desk with a note the next week. Margaret hadn't missed the symbolism of the daisies, which were also known by the name marguerite in Europe.

I MISS YOU.

THAT'S ALL the card had said. It hadn't been an apology, but Margaret wondered if they were past apologies. At the time, Margaret had rolled her eyes at the card and shoved the note far into the depths of her desk, but the daisies had commanded a spot on her desk for the following week, where their cheerfulness seemed to poke at the sullenness that cloaked her.

The next week it had been roses and some expensive bath soaps. Margaret had stared in confusion at the gifts on her desk, wondering if Sean had gone off the deep end.

This time the note read:

I ALMOST WISH that you hadn't stepped back into my life, for I wouldn't feel your absence so strongly then.

. . .

"It's not my fault you don't have me," Margaret had said angrily, surprising her assistant and causing Margaret to blush. It wasn't typical for her to display emotion at work, which made her even more infuriated with Sean.

And the gifts hadn't stopped. Every couple of weeks a new gift showed up on her desk, a new card entreating Margaret to reconsider.

To give him a chance.

As the time grew longer since she'd last seen Sean, his gifts became more serious. Just a few weeks ago he'd sent her a stunning necklace of intricate crystals, twisted around golden wires. It was an elegant statement piece and the card held an even more stunning proclamation.

I hope that when you wear this, you'll think of me – my lips at your throat. My heart pressed to yours. Our love tangled together like the threads of this necklace.

Margaret was quite certain her face had turned sixteen shades of red before she stuffed the card into her desk drawer.

But she found herself wearing the necklace every day, running her hands over the stones, daydreaming of his touch. She always felt foolish when she caught herself in a daydream, and worked even later hours to make up for her lapses in concentration during the day. As the days wore on, Margaret worked harder, ate less, and slept in spurts.

Her clothes began to hang on her; Margaret wondered if she needed to take them to a tailor.

"Did you open it?" Katie, her bubbly assistant, peeked into her office.

"No," Margaret said, turning to look at her.

"Do you need some scissors?" Katie asked, tucking her stick-straight blonde hair behind her ear, her eyes wide and excited. It had been hard to keep the fact that she had an admirer from afar from Katie, and soon Katie had been rushing to greet the UPS man each week, hoping for another installment in the long-distance love affair.

"No, I don't," Margaret said. What she needed was some gumption to open the huge package that sat across the office from her. Margaret knew her walls were beginning to crumble, but she wasn't sure if she was ready for whatever lay beneath the brown paper.

"Have you called him yet?" Katie asked, leaning against the wall and crossing her arms over her chest as she eyed Margaret.

Margaret just shook her head sadly, not knowing what to say.

"You need to call him. That necklace alone had to have been really expensive. The least you can do is thank him," Katie admonished her and Margaret felt her shoulders hunch.

"I've sent him a thank you note for every gift," Margaret protested.

"A politely worded thank you note. He sends you declarations of love and you send him a corporate thank you," Katie pointed out, having been privy to a few of Sean's messages.

Margaret felt guilt creep up her spine.

"I don't know what to say," she finally said.

"Say what you feel," Katie insisted.

"That's what I'm having trouble figuring out," Margaret murmured. It was true. Her feelings for Sean were so conflicted she didn't know what to say to him. And as time went on and more gifts and sentiments rolled in, Margaret found herself being swayed by his pleas. But then she wondered if it was just the distance between them that was making her soften her outlook on things. It was all so confusing and jumbled in her head. She'd never felt like this before – in her orderly world, messy emotions had no part.

"Why don't you hold my calls for a bit?" Margaret asked.

"I will. But make sure you open this, and take some time to think about what you want to say to him. I suspect this is going to be even more dramatic than your last gift, judging from the size of it alone," Katie said as she closed the door behind her.

"Now or never, I suppose," Margaret said, standing and wiping her suddenly sweaty palms on her now-baggy black dress pants. Crossing the room, she examined the package, finding the plastic slip where a card and shipping note were concealed. Pulling the card out, she couldn't help but feel the pulse of love that came from the envelope.

Yes, she could feel things from inanimate objects, too. Margaret wondered how Sean would feel if he knew the extent of her abilities. Sliding her fingers beneath the envelope flap, Margaret pulled the card out.

This is us. I know what this means.

'This is us'? Margaret felt her heart begin to pound harder in her chest as she put the card down. She pulled at a corner of the brown paper, the sound of the tear seeming to echo across her office as she pulled the paper away from what she now saw was a painting.

"Oh...I just..." Margaret held a hand up to her mouth as tears leapt to her eyes.

The painting was done in dramatic acrylic paints, the blues of the water and the sky contrasting with the tan sand of the beach and the greys and greens of the cliffs jutting out proudly above the water.

It was the cove, glowing brilliantly for all to see, with the faint outline of a couple locked in an embrace on the beach.

Margaret knew instinctively that it was Aislinn's work, and she wondered when Sean had asked her to paint it.

How oddly appropriate that her daughter's half-sister would paint the most important moment in Margaret's life for her. The irony wasn't lost on her. But in it, there was beauty as well. The painting wouldn't have had the same impact if it had been done by another artist. It seemed to scream to her – *see? Can't you see that we are all connected?*

I get it now, Margaret thought. I get it.

None of it really mattered, the past, what had come of it. What mattered was the now, and who they were. Had they not tumbled onto the beach that night, none of this would have happened.

A soft knock at the door had Margaret's head whipping around and she quickly dashed the tears from her eyes.

"I asked to not be disturbed," she called.

"I know; it's just that you have a visitor. Oh wow," Katie breathed as she caught sight of the painting. "That's fantastic."

"Yes, it is," Margaret said, not knowing what else to say. "Can you tell my visitor to schedule an appointment? I would like to be alone this afternoon."

"Um, I can't really do that," Katie began and then Margaret's eyes shot to the door when she heard a voice.

"Sure and you don't think she'll turn her own mother away?"

CHAPTER 39

"WELL, ISN'T THIS lovely?" Fiona said, pushing past Katie to stand by the painting, hands at her hips. Her grey hair was combed neatly and she wore a white button down and khakis, much like every other day in her life. The only thing missing was her straw hat on her head and a bag of garden tools at her side.

"Mother!" Margaret said, feeling as though the wind had been knocked out of her. She rushed across the room to bend and give Fiona a hug, struggling with tears again as they embraced.

"I'll just leave you two. Would you like some tea?" Katie asked.

"That'd be lovely," Fiona said with a bright smile as she pulled away and scanned Margaret. A furrow formed in her brow as she examined Margaret's face.

"Why didn't you call me? It's clear that I'm needed," Fiona admonished.

"I'm fine," Margaret said automatically, causing Fiona to bark out a laugh.

"Fine? You've easily lost a stone. Your clothes are all but hanging on you. And I walk in to find you sobbing over a painting of the cove. You, my dear, are anything but fine."

"I'll just leave this here?" Katie asked tentatively from the doorway, crossing to set a tray with two cups on a small side table.

"Thanks, Katie," Margaret said, striding after her to close the door. "Mom, you can't just say stuff like that. I don't want the people at my company to think I'm losing it."

"Well, you're human aren't you? You're allowed to have a crisis once in a while," Fiona said as she sat in one of the soft grey leather chairs by the tea. "Come, sit."

And I'm being ordered around in my own office, Margaret thought with a sigh. Realizing that she actually wanted nothing more than a cup of tea with her mother, though, she sat and accepted a mug from Fiona gratefully.

"Beautiful office," Fiona said cheerfully and Margaret had to smile.

"It is. I love this building," she agreed.

"Yes, it's quite welcoming, while also making clear how powerful you are."

"Thank you – wait, back up. Why are you here?" Margaret asked, shaking her head in confusion at Fiona.

"You needed me," Fiona said simply and Margaret rolled her eyes.

"I would have been happy to fly you over – first class in one of those new sleep pods, too. We could have had Keelin come and done a nice girls' trip. I have no problem with you coming to visit. I just would have planned for it."

"You told me to come whenever. So I came whenever," Fiona said, smiling contentedly at her daughter.

"Well, I'm happy to have you, even unexpectedly. I'll have to rearrange a few appointments is all," Margaret said, crossing to her desk. "How long are you here for?"

"Two days."

"Two days? Why so short?" Margaret said, growing increasingly confused.

"I've herbs to cultivate. Things to do," Fiona shrugged, not really answering the question. One thing that Margaret knew is that Fiona was the queen of evading questions if she so chose. Shaking her head, Margaret scanned her appointment book for the next two days.

"Katie, can you clear me for the next two days? Except for the appointment on Thursday with Jan." Jan was the vice-president of Margaret's real estate company, and had also grown to be a close friend through the years. Margaret never canceled meetings with Jan.

"Will do," Katie sang back through the intercom. Margaret straightened and looked at her mother beaming at her.

"What?"

"I'm so proud of what you've built up," Fiona said.

Margaret immediately felt self-conscious. The part of her that had always wanted to prove to her mother that she could be successful on her own crowed in delight, and then the other part of her that had difficulty accepting compliments blushed.

"Thanks, Mom. That means a lot," Margaret said softly, crossing the room to sit and pick up her mug of tea again.

"I've always been proud of you, Margaret. But sometimes as a mother, you have to know when to let the birds fly on their own, so to speak," Fiona said, reaching out to pat Margaret's arm.

"Is that why you've never come to visit?" Margaret had asked this question before, but for some reason it still bothered her.

"You never wanted me to," Fiona said gently and Margaret knew that she was right. Too many buried feelings that Margaret hadn't had time to deal with when she was building up her empire and raising Keelin.

"I suppose you're right," Margaret said, as she smoothed a wrinkle in her pants.

"We can't change the past, my dear. All we have is now," Fiona said, her eyes crinkling at the corners.

"Speaking of now. Would you like to come to my place? I can get you set up in the guest bedroom and then we can explore a bit."

"Yes, that'd be nice."

Already thinking about where they should go for dinner, Margaret stood and caught sight of the painting again. It seemed to hum with energy, the sway of the waves and the thrust of the light seeming to brush against her skin. She itched to be back on that sandy shore, cradled in her lover's arms, the exuberance of youth shrouding her good sense.

"That's quite a gift," Fiona murmured, coming to stand next to Margaret as they examined the painting.

"It is at that," Margaret said, her heart beating faster even as she looked at the painting.

"This is a gift of love," Fiona observed.

Margaret shrugged, unable to deny her claim, but not quite ready to say the words.

"He's backed you into a corner," Fiona said on a laugh.

"Excuse me?"

"Sean. He's backed you into a corner. There's no way you can ignore something like this."

"Try me," Margaret grumbled, striding over to her desk to grab her purse from the bottom drawer. "Let's get out of here."

"If you insist," Fiona said with a smile, casting one more glance over her shoulder to where the painting stood, a clash of color and movement in the serene office.

Margaret suspected that Fiona would have more to say about the painting. Pulling the door closed behind her, Margaret shot Katie a look.

"Nobody is to go in my office on penalty of being fired."

"Yes, ma'am," Katie said, all but saluting as they breezed past her, Fiona's chuckle making Margaret's cheeks burn.

So what if she wanted to protect the painting? It was a nice piece of art. It certainly had nothing to do with her employees prying into her love life.

She didn't *have* a love life, Margaret reminded herself. Period.

CHAPTER 40

"Do you mind walking? It's about a mile and half," Margaret said, then caught herself trying to convert the distance into kilometers for her mother.

"I walk every day, Margaret," Fiona said and Margaret imagined her mother striding across the hills and climbing into the cove. A walk across downtown Boston wasn't going to faze her.

"So, this is the Charles River. My apartment is on Beacon Hill which overlooks the Commons, a main park here in town," Margaret rattled off as they began to walk from her office down a crowded sidewalk, where everyone was finishing up their day and leaving for after-work happy hours in the sun.

Margaret tried to see Boston through her mother's eyes. The crush of the after-work rush of people on the sidewalks, the honking from impatient cars stuck in traffic, and the distinct smell of city all combined to make this early spring day a chaotic image of a bustling metropolis.

Where Margaret saw the latest in street fashion, Fiona probably saw the annoyance of having to push past people on the sidewalk.

"It's happy hour," Margaret explained as they walked past a cabbie leaning against his car and talking into a Bluetooth headset, a Red Sox hat pushed low on his head.

"It's a lively town," Fiona said.

"That's a kind way of putting it," Margaret said with a smile as they came upon the Commons. "Much busier than you're used to."

"Different people crave different lifestyles. I've always found great comfort in being close to nature. Not all do," Fiona said, smiling as they waited for a walk signal at the intersection.

"I guess I was just always drawn to a busier way of life," Margaret said as they crossed the street and entered the gates of the garden side of the Commons.

"Nothing wrong with that," Fiona said, turning to marvel at the flowers in the gardens. Concrete pathways roamed through manicured lawns, past ponds, and through carefully landscaped beds of flowers.

"This is my favorite part of the Commons," Margaret said as they walked.

"I can see why," Fiona said. She gestured to where a bench sat across from a small pond. "Let's sit."

Margaret couldn't help but think about the last time she had sat on this exact bench. Keelin had come to her for answers about her past. Now she wondered if she would do the same with her own mother. Stretching out her legs, she leaned back and let herself absorb the tranquility. It seemed like she hadn't slowed down or left work early in months. This was a welcome break.

"Thanks, Mom. For coming here. I don't think I realized how much I needed you until I saw you," Margaret said, surprising even herself with her words. She kept her eyes trained on the pond, nervous about what Fiona would say.

"I think we've left some things unsaid that need to be worked through," Fiona said and Margaret jerked her head up to meet Fiona's eyes.

"I thought you were here to talk about Sean."

"I'm here to talk about a lot of things," Fiona demurred, watching Margaret's face.

"I don't know. I thought we had a pretty good talk at the cove," Margaret said, shrugging her shoulder.

"We did. But there's more to that talk that we didn't get through. Most notably one of the reasons you ran at the time – your power. My power. And, now, Keelin's power."

Margaret grimaced, not wanting to have this conversation, already working to put her mental shields up. She looked up when Fiona's hand touched her arm. Instantly, a wave of comfort washed through her, and she smiled at her mother.

"Thanks," Margaret said.

"I see you've come to terms with the power of touch," Fiona said, referring to her gift of healing.

"What other choice do I have? Both you and Keelin have this ability. I've fought it for a long time, but at some point, you just have to accept it."

"Why fight it at all?" Fiona asked, tilting her head to study Margaret.

For the first time, Margaret felt like her mother was seeking to understand why Margaret had reacted the way she did, instead of just trying to force a way of life upon her.

"It scared me. There's always been a part of me that craved a normal life. That was before I even understood how you could heal, though. Just knowing about my own ability – that I was different – made me desperately crave the normal. I used to pore over magazines about the States, and dream of one day leaving the tiny cottage in the hills and becoming this fancy metropolitan woman. And, well, here I am," Margaret said on a half-laugh as she looked down at her baggy pants. "Typically more well-presented than now, of course."

"What was it about accepting your gift that scared you so much?" Fiona leaned back, bringing her arm to lie across the back of the bench so her hand brushed lightly across Margaret's shoulder.

"I...I'm not good with feelings. Surprise, since I'm the empath," Margaret shrugged. "I find emotions to be messy. I'm not good at communicating them, I'm not good at responding to them, I'm just...closed down, I guess. So being handed this gift where I feel so much – well, it was hard to swallow. *Is* hard to swallow. I did my best to hide it, tack it down, not use it. I'm not sure if I will ever really accept it."

"Why do you have to accept it?" Fiona asked, causing Margaret's head to whip up.

"You always told me we have to use our gifts. That we mustn't turn our back on our powers," Margaret shot out.

"Maybe you don't have to accept it to use it. Maybe this is more about learning to live in peace with it," Fiona said gently, and Margaret turned back to study the water again.

"But I thought Grace O'Malley gets all angry if we don't use our power."

"Grace is but a spirit. She's only love. You have to know that. Whatever choices you make in this life – so long as you can live with them – are yours to make. Not mine, not Keelin's – not anyone's but your own. If you feel that you don't want to explore your gift and would rather not actively use it, by all means, go on with your bad self."

A laugh bubbled up in Margaret's throat as her mouth dropped open. "Go on with your bad self?"

"Ah, Keelin says it sometimes. Must be something the kids say these days," Fiona laughed with Margaret.

"So you're saying that if I just want to be – and am happier without exploring that side of myself – you're okay with it?"

"Of course," Fiona said simply, and Margaret felt a weight ease from her soul.

"Because I always felt like I made you angry by not following in your footsteps," Margaret pressed the issue.

"You made me angry when you left without giving me the dignity of a conversation. You hurt my feelings by not allowing me near my granddaughter. But you would certainly not make me angry if exploring your power makes you so wildly unhappy."

Margaret nodded.

"It does. I think one of the things I've learned about

myself is that I'm actually okay with not exploring more of that side of me. I like living a more normal life. I'm happy to shield that power as much as I can. I feel like I've finally come to really know myself – and that is me. Do you get that? Me is the person who has no interest in her power. I hope you can accept that about me. I do," Margaret said, meeting her mother's eyes.

"Oh darling, I do. I only want you to be happy. If you know your own mind on this, then so be it. I'm not going to hide who I am from you. I certainly don't expect Keelin to do so either. So, that is something you'll need to make clear to your daughter. She needs to understand your acceptance of where she is in her life. Especially as she starts forward in her new life with Flynn and working with me as a healer. She needs to hear that from you."

"Well, of course I accept her," Margaret stuttered out, crossing her arms over her chest. Hadn't she paid for the wedding? How could her daughter not know she accepted what Keelin did for a living?

"Then you need to tell her that."

"I will. I hadn't realized she didn't know. I suppose I haven't made that very clear, either," Margaret pursed her lips as she thought about it. "Okay, talk with Keelin this week. We're good on the whole using our powers thing?"

"We are right as rain, my dear. Now, I'd love to see that pub where they filmed the show Cheers."

"You know Cheers?" Margaret asked, laughing as she and Fiona stood.

"Of course. I do have a television, you know."

Margaret looked down at her mother's smiling eyes

and felt a pang for all the moments she had missed with her. Reaching out, she ran a hand down Fiona's cheek.

"I'm sorry we didn't have this conversation earlier," Margaret said.

"Everything in its own time," Fiona said, pulling her in for a hug.

And wasn't that just the truth of it?

CHAPTER 41

MARGARET SHOOK HER head as her mother ordered another round of pints. The tourist bar that had inspired the hit television show Cheers was a far cry from what she'd had in mind for an elegant dinner. Instead of linen tablecloths and a glass of wine, she was eating a burger and drinking an icy cold beer.

"If only Keelin could see me now," Margaret laughed at Fiona, surprised to find herself having a good time.

"This is good for you. Break out of those suits and fancy restaurants," Fiona observed as she took a sip of her beer.

"Looks like I'm making all sorts of changes this week," Margaret said, discreetly checking her phone.

"You check that phone a lot," Fiona said.

"Ah, yes, I suppose I do. Habit," Margaret said.

"It must be tough running your own business," Fiona said, stealing a fry from Margaret's plate.

"Well, I wouldn't say it's easy. But it is easier than it used to be. God, I remember when I was first starting out.

I'd have a toddler screaming at my feet while I tried to talk on the phone to potential clients. It's come a long way since then. Now I have Jan who takes care of a large share of the work, and a really great group of real estate agents working for us. Plus, our admin staff is wonderful. I feel like we've created a good culture. I try to offer the best of benefits to my employees and never pay a man more than a woman. I think it shows in the longevity of my employees as well. I have a fairly low turnover rate," Margaret looked down at her hand, surprised to find her pint glass empty.

"It sounds like you've done a wonderful job. Your office is beautiful, Katie's a doll, you're clearly successful – so why do you seem so unhappy?" Fiona asked.

"I'm not," Margaret said automatically and then paused, putting her hand up. "Okay, obviously I look like I'm unhappy because I've lost a little weight and haven't been sleeping well."

"Because of Sean," Fiona said, signaling the bartender for another round.

"No, most certainly not," Margaret argued.

"If it's not Sean then it's because you're unhappy with your work," Fiona said.

"I'm not. I love my job," Margaret said and then paused. Did she?

"Do you?" Fiona echoed her thoughts and Margaret glared at her.

"Stay out of my head."

Fiona chuckled and took a sip of her fresh pint. "I wasn't in it. But clearly I asked a question you were thinking."

"I suppose I am – I don't know. I'm not dissatisfied. I'm just not as hungry as I once was. It used to be a lot more exciting to solve the problems of a new business or work on organizing new processes. But now everything runs so smoothly that I'm not sure what else there is to do," Margaret admitted, surprised to realize that it was true.

"Can you sell it to Jan?" Fiona asked, turning to meet Margaret's eyes.

"Sell?" Margaret asked, genuinely shocked. She sputtered a bit and took a sip of her beer to calm herself down. The thought of selling her business made her palms sweat.

"Yes, sell. You could do something else."

"Something else? Are you crazy? I've spent my whole life working for this," Margaret argued, growing heated. "Don't you understand how hard I've worked to get here?"

"I do. And yet here you sit, a stone underweight, in wrinkled clothing, alone in a prestigious apartment in Boston. You can't tell me this is what you've worked so hard for."

It was like a punch to her gut – but who was she kidding? Fiona rarely pulled her punches. Margaret's mouth worked as she tried to process what her mother was saying. For every defense that popped into her mind, something else contradicted it.

"I don't think I ever thought it would work out like this," Margaret finally admitted.

"What did you want to happen?"

"I don't know. I guess I just saw myself falling in love with one of the doctors or lawyers that I dated, having someone to travel the world with, watching Keelin as she got through school...

"And now Keelin's gone and I haven't dated in a year or two and here I am," Margaret said, clinking her glass against Fiona's. "Cheers!"

"Sláinte," Fiona said quietly, watching her daughter carefully. "I just don't understand," Fiona said finally.

"Understand what?" Margaret said, staring morosely across the bar at a Sox fan cheering on the game.

"You've never been one to go down without a fight. You picked up and moved to another country when you didn't like what was happening. You started your own business from scratch. What in the hell is stopping you from living the life you want right now?"

Margaret gaped at her mother.

"I...I guess I don't know what it is that I want," she admitted.

"Well, I suggest you figure that out before you wither away," Fiona ordered. "Now, eat."

"Yes, ma'am," Margaret said, stuffing a French fry in her mouth and letting the salty goodness of fried potatoes melt on her tongue.

Suddenly, she was ravenous.

CHAPTER 42

"What do you want to do today?" Fiona asked from where she sat in the gilded front room of Margaret's apartment. Margaret had slept well for the first time in ages, and she wondered if she could attribute that to the beer she had drank or the first real meal she'd eaten in months.

"I was thinking we could walk around Faneuil Hall and maybe go to the aquarium? Or we could hit the shops?" Margaret asked, dropping a kiss on her mother's cheek and sitting on a settee done up in cream and gold fabric. She reached over for the mug of breakfast tea her mother had poured for her.

"Can we do one of those duck boats?" Fiona asked, her eyes lively with enthusiasm.

"You want to go on a duck boat?" Margaret raised her eyebrow at her mother. In all of her time living in Boston, she'd never gone on a duck boat. These crazy contraptions were half-boat, half-car. The passengers sat on top and were whisked around the city learning about the Freedom

Trail and other historical aspects from tour operators with thick Boston accents. The culmination of the ride came when the car/boat was driven into the water, touring along the Charles River. Margaret had always considered them to be tacky.

"Sure, it looks like fun."

"I suppose we could try that out. Not something that I've ever done, but I guess I could use a little fun," Margaret said, throwing her hands up.

"When do you want to leave?"

"I'll just change into jeans," Margaret said. The way she was going she'd need several new pairs of jeans. It seemed more and more she was finding herself in places that didn't require her dressy clothes.

HOURS LATER, Margaret laughed as her mother wore a lobster bib tied around her neck and cut into a garlic and butter soaked lobster. The duck boat had proven to be a wild ride, and Margaret had found herself enjoying every moment of the ridiculous tour. It had also given Fiona a chance to see a small snapshot of Boston. When Fiona's eyes had lit up with glee when they'd taken to the Charles River, Margaret found herself happy she hadn't tried to control their day.

After the duck boat tour, they'd wandered through the small aquarium on the harbor, shopped at Faneuil Hall, and now found themselves tucked at a casual seafood restaurant by the water.

"You should try the clam chowder. They say it's award-winning," Fiona said and Margaret laughed at her.

"Every restaurant in Boston claims to have award-winning chowder," Margaret said with a smile.

"Hmpf. Well you should try it anyway," Fiona prodded. Margaret had ordered just a crab cake, since she was used to not being very hungry these days.

"You know what, I will," Margaret said, flagging down their waiter and ordering a bowl of the clam chowder along with another glass of white wine.

"There you go. Need to put some weight back on you," Fiona observed.

Margaret sighed.

"It wasn't intentional."

"A broken heart will do that to you," Fiona observed.

"I am not broken-hearted," Margaret exclaimed.

"I would know, seeing as I'm the one looking at you. You seem to forget that I went through this once before," Fiona pointed out.

"Mom, I was just a kid then. Of course I was dramatically upset over Sean."

"I'm talking about me. When I lost your father," Fiona said quietly, her eyes meeting Margaret's.

"Oh, of course," Margaret said. "Sorry, I know not everything's about me. I get a little caught up sometimes."

"It's okay."

"Mom, I barely remember that time. I just know how distraught you were. It was like being sucked under by a huge wave of sadness. I almost couldn't breathe."

"And I'm sorry for that. I should have shielded you better. What was I thinking? Of course my empath daughter would be hit hard by my emotions."

"I wish I remembered more of him," Margaret said.

"Ah, he was a good man. Larger than life. Stubborn as all get out. And loved with the purest heart I've ever known. I was lucky to have him for the short time that I did," Fiona said.

"You never wanted to remarry?"

"No. That was a choice that I was given," Fiona shrugged.

"What do you mean, you were given a choice?" Margaret asked, genuinely curious. She'd never heard her mother talk this way about her father.

"Ah, that's a story for another time, child. Suffice it to say that I chose well, but another husband wasn't in the cards for me. I've made peace with that. And, I'm happy."

Margaret knew what it was like to live alone, and now she wondered if her mother was just as lonely as she was.

"Aren't you lonely?"

"Probably not as lonely as you are. I have friends, the village, my work; Flynn and Keelin are right over the hill. And Ronan. I'm busier than most could expect to be at my age."

"I suppose you're right," Margaret said, beginning to ask another question before she was stopped by her mother's finger pointing at her.

"Stop changing the subject. The point is, I know a broken heart when I see one. Tell me what happened with Sean."

Margaret opened her mouth to protest but then stopped.

"He was dating someone else," she shrugged and looked away, taking a sip of her wine to wet her now-dry throat.

"He was most certainly not," Fiona insisted. "That man is not a two-timer."

"I don't know. We had a big fight, I could tell he was lying about dating her, and I stormed out," Margaret said miserably, pushing her crab cake around on the plate.

"So you ran."

"I ran," Margaret said, looking up to thank the waiter for her bowl of chowder.

"Fix it," Fiona said.

"I don't know if I can," Margaret pleaded.

Fiona drew back and glared at her, making Margaret feel like she was ten years old again.

"That man sends you gifts. How many months later? The only thing you need to fix is your damn head," Fiona said.

"Mother! He lied to me about being involved with someone."

"Oh, please. He wasn't involved with her. And even if he had been, that man has eyes for nobody but you."

"How do you know that?"

"I've got eyes of my own, don't I?"

"I don't think it's as easy as you think it is, Mother. There is a lot of history between us. So much buried anger and hurt feelings. We keep cycling around and arguing about past hurts."

"Bah," Fiona waved her hand at Margaret, "you waste precious time arguing about the past. For what? To make you more miserable. Stupid. If only you could understand how fleeting this life is – you would embrace love with everything you had and fight for it. No matter what."

Margaret saw the emotion in her mother's eyes and knew that she spoke of her husband.

"I'm sorry, Mom. I'm sorry if this seems foolish to you. But they're my feelings."

"So work through them. You hold on to stuff for so long you'll end up dying alone, withered to a stringbean in your gilded cage of an apartment."

Anger flashed through Margaret.

"You don't get to come here and tell me what to do," she leaned across the table and hissed at her mother, glancing around to make sure the other diners didn't hear her.

"I most certainly do when you're all but killing yourself over a man that you're too stubborn to love," Fiona shot right back.

"I am not too stubborn to love him," Margaret all but shouted.

"So what's stopping you, then?"

CHAPTER 43

The question echoed through her head on the walk home. Margaret hadn't been able to answer Fiona's question and, to Margaret's relief, Fiona had eased up on her interrogation when the waiter came around with the dessert menu.

"Would you like an after dinner whiskey?" Margaret asked stiffly, as they entered her apartment door.

"Yes, please," Fiona said, moving to turn on the lamps around her sitting room.

Margaret crossed to her wet bar and poured a glass of Middleton Rare for both of them, then walked across the room to settle into a chair. The ringing of her cell phone from her purse jolted her and she moved across the room to unzip the flap and pull her iPhone out.

"Keelin, at this hour?" Margaret said with a raised eyebrow, calculating that it would have to be after midnight in Ireland. Her heart began to race as she wondered what could be wrong.

"Keelin, baby, are you okay?" Margaret asked immediately, turning to meet Fiona's concerned eyes.

"Mom, I'm great. Everything's okay," Keelin's voice rang out. Margaret could feel her joy through the phone so her panic instantly subsided.

"It's awfully late there. I'm just sitting down with a whiskey with your grandmother," Margaret said, moving to sit down. She reached across the table and gently clicked her glass against Fiona's.

"Oh good, you're both there. I was hoping she would still be up."

"I'm not that old," Fiona grumbled, having heard what Keelin had said.

"She says she's not that old," Margaret said with a smile.

"I have to tell you something," Keelin said.

"Go ahead, love," Margaret said, smiling over at Fiona.

"I'm pregnant! I'm not that far along. Maybe even a matter of weeks. I know I'm not supposed to say something this early but I just took a test and Flynn and Ronan are the only ones I can tell and I'm just so excited and I just had to tell you and since I couldn't run across the field to tell Fiona…" Keelin rambled on, gushing with excitement.

"You're pregnant?" Margaret's mouth dropped open and she turned to Fiona. "She's pregnant!"

"I know," Fiona said simply and Margaret glared at her.

"Fiona says she already knows."

"I knew it! I knew she knew when she told me to start

drinking more milk," Keelin fumed. Margaret gave her mother the stink eye.

"I can't believe she didn't tell me," Margaret complained, looking at her mother.

"It wasn't my news," Fiona said gently, holding her hand with the glass up to toast her granddaughter through the phone.

"She's toasting you. And so am I. I'm so happy for you, darling," Margaret said, finding tears had crept into her eyes.

"You'll come. Right? You'll come out and help won't you?" Keelin said, fear slipping into her voice.

"Of course I'll come. We'll both be there for you," Margaret insisted.

"Okay, Flynn is making me get off the phone since he has to get up at five in the morning. Give Fiona a kiss for me. I love you!" Keelin sang out and Margaret ended the call with a sigh.

"A baby!" she squealed and then blanched. "I'm going to be a grandmother!"

"Old woman," Fiona cackled at her.

"Hey, that makes you a great-grandmother," Margaret pointed out and Fiona stilled.

"Damn it. You're right."

"Is it a girl?" Margaret asked, raising an eyebrow at her mother.

"Now how would I know such a thing?" Fiona stuck her nose in the air.

"Oh like you didn't know what Keelin was? Please, you told me when I was four weeks along that she was a girl." Margaret laughed at her mother, surprised to find they could talk about that time without pain or resentment.

"It's a girl."

"Woohoo!" Margaret crowed and then stilled, a worried look crossing her face. "So she'll have a power."

"Aye. It'll be fine. She's got all of us to help her," Fiona said gently.

"You're right. It will be fine," Margaret said.

Except she wouldn't be there – at least not all the time. Margaret had her business to run, after all.

She stared into her whiskey glass, Keelin's news kicking around her head.

"What are you thinking about?"

"Just how often I'll be there to help her, I guess," Margaret shrugged and sipped her whiskey.

"It's not that bad of a flight," Fiona pointed out.

"I know. It's not always easy to get away from the business, is all," Margaret said.

"Isn't that the point of owning your own business? To be able to leave when you want?"

Margaret huffed out a short laugh. "One would think so. I just feel like I always need to be checking in with things, I guess."

"Tell me something – do you have savings? An investment portfolio?"

"What do you know of investment portfolios?" Margaret laughed at her mother.

"I have one. A very nice one. How do you think I've been able to give away so many of my healings for free over the years?"

"You have an investment portfolio? Really?" Margaret

asked.

"I do. It's diversified and everything. I live off the distributions. I don't need much to live on anyway – I have no debt."

"I suppose that's true," Margaret said, marveling at this new aspect of her mother she had never seen before.

"So? Have you saved money over the years? Or spent foolishly?" Fiona asked, raising an eyebrow as she looked around at the lavish furnishings of Margaret's sitting area.

"I've saved. Yes, I've spent my fair share of money. But you'd be surprised how much I've been able to put away over the years. I'm all set financially," Margaret said.

"So you don't need the business for money anymore," Fiona stated.

"No, at least not really. It's a nice extra cushion but, yes, I could certainly live off my investments and savings," Margaret agreed.

"Then it seems like you have some thinking to do," Fiona said as she rose, taking her whiskey glass across the room to set it by the wet bar sink. "I'll leave you to that. I'd like to get some sleep now. I'm still on Irish time."

"Sleep well. We can talk about plans tomorrow. I just have that meeting with Jan and then I'm all yours."

"I can't wait," Fiona said with a smile as she left the room, heading down the narrow hallway towards Margaret's luxurious guest room.

"Now, if only *I* could sleep," Margaret murmured, turning to stare out of her window at the Commons lit up at night. Time passed as she stared into the night, her whiskey glass clutched in her hand and her future laid at her feet.

CHAPTER 44

"You look tired," Fiona observed from where she sat with a cup of tea and the paper. Margaret tucked her hair behind her ears and smiled brightly at her mother, though she felt like her smile was probably bordering on manic. She certainly felt that way inside.

"I didn't sleep much, or at all really. I've moved up my meeting with Jan so we'll have the rest of the day. I'm just not sure how long it will take," Margaret chattered as she stormed around the room, collecting her purse, a few file folders that she had spent the night reviewing, and a notepad. Grabbing a to-go cup, she bypassed her mother's tea and poured steaming coffee into her cup. Bending over, she kissed Fiona's cheek quickly.

"Call you in an hour or two. Relax. Take a bubble bath. Or walk down Charles Street. There are some lovely boutiques. Key's in the Hermes dish by the door."

"Good luck," Fiona called, just as Margaret hit the door at almost a dead run.

"Why do you say that?" Margaret asked, turning to look at her mother.

Fiona smirked and just sipped her tea quietly, turning the page of the paper.

"Fine, forget it. Bye," Margaret said, hurrying from the door to her elevator. After waiting impatiently for the elevator doors to open, Margaret decided to bypass the elevator. She took the stairs two at a time until she bounded into the lobby, almost running over her doorman in the process.

"Sorry, Frank!"

With a little laugh, she let herself onto the street, hurrying past people on the sidewalk, their faces but a blur as she ran through details in her head. Her body buzzed with adrenalin, the nervous jitters making her hand that gripped the folder shake a bit. In record time she reached the front stoop of her office. Standing back, she made a slow perusal of the brownstone building, with red begonias in pots out front and black shutters lining the windows. Margaret had a right to be proud of what she'd built up, she thought as she breezed through the doors with a quick wave at the receptionist.

"Margaret, I have some phone messages for you," Katie called as Margaret made her way back towards her office.

"Not right now, please," Margaret sang and bypassed her office to head toward the conference room in the back. Pushing the door open, she was pleased to see Jan already working on a laptop at the long mahogany table. Margaret had always loved this conference room. With cushy chairs, a gorgeous table, and an entire wall of windows that showcased the view of the Charles River, it always made an impression on their clients.

"Morning," Jan looked up from her computer with a smile. With short cropped dark hair, brilliant blue eyes, and an eye for perfectly tailored business suits, Jan was a no –nonsense businesswoman with a heart of gold. She'd been a pleasure to work with through the years and had deserved every promotion she'd gotten.

"Hi Jan, how are you?" Margaret asked, moving to sit in her spot at the head of the table.

"I'm good. I have this quarter's sales reports here. We've outdone ourselves again," Jan said, slipping right into business mode as she flipped open her folder. It was something that Margaret had always appreciated about her – she was never one to waste business time on gossip and personal life. That was for happy hour, naturally.

"Tea? Coffee?" Katie asked, poking her head in.

"Tea, please," Margaret said and Jan nodded her agreement.

Margaret turned her chair away from the table and steepled her fingers on her knee, looking out the window at the river. A rowing boat, out for practice, zipped past the window, the girls cheering in the boat. It looked like fun, Margaret thought.

"Margaret?" Jan said, pulling her attention back to the table just as Katie came through the door with a tray and pot of tea. Margaret waited while Katie poured mugs for them both.

"Anything else?" she asked brightly.

"No, thanks Katie. Love your blouse, by the way,"

Margaret said, and Katie beamed at her in thanks before slipping from the room.

"Okay, so back to these figures," Jan said and then stopped when Margaret held up her hand.

"Jan, I've been up all night."

"Why? What happened? Is something wrong?" Jan asked, her face immediately creased in concern.

"No, actually, I think everything is right," Margaret said, turning from the window and taking a sip of her tea before flipping her folder open. Silently she handed Jan a stapled packet of papers.

"What is this?" Jan asked and then began to read. "Wait…"

Margaret laughed as her friend's face flashed quickly from concern to joy.

"I'd like you to buy out the company," Margaret said simply, and watched as Jan's mouth moved but no sound came out.

"I spent all night reviewing the assets, had a very early morning phone call with my disgruntled and annoyed accountant, and I'm prepared to sell the entirety of my interest for that number."

"But…but this is below what it's worth," Jan protested.

"I know. But it's still more than I started with," Margaret said, rolling a pen between her hands.

"Margaret, as your friend, I would have to advise you against selling for this price," Jan began and Margaret raised her hand again to stop her.

"Jan, you've been with me every step of the way. Even months I could barely afford to pay you or had to pay you a smaller paycheck in order to keep the lights on here. Not only are you a dedicated employee, but you are a loyal friend. There is simply no one else I would trust to hand my business to. I know you'll take care of everyone here. I trust you'll continue to run the business with the same ethics and values that have made it what it is today. The price I am offering it to you reflects all of that. I hope you will accept it," Margaret said.

Jan swallowed and Margaret saw a sheen of tears in her eyes. She was surprised to feel emotion welling up in her own throat.

"But what are *you* going to do? I can't imagine you not being a part of this business," Jan whispered.

"I'm going back to Ireland. It's time. Keelin's pregnant and I have unfinished business there," Margaret said, surprised to find that the words felt good. This decision felt good; her gut told she was doing the right thing.

"Oh, this is even worse. You're leaving the business *and* the country." Jan covered her face with her hands and Margaret stood up, moving around the table to crouch and put her arm around her friend.

"It'll be okay. It's only a six-hour plane ride. You love to travel. It'll be an excuse to come visit me. Plus, you haven't finished reading the contract. I have a stipulation in there."

Jan sniffed and turned to hug Margaret quickly before paging through the contract. When she saw the stipulation, she let out a hoot of laughter.

"Of course you can always stay at my house when you come back to visit. And since it's in the contract – I suppose that I'll be on a plane to Ireland once a year as well."

"So is that a yes?" Margaret asked, finding her stomach had twisted into knots. This was a huge decision, and part of her was surprised to find that she was making it so quickly.

"Are you sure you don't want more time to think about this?" Jan asked, reading Margaret's thoughts easily.

"No, I know what I want," Margaret said.

"Then let me get on the phone with the bank," Jan said, flipping to the back page and signing the contract with a flourish. She pushed it back over to Margaret.

Margaret held her favorite pen for a moment, looking at the last page with her name typed neatly under the signature line. Funny how years of hard work could be signed away in a moment, she thought.

Taking a deep breath, Margaret put pen to paper and rolled the dice on a new life.

CHAPTER 45

"I've brought lunch," Margaret sang as she bounced into the apartment two hours later. She had spent some time with Jan going over processes, as well as calming down a tearful Katie. She'd also promoted Katie and given her a handsome bonus to pack up her office and ship everything to Dublin once Margaret called for it.

Including the glorious painting Sean had sent.

"I'm in here," Fiona called and Margaret pulled up short to find her mother in the kitchen, wrapping dishes in newspaper and placing them gently in boxes.

"Mother, what are you doing?" Margaret asked, placing the box of pizza down on the table.

"I'm helping to get you packed. You'll need to decide what you want to donate and what you want to ship over. Is there a service that can come help?" Fiona asked, turning to smile brightly at her daughter.

"Jesus. You don't miss a trick, do you?" Margaret sighed, brushing a kiss across her mother's cheek before pulling out two plates. "Sit. You're about to have some of the best pizza you'll ever eat."

"I'm in," Fiona said, stopping what she was doing and plopping down at the table as Margaret reached into the box and pulled gooey slices of pepperoni pizza out and heaped them onto the plates. Reaching for paper towels, she plunked the roll between them on the table and sat down with a sigh, savoring the heavenly scent of pizza.

"I should've bought this pizza more often," Margaret mumbled over a mouthful of cheese and garlic.

"It's excellent," Fiona agreed, looking up at Margaret. "So? How'd it go?"

"Well, obviously you've used your super-secret psychic powers to already figure out that I sold the business," Margaret said grumpily.

"Or I overheard your conversation with your accountant this morning on my way to the bathroom," Fiona said sweetly and Margaret laughed.

"Fair enough. It went well. Jan's over the moon about it and I'm moving too fast to let it all settle in. I'll probably have a good cry on the flight over tomorrow with you but for now – I'm in action mode."

"Tomorrow? You're coming back with me?" Fiona said, delight flitting across her face.

"Yes, and I've upgraded us to first class. I love those little pods that let you stretch out and sleep."

"Thank you. Are you sure you're okay with this, though? It *is* moving a little fast," Fiona asked, worry lacing her voice.

"I've always moved fast, Mother. When my mind is made up – I move on it. Period. I'll deal with the emotional fallout later. But this time, I'm trusting my heart and my gut. Both say I'm making the right decision for me at this time. And even if Sean laughs in my face or we can never be in a relationship again – there are so many other things I can do. I want to be in Ireland not just for Keelin – but for you as well. I feel like we are finally building a friendship and…well, I don't want to lose that," Margaret admitted softly.

Fiona reached across the table and squeezed her hand.

"Then welcome home, my love. I couldn't be happier to have you back."

"I love you, Mother," Margaret whispered, realizing how rarely she said it.

"I love you too. Now, what needs to get done before our flight tomorrow?"

Moving out of emotional mode and back into take-action mode, Margaret stood from the table.

"I have a huge pack of stickers in my purse. Basically we need to label everything as ship or donate. I'll pack a few bags of clothes to come with me right now, and the rest can be shipped over later. Jan and Katie are taking care of it, as a going-away gift for me."

"They are good friends. I'm glad you've had them in your life," Fiona said, holding out her hand for the stickers.

"I know. I've already stipulated that I'll fly them over once a year, so it won't be so hard to miss them. I think my biggest struggle will be that I am going to feel like a fish out of water! No need to check my phone constantly. I can't imagine what I'm going to do with my time,"

Margaret said, stepping to the hallway that led to her bedroom.

"I suspect you'll figure that out pretty quickly," Fiona called after her.

"I can only hope you're right," Margaret said as she opened her closet and began the task of picking out what she would need for a new life in Ireland. Nerves trickled up her spine as she stared at a row of business suits. Would she ever even need a business suit again? Taking a step back, Margaret sat down on her bed and thought about her dilemma for a moment.

"Three good suits. The rest can be donated or Jan and Katie can take them. On to more casual wear," she decided, stepping to the closet to pick out a black, grey, and cream business suit. Laying them on the bed, she turned and pulled open a closet full of her shoes. Groaning, she wondered how she would choose between her favorite shoes.

And refused to let the worry that wanted to trickle in sway her from her decision.

CHAPTER 46

"I can't believe I'm here," Margaret marveled as they bumped along the lane in Fiona's SUV on the way to her cottage.

"It'll set in soon enough," Fiona said cheerfully, reaching over to pat her daughter's leg before pulling to a stop in front of her cottage.

Margaret had decided to come back to Grace's Cove first before figuring out her plan of attack for Dublin. First, she needed to squeeze her baby girl. Then she'd figure out the rest of her life.

"I still can't believe I just up and sold my business and came back to Ireland," Margaret said again, feeling a little shell-shocked now that her rapid-fire decision making had come to a stop and the dust was settling a bit.

"Change is good for the soul," Fiona said serenely.

"Says the woman who has lived in the same cottage for over forty years," Margaret said, raising an eyebrow at her mother as they got out of the truck.

"Ah, well, there are other ways to change that don't

involve a location change, you know," Fiona sniffed and hauled her small bag from the back of the truck, leaving Margaret to carry her own luggage to the cottage.

"You've got wifi in this place, right?" Margaret asked, looking around the main room before taking her first bag back to her childhood room.

"Of course. What do you think I am? Ancient?" Fiona sniffed and Margaret covered a smile as she went to get the rest of her luggage. An internet connection was all she needed to get started on an apartment search in Dublin. She was also seriously considering doing some volunteering so as not to be stuck with too much free time. Margaret wasn't comfortable with being idle.

Margaret settled her bags in a corner. Stretching, she worked out the aches from the flight, stopping to make use of the little bathroom before joining her mother in the main room.

Fiona moved to the sink and pushed the window open, encouraging a spring breeze to sweep through the house. A joyous bark had her jumping back from the sink.

"Ronan!" Fiona squealed and dashed out the door, Margaret following in her wake with a smile on her face. She turned the corner of the house to see Fiona on her knees, hugging an ecstatic Ronan as he wiggled in her grasp, desperately swiping his tongue across Fiona's face.

"I think he may have missed you," Margaret suggested, laughing at the pure joy on Fiona's face.

"I just love this dog," Fiona agreed.

Margaret's head popped up at a shout from the hill. Looking up at the ridge that separated Flynn's land from Fiona's, Margaret saw Keelin standing there with another dog. Waving, she found herself starting to half-laugh, half-cry as Keelin stumbled down the hill and raced to her. In moments they had their arms around each other and were doing their best to not turn into a weepy mess.

"I'm sorry," Keelin gasped out, pulling back to wipe her eyes. "I'm just so emotional."

The dogs raced in circles around them, barking out their joy.

"Hormones," Margaret said, wiping her own eyes with a laugh. "Oh, let me look at you." Holding Keelin at an arm's length, she examined her daughter for any changes. Other than the slightest of curves at her waist, nothing would have given away the fact that she was pregnant.

Aside from the pulse of love that Margaret could read coming from Keelin's womb. She stopped for a moment and studied the feeling, realizing that it comforted her to be able to feel her granddaughter's emotions from within the womb. It was an unexpected twist to her ability that she had never really realized she had.

"I can feel her," Margaret said in awe, itching to reach out and touch Keelin's stomach, but not wanting to be rude.

"Her?" Keelin gasped and Margaret slapped a hand over her mouth.

"It, I mean, it," she rushed to correct her slip.

Keelin began to laugh, dancing around her mother and Fiona.

"Fiona! Is it a girl?"

"Aye, it is. Though this one should learn to keep her mouth shut," Fiona said, glaring over at Margaret.

"That's okay. I wanted to know. I already suspected. I swear I can hear her whispering to me in my dreams."

"Sure and this one's going to be a powerful one," Fiona agreed. Margaret stiffened as she imagined what difficulties the baby could put Keelin through.

"That's okay. Flynn and I can handle it," Keelin said, easing the tension that had worked its way into Margaret's shoulders.

"I'm so happy for you," Margaret said and Keelin whirled to dance over to her mother again.

"I can't believe you're here! How long is your stay?"

Margaret cast Fiona a look before smiling at her daughter.

"That's undetermined."

"What do you mean?" Keelin asked, confusion crossing her pretty face. "Is something wrong?"

"No, of course not. I sold the business is all. I'm here for the foreseeable future. Well, probably up in Dublin, but much more accessible than if I was in Boston," Margaret said, hurrying through her explanation in order to ease Keelin's worry.

"Shut. Up. You sold the business? I can't…I don't even know who you are!" Keelin exclaimed dramatically, causing Margaret to laugh.

"It was bound to happen at some point. I couldn't keep running it my whole life," Margaret said gently.

"Yes, but the business is your baby. Did you sell it to Jan? Oh, I hope you did. Or Katie. I love them both," Keelin said eagerly.

"Yes, I sold it to Jan. And promoted Katie. They are ecstatic and under strict orders to visit once a year."

Keelin squealed and danced again. "Yay! I can't wait to show them my world. So, how long are you in Grace's Cove for?"

"Probably a week. Then I need to get settled in Dublin."

Keelin stopped and gazed at her mother, a knowing expression crossing her face.

"You're going after Dad, aren't you?"

Margaret blushed. It sounded so unladylike when Keelin put it like that.

"We'll have to see what happens."

CHAPTER 47

"I'M REALLY PROUD of you, you know," Margaret said to Keelin as they sat in the sun on Fiona's picnic table. Typical of Ireland in the spring, the week had been full of moody days and this was the first chance they'd had to enjoy the sun. Fiona and Keelin had spent the week working on their craft, while also bottling and creating new elixirs and tonics. Margaret had even found herself dutifully labeling jars at the table, her old resentment over doing this type of work gone.

"You are? I was worried that you weren't happy with me coming back here to learn about healing," Keelin admitted.

"I can't say that I was ecstatic about it. I'm in a better place with it now. More accepting. More understanding, I suppose. I don't want you to think I wouldn't be supportive of anything you do. I'm your mother and I'll always love you," Margaret said truthfully, realizing she probably should have said this to Keelin a long time ago.

"Thanks Mom. That actually means a lot to me,"

Keelin said, blowing out a big breath in relief as she stretched her legs out from the table and lifted her face to the sun.

"Well, I should've said it sooner. I think I've been caught up in my own unhappiness," Margaret admitted, surprised at her admission to her daughter. She supposed it was her month to learn and grow.

"You have been unhappy. For a long time, actually. I'm just glad you decided to shake it up a bit," Keelin said, turning to meet her mother's eyes. "All I want for you is to be happy too."

"Oh honey, I'll be fine. No matter what. You don't have to worry about me," Margaret said, reaching out to squeeze Keelin's hand.

"Being fine and living your life to the point of happiness are two totally different things," Keelin pointed out. "Grace showed me that."

Margaret stilled.

"Excuse me? Grace did? Is that a friend of yours?" she asked hopefully.

"No, Grace O'Malley. She appeared to me, you know. She's appeared to all of us. Except you…unless you haven't told me?" Keelin asked, raising her brow at her mother.

"The Grace O'Malley appeared? As a ghost? No, I'm sorry, I can't say I've had that specific delight," Margaret murmured, shaking her head in disbelief at her daughter. Maybe hormones were making Keelin a little loopy, she thought.

"She did. When I tried to heal Flynn and almost lost my life. She let me make a choice about choosing love.

I'm surprised she didn't show for you, back when you moved to Boston," Keelin mulled, dismissing the craziness of her encounter as she tried to figure out why Margaret hadn't had a sighting yet.

"Keelin. You know this sounds a little crazy, right?" Margaret broke in.

"It's true, though. You should know by now that anything goes in the cove," Keelin said simply.

"I suppose," Margaret murmured, unsure what to do with this new information.

"Listen, I have to go get the horses fed and dinner on for Flynn. We'll come over for breakfast tomorrow before you head out, okay?" Keelin said, jumping up to bend and give her mother a hug.

"Should you be feeding the horses? Don't the stable hands do that?" Margaret asked in concern.

"I like to help. There is one who's close to foaling; she likes it when I come around. I'm able to soothe her," Keelin explained.

"That's sweet. Can I come by tomorrow and see her before I go?"

"Sure, we'll do breakfast at our place," Keelin beamed at her before whistling to Teagan, Flynn's Irish setter, and setting off across the hills. Margaret marveled at her ease in this world, surprised to find that her daughter fit into the fabric of this community far more naturally than she ever had.

"Grace O'Malley's ghost," Margaret said out loud with a huff. It kind of annoyed her that she had never been singled out for a visitation from the mighty Grace O'Malley, yet everyone else and their mother seemed to be on chatting basis with the ghost.

"That's it," Margaret said on an oath, standing up and striding across the fields towards the cove.

It was time to tackle her destiny head on.

CHAPTER 48

Fuming, Margaret made her way down the cliff path, collecting rocks and flowers on the way down, Ronan racing ahead of her towards the beach. She'd never been much of a dog person before, but between Baron and Ronan, Margaret was now sold on the animals. They provided great companionship, and Margaret was happy to have Ronan's company as she descended into the cove.

It felt weird being back here on her own. Rarely had she come here without Fiona because the cove had creeped her out, even as a child. Reaching the bottom now, she stood for a moment, surveying her surroundings.

The sand beach stretched before her, the sand dark with the remnants of yesterday's rain. The rocky cliffs jutted into the sky around her, the sun beginning its descent into the sea, the rays piercing through the opening where the two cliffs almost met. Today the water was anything but peaceful, raging in waves that battled each other before crashing onto the beach, mirroring the painting that Sean had given her.

"How appropriate," Margaret said drolly, before stepping onto the sand and drawing a circle around her with the toe of her shoe.

"Ronan, come here," Margaret ordered, unsure if she needed to protect the dog or not, but knowing that Fiona would be devastated if anything happened to him. Ronan ran over to her side and sat inside the circle, seeming to know the drill.

"Um, we come in peace," Margaret began and then laughed at herself. It wasn't like she was on an alien planet. "I mean, we come here for the purest of purposes and mean no harm. Please accept these gifts," Margaret said, pulling her hand back and launching the rocks and flowers into the water. Margaret watched as the sea seemed to reach up and accept her gift, swallowing the rocks and dragging the flowers under. Deeming her work done, Margaret stepped gingerly from the circle.

And immediately jumped when a huge wave slammed the shore, water rolling close to the tips of her shoes. Ronan whimpered and jumped back.

"Oh, knock it off. I know you're mad at me. But guess what? I'm mad at you too!" Margaret shouted, then felt ridiculous as she realized she was screaming at a big pool of water.

The waves subsided gently and Margaret sniffed.

"Thank you," she said, beginning to walk gingerly down the beach. She knew where she was headed.

Directly to the small alcove sheltered by rocks where she and Sean had forever changed their lives.

Reaching the rocks, she sat on one and watched the play of the light on the waves and the rocks, feeling the undeniable press of power against her skin. There was no way she could ever hide from what she was or whence she came. Anger rose unbidden into her throat.

"Grace O'Malley! Show yourself this instant. I will not put up with you trying to mastermind my fate!" Margaret screeched, standing and putting her hands on her hips.

"Grace O'Malley! I know you're here. Stop hiding. You're a better woman than that, aren't you? Oh powerful and mighty pirate queen?" Margaret shrieked again, her voice echoing off the cliffs. The waves built in intensity as her words crashed through the cove and Margaret turned her gaze on the water.

"I said Knock. It. Off!" The waves died instantly and a cool, placid blue water greeted her.

"Thank you," Margaret acknowledged, her nose in the air.

"You've always been a stubborn one."

A voice like honey on razor blades sliced through her and Margaret straightened, a chill racing down her spine. Turning, she greeted Grace.

"Great, great, great, great grandmother? So nice to finally be acquainted with you," Margaret said stiffly, though her body hummed with adrenalin from being this close to Grace.

Grace stood by the rock wall, the sun's rays slicing through her figure and illuminating her, making her seem to glow in vivid colors. A ruby red dress with miles of lace and pleating covered the ghost. Gold winked at her throat and her wrists, and Grace held her head proudly.

Pirate Queen indeed, Margaret thought, worry beginning to ratchet through her as she realized just how powerful Grace O'Malley was.

Grace's mouth quirked in a small smile at Margaret's words.

"Well, what is it, child? You seem quite angry."

"Why did you show yourself to other people and not me? Don't you have great words of wisdom to impart to me?" Margaret realized her tone sounded petulant, and she wanted to kick herself.

"It wasn't time to show myself to you," Grace shrugged delicately.

"It wasn't *time*? You don't think you could have been of help – oh, I don't know – twenty-eight years ago or so? You ruined my life with your little light show," Margaret spat out.

"The cove is charmed. It wasn't me who ruined your life. And even if it had been, you can't blame your choices on anyone else. You have free will, after all," Grace said.

"That's not fair. You knew what would happen with the light. You knew Sean would leave me." Margaret felt herself digging her nails into her arms as she tried to push down on the anger that clawed its way up.

"So? We all have lessons to learn in this life. It wasn't my job to make things easy for you," Grace said, her chin high, regal as ever.

"You've got to be kidding me. You can't make things easy for me? Your own offspring? That's ridiculous," Margaret scoffed.

"My own offspring who refuses to accept the gift that I have bestowed upon her. One who judged her very own mother – one of the greatest natural healers this world has known. Your mother saved thousands of lives over the years, after making the ultimate sacrifice – choosing to stay with you and heal others over her own love life. And you expect me to help you, selfish child? No," Grace said, shaking her head, "I don't think so. Sometimes the hardest lessons must be learned without interference. That is a mother's love."

Margaret felt shame wash over her and her heart began to pick up speed.

"What do you mean, my mother made the greatest sacrifice?"

"She chose you, child. Over saving your father. Over the love of her life. Someday you'll know the story," Grace said gently.

"But…I thought he died of a heart attack."

Grace just shook her head at Margaret, refusing to speak.

"Okay, fine, I'll ask my mother someday. But you can't blame me for how I felt when I was younger. Or how I acted. I was just a kid. I'm not that person anymore," Margaret protested.

"I don't blame you for who you were. You had to learn the tough lessons to get to where you are now," Grace said.

"But you still don't want to help me, because I won't accept my gift," Margaret said.

Grace just shrugged again and looked out over the water. Margaret recognized the tactic; it was one she often used in negotiations. Silence is a powerful tool.

"Look, I admit I'm not comfortable with my gift. But can't you support me in knowing my own mind? Maybe I am not the person you think that I am. Maybe I am happier when I can shield myself from everyone's emotions and live my life normally. Isn't that the real definition of accepting myself? Knowing what works best for me?" Margaret asked, beseeching Grace to understand her point of view.

Grace considered Margaret's words for a bit, before nodding once.

"Your power will leave you when you've learned the final lesson you were put on this earth to learn," she said finally.

"Wait, what? Really? You'll take it away?" Margaret asked in astonishment and then realized that she was talking to the cliff wall of stones. Whirling, she looked out over the now calm water. "Grace? Hello?"

Silence greeted her.

"Well, what the heck does that even *mean*?" Margaret seethed, finding herself just as unsettled as she had been when she first came down into the cove. Grumbling, she whistled to Ronan and began the hike out of the cove, wondering just what else it was she was supposed to learn.

CHAPTER 49

*S*HE WAS STILL pondering that same question the next day as she sat on the train, her luggage in storage above her head. Margaret hadn't considered the fact that she would probably need to buy a car, so she'd booked a last minute train ticket to Dublin and had waved everyone goodbye from the station.

Margaret hadn't told anyone about her meeting with Grace. It still felt too raw – too undecided – to her. But now she was kicking herself – because what if that was her last lesson? Maybe she was supposed to be more open about sharing her troubles with her family.

Sighing, Margaret sat back and watched the countryside flash by her window. It was another rainy day, the broody grey sky matching her mood perfectly. Margaret pulled out her folder and began to review some of the apartments she had looked at online this week. She wasn't quite ready to make a decision, so she'd booked a lovely-looking boutique hotel right by Christchurch Cathedral in downtown Dublin. She planned to stay there a week and take her time touring the city before she decided which area she would prefer to live in.

And decide just how to let Sean know she was back in town.

He needs your help, you know.

Fiona's words echoed in her mind. Her mother had issued that statement on the flight over from Boston, jerking Margaret out of a dozing state.

"Excuse me?" She'd asked.

"Sean. He needs your help. He won't tell anyone, but his business is failing. Flynn told me he'd been up to Dublin just last week and the office was a mess, Sean has lost weight, and they were behind on shipments," Fiona had said evenly as she'd unfolded her blanket.

"I'm not sure what that has to do with me," Margaret had said, honestly confused by the way her mother's mind worked at times.

"You'll figure it out," was all Fiona had said on that matter.

Margaret circled back to the conversation, sipping from her water bottle, as the countryside raced by. She could only conclude that Adeline had run the business into the ground. It wasn't like Margaret could do much about it, though. Not only had she and Sean parted on bad terms, but she'd never worked in the fishing industry before. She'd be like a fish out of water.

Margaret groaned at her pun and shook her head.

But she found herself flipping the sheets of paper that held apartment listings and scribbling on the backs. Soon a plan began to form.

An hour later, Margaret breezed into the lobby of her

hotel. She nodded her appreciation of the grey and neon green accents, along with the bright white orchids on the white marble counter of the front desk.

"Hello, welcome to Crocket and Harrington, how can I help you?" The front desk woman beamed a chipper smile at Margaret.

"I have a reservation, but I have to ask. Do you have any business suites? With a desk and a printer?"

"We do. I'd be happy to change that up for you, let me just pull your details up."

Margaret waited as the woman scanned the computer, her mind whirling as she considered possibilities.

"And you're booked for a week. Is that still the same?"

Margaret leaned on the counter and smiled at the woman.

"Do you have monthly rates?"

The woman raised her eyebrow but only nodded as she clicked the keyboard a few more times.

"We do have one of our business suites available for the month." The woman quoted a rate that would have normally had Margaret's stomach dropping, but with the sale of her business, she was feeling a little flush with cash.

"That's fine. I'll take it," she said easily, feeling the pressure of needing to immediately find an apartment ease from her shoulders. "Oh, and can you recommend a place nearby to buy a car?"

"To rent a car, you mean?" the woman asked, clarifying for Margaret.

"Nope, I need to buy a car."

"My cousin's in the business. He'll give you a discount

if you say you know me," the woman said cheerfully, opening her purse and pulling a card out.

"Thank you. You're quite kind," Margaret beamed back, the two women in perfect accord as women who liked to get things done.

"Henry will take your bags up. Let me know if I can help with anything else at all," she said with a smile, sliding the key across the counter.

"Thank you."

Margaret rode the elevator up, all but buzzing with nerves and excitement. She barely noticed her bags being delivered, stepping briefly away from her laptop to hand Henry a tip. Sitting back down, she opened a word document.

Typing the word 'RESUME' across the top, Margaret got down to business.

She could only hope she was making the right decision.

CHAPTER 50

MARGARET PULLED HER new car – a VW convertible Bug – up to the gates of Sean's warehouse and waited for the gate operator to open the chain link fence and wave her in. Margaret drove her car to the visitor parking, nerves clenching at her stomach as she parked.

She'd had great fun negotiating her car purchase that morning, the salesman honoring the discount she'd been promised. Though her business sense told her to buy a more practical car, she'd been drawn to the cheerful red VW Bug. Deciding to throw caution to the wind, Margaret had passed by the more sensible sedans and plunked money down for the happy-looking convertible.

Facing the door into Sean's warehouse, Margaret wiped suddenly sweaty palms on the trousers of her black Prada business suit. She'd accessorized with a black and white polka dotted blouse and screaming red pumps that matched her new car. Her hair was pulled tidily back and she'd taken extra time with her makeup. Unsure of how she would be greeted, Margaret counted to ten before she got out of the car, pulling a leather portfolio and Prada purse with her.

Steeling her nerves, Margaret walked confidently into the warehouse, ignoring a whistle from where trucks were being loaded across the warehouse. Her back ramrod straight, she clipped across the cement floor to the line of glass offices, bypassing Adeline's to where she knew Sean's office was situated. Arriving at the door, she paused for a moment, suddenly nervous about knocking. The blinds on his windows were closed, but she could see light behind them. Someone had to be in there.

Taking a deep breath, she knocked loudly.

"Come in," Sean called and Margaret gulped, swallowing past her dry mouth.

"You can come into my office any time," a worker called from across the room, cementing Margaret's determination to open the door.

Fluorescent light washed over her as she pushed the grey door open, and she stopped mid-stride, her mouth gaping open at the sight that greeted her.

"Sean!" Margaret exclaimed.

"Maggie?" Sean asked in confusion from where he sat at his desk.

Fiona was right, Sean had lost weight, Margaret thought as she stared at a visibly smaller version of the man she had last seen six month ago. Dark circles ringed his eyes, and his clothes looked rumpled and slept in.

And his office…

Well, his office was disastrous, Margaret thought as she looked around, her mouth still gaping. Piles of folders covered every square inch of available space – the floor, the visitor's chairs, the tops of file cabinets. They were piled on the table behind Sean's desk, and towered precariously high on his actual desk, all but hiding the man behind it.

Sean stood and crossed to her, slamming the door closed behind her before dragging her under with a mind-numbing kiss that all but made her forget why she was there.

"Wait, wait," Margaret gasped, pushing back from Sean as she panted for breath. Reaching up, she wiped lipstick from his lips gently.

"You came," Sean whispered, his eyes alight with hope.

Margaret wasn't sure where to start. She hadn't exactly come to jump straight into his arms, but he looked so pitiful she couldn't bring herself to contradict him.

"I did," she said cautiously, pushing him lightly back another step, "and I see that it's not a moment too soon."

Margaret gestured to the folders and Sean winced, running his hand through his hair, causing it to stand on end and making him look a little crazy.

"Sorry for the mess. I'm kind of doing damage control," Sean said sheepishly, his cheeks pinking as he looked around at the disarray.

Margaret sighed, knowing just who was to blame for the chaos she was looking at.

"Adeline?"

"Adeline," Sean concurred.

"Sean, sit down. I have a proposal for you," Margaret said, marching over to Sean's visitor's desk and sweeping the file folders off of one of them. Gingerly wiping the seat clear of a layer of dust, she settled onto it, keeping her nice purse on her lap and reaching into her portfolio.

Sean's eyes narrowed at her as he rounded the desk and sat. Moving a pile of papers and folders aside, he crossed his arms over his chest and leaned back in his chair.

"Go ahead."

"First of all, I want to thank you for all the lovely gifts."

Sean raised his hand to stop her.

"Are you here for business or personal, Maggie?" Sean asked, reading her correctly, hurt washing across his face.

"Both, actually, but I'd like to start with business," Margaret said.

"Then don't lead with the personal," Sean suggested bitterly and Margaret realized her mistake.

Sighing, she leaned back in her chair and contemplated her words carefully.

"I want to talk about the personal. And I believe I owe you – well, we owe each other – an honest discussion about that. However, since it looks like you're in crisis mode here, let's start with business."

Sean considered her words before nodding.

"Fine, continue on."

"Great, okay," Margaret blew out a breath and then reached into her folder to hand Sean a piece of paper.

"Resume?" Sean asked, reading the top line of the paper and then looking over the top of the page at her. Looking back down, he began to read, his eyebrows shooting up in surprise. "From what I am gathering – this is your resume?"

"Yes. I'd like to come work for your company," Margaret said, excitement racing through her as she thought about the unique challenges that would come with hauling his company out of near-disaster.

"You want to work in the fishing business?" Sean asked in confusion. "I thought you loved real estate. What about *your* business?"

"I sold my business," Margaret said, the words coming out more easily each time she said them.

"You sold your business?" Sean asked in surprise and then narrowed his eyes at her. "Hey, I don't know what you've heard, but I'm not some damn charity case, okay? I can take care of my own business."

Margaret almost lashed back, but then bit her tongue, thinking about how she would feel if someone had come to her business and offered to save it. She imagined she would be hurt and embarrassed. Taking Sean's feelings into consideration, Margaret proceeded carefully.

"I'll expect to be paid, of course. And this really has nothing to do with you and everything to do with me," Margaret said, pointing her nose in the air.

"Is that right?" Sean said sarcastically, raising an eyebrow at Margaret.

"It is. I realized I was bored. I miss being back in the thick of things and building a business up. Mine was up and running, smooth as could be. There were rarely any problems. Nothing to fix," Margaret looked around at the pile of folders again. "I realized I'm a fixer. I want to solve problems. So, here I am."

"And you heard my business had a problem how?"

"Fiona," Margaret said simply, seeing no reason to lie.

Sean groaned and rubbed his hands over his face. "Which means Flynn knows."

"Listen, they care about you. It's not your fault some trashy gold-digger ruined your company," Margaret said pointedly.

"She *was* a trashy gold-digger," Sean agreed, causing Margaret to break out in a smile.

"You're the one who dated her," she joked.

"Hardly. You know that was never really a thing, right?" Sean asked, his eyes searching hers.

"I suppose I do now. I just felt like we were walking on stilts with our new beginning and anything could push us over. Adeline pushed us over," Margaret said softly.

"So does that mean you'll give me another chance?" Sean asked, hope filling his voice.

"Am I hired?" Margaret countered.

"You're hired."

"Then, no. I don't sleep with my boss," Margaret said primly.

She ducked as Sean chucked a ball of paper at her and then they both burst out laughing, tears leaking down their faces.

"Oh, I needed that," Sean gasped. "I've missed you, Maggie."

"I've missed you too. Now, let's get to work."

CHAPTER 51

And work she did, Margaret thought gleefully three weeks later as she pulled up to what was now known as her spot at the warehouse.

"Morning Ms. O'Brien," a worker called respectfully, and Margaret waved cheerfully back at him.

"Good morning, David. How was your date last night?"

"Great. I'm taking her out to dinner this weekend. Any suggestions?"

Margaret paused and looked through her phone, finding the name of a florist and a nice restaurant for David to take his date to.

"How's the baby, Matthew?"

"She's teething, but doing as well as can be," Matthew said ruefully. Margaret patted him on the shoulder.

"It'll pass soon enough. Try some whiskey on her gums," she called over her shoulder as she headed into her office, already checking through her email on her phone. In a matter of weeks, Sean's employees had gone from catcalling strangers to friends, and she felt like a surrogate mother/girlfriend/best friend to them all. Sean had good employees; he'd just needed a good manager.

And hadn't he found one, she thought as she entered her office and put her purse in her desk.

She'd done a very quick renovation of the space, painting the wood-planked walls a pale grey, and adding several lamps around the room so she never had to turn on the awful fluorescent lights that lined the ceiling above. Margaret had installed a new desk, and fresh flowers sat on the side table. Switching on the radio, she moved behind her desk and buzzed the intercom.

"Susan, will you come in please?"

Susan O'Leary had been a hire Flynn had recommended and she'd been worth her weight in gold. Staying late every night, Margaret and Susan had quickly categorized the folders, and had installed a new software system to track orders. Her first meeting of the day would be to discuss the new website that she'd solicited a design team from downtown to handle; they were already back on track with their orders. The employees had taken to the new software system easily, and more than one had thanked her for streamlining the process.

Sean had learned within a day or two to get out of her way; now she just saw him when he stopped to drop lunch on her desk and insist she take a break.

"Hi Margaret," Susan said as she stepped into the office.

"Susan, you look lovely today," Margaret complimented her assistant's new blouse as she turned to her laptop.

"Thank you," Susan said, sitting down with a notepad.

"Okay, today we need to respond to New York on that proposal that got botched a few months back," Margaret began, rolling her eyes.

"I swear…what didn't that woman mess up?" Susan wondered.

As Margaret had began to shovel out the mess Adeline had created in her brief time at the company, she'd found more than the markings of an inefficient manager. Adeline had also been embezzling funds. Margaret and Susan had been able to piece enough evidence together that Sean was with the local authorities this morning. Margaret would never admit that she took satisfaction knowing Adeline would likely be going to jail for a bit. But…secretly a part of her did.

"Nothing we can't fix. And, speaking of that, I'd like to thank you for all the extra hours you've put in over the last few weeks," Margaret said, handing Susan an envelope.

"You don't have to thank me," Susan waved Margaret's words away. "I like a challenge."

"I understand, but you still have children to feed. I know your mother and your husband have been helping while you were here late," Margaret said. Susan opened the envelope and her mouth dropped open at the numbers on the check inside.

"This is…this, no, I can't take this," Susan said, sliding the check back across the desk, further cementing Margaret's belief that she was a great employee. "It's too much. That's more than two months' salary!"

"You've earned it. Consider this a bonus and a thank

you. Take it or I'll mail it to your husband and insist he deposit it," Margaret threatened. She knew the family could use the money, and watched as the decision to accept battled across Susan's face.

"Then, I'll accept. Thank you. This will go a way towards relieving a few of our debts," Susan said gratefully, slipping the check into her pocket.

Margaret smiled at her, happy that she would take the money.

"Website meeting in an hour. Will you sit in on that?"

"Me? I don't know the first thing about websites," Susan admitted.

"Do you ever go on the internet to order things?" Margaret asked.

"Sure, here and there."

"Well, then you have the right qualifications. I want the website to be easy to navigate. You'll offer good insight," Margaret insisted. She paused as Sean stuck his head in the door.

He'd already put some of his weight back on, Margaret noted, and his skin looked less grey. She couldn't help but feel a low tug of lust when she looked at him. Working around him these past few weeks had certainly proved challenging, as she was constantly forced to tamp down on her libido.

"Susan," Sean nodded at Susan, then looked at Margaret. "I'd like to talk to you, please."

"I can leave," Susan said, jumping up and breezing past Sean with a "thanks for the bonus" comment on the way out.

Margaret grimaced. She hadn't wanted Sean to know about the bonus, as she'd paid for it out of her own funds.

"What bonus?" Sean said, closing the door and coming to sit in the chair across from her.

"Oh, I just gave her a small bonus as a thank you for all her hard work," Margaret said quickly, ducking to dig in a drawer so as not to meet his eyes.

"Interesting. I didn't see anything about a bonus on the books when I went through payroll this morning," Sean said, his voice carrying an undercurrent of anger. Margaret popped up and met his eyes, realizing that he thought she was lying to him. She supposed he had a right to be angry, as he had just come from dealing with an embezzling employee.

"I paid for it out of my pocket," she said stiffly.

"And why is that?" Sean's voice was low, causing the hair on the back of her neck to stand up.

"Because I've looked at those same books and I know you can't afford a bonus right now, seeing as you're coming out of a financially precarious time."

Sean sighed and looked up at the ceiling, clearly counting to ten.

"If you want to give an employee a bonus, please come to me," he said stiffly.

"But Sean, I know you can't afford it. I can. And I wanted to do this. She deserves it," Margaret pleaded her case.

"Yes, I know you can afford it," Sean exploded, standing up and pacing her office. Margaret drew back, clamping her mouth shut as she watched him pace. "I understand that you're rich. That your business was so damn successful, and mine isn't. I get it. But you don't need to wave it around in my face."

Sean slammed the door as he stormed out of the office, blinds banging against her window.

"Well, I never!" Margaret fumed. "Ungrateful man! After all I've done to help."

Her intercom buzzed.

"Everything okay?" Susan asked.

"I have no idea," Margaret answered honestly. "I suppose I'll have to find out. See you at the meeting."

Getting up, Margaret smoothed her jeans and straightened her blouse. She'd learned quickly that Sean's business was not one that required suits and heels. Especially if she didn't want her Prada smelling like fish. A few days in, she'd switched to wearing jeans and a nice blouse to work.

Margaret tapped tentatively on Sean's door. When there was no response, she peeked her head in to find his office empty.

"Out by the water," David called helpfully and Margaret smiled her thanks. "I think you'd better let him take you on a date soon," he added.

Margaret stopped and tilted her head at him in question. "Excuse me?"

David smiled and pushed his cap up, jerking his thumb towards the field outside.

"The bossman. He's been mooning after you ever since you left. It hasn't gotten better since you've gotten back, either. You'd better take pity on him soon before he blows a gasket," he offered cheerfully.

Margaret supposed that, since she gave David dating advice, she couldn't exactly reject his opinion.

"Thanks, I'll take that under consideration," Margaret said dryly as she moved past him and out towards the picnic table.

"Go get 'em, boss!" David called cheerfully and Margaret waved over her shoulder, half amused and half annoyed that her private life was on display.

Stalking across the grass, she found Sean sitting at the picnic table where she had last sat when she'd not wanted to go back into the warehouse and deal with Adeline. Squaring her shoulders, Margaret came to stand over him so her shadow blocked the sun.

"Do you have a problem with me?" she asked, ready for battle.

"Maybe I do," Sean said, looking past her, out toward the water.

"I refuse to apologize for being a successful businesswoman," Margaret said, her voice cracking. "I worked really hard for that. I would think you – of anyone – would understand that."

Sean sighed and shook his head. Turning, he patted the bench next to him.

"Sit, please."

Margaret sat, her arms crossed and back straight.

"I'm sorry. I know you worked really hard and were wonderfully successful in your business. I guess it's just a little...emasculating to have you come in and clean up the mess I've made of things," Sean admitted sheepishly.

Margaret felt her heart immediately softening.

"Sean, I'm really impressed by what you've built up. You have a quality operation with long-term employees who care about you, and you run wonderful tours. I am in awe of what you've done. It's not your fault things fell apart. You trusted an employee who screwed you over. I've had to fire employees before and deal with difficult times in my business. Things didn't always run smoothly for me either. That isn't a reflection on you. That's just business. Problems come up. You fix them. That's all."

Sean surprised her by reaching out and running a finger down her cheek.

"It's not just you coming in to fix everything," he admitted softly.

"It isn't?" Margaret said, finding herself breathing a little faster as she met his eyes.

"No, it's you. You're driving me crazy!"

"I am?" Margaret asked, her heart clenching a bit.

"Yes!" Sean shouted, shoving away from the picnic table to pace in front of her. A lot of yelling and pacing this man was doing this morning, Margaret thought as she watched him carefully.

"You just come back here, clean everything up in my life, looking gloriously beautiful while you do so. And I'm left drooling after you every day. Making excuses to stop in your office. Keeping my blinds open so I can catch a peek of you zipping around the warehouse. Wanting to punch David and Matthew and everyone else as you laugh and joke with them every day. *I* want to laugh and joke with you," Sean steamed.

"You *can* laugh and joke with me," Margaret ventured.

"I can't! You were the one who put up the 'no flirting with the boss' rule. You've swept back into my life, but you keep me at a distance with a ten-foot pole," Sean shouted.

Margaret glanced over her shoulder to make sure there wasn't anyone nearby.

"I'm not keeping you at a distance," she began.

"Bullshit," Sean said, bending over and bracing his arms so that Margaret sat caged between them. Her pulse picked up and she found herself unconsciously wetting her lips.

"I am just really trying to work hard and help you. You looked so lost when I came back, like you were fading away," Margaret whispered.

"I was fading away. Without *you*. Not because of the business. Why can't you see that?" Sean begged, and Margaret's heart all but skipped a beat.

"Really?" she asked.

"Really. I swear, I've been a lovesick puppy with you gone. Half the reason I've let business go is because I've been obsessed with finding out how you're doing, if you'll come back, what gift to get you. And you kept sending back these politely worded thank-you notes. I wanted to throttle you!"

Margaret gulped.

"I didn't really know what to do. How to respond. I thought that I was being kind."

"Margaret, if you don't want to be with me, then let me down easily. I can't deal with this hot and cold act. I'm too old for these games."

Margaret stilled. Had she really been playing a game? Was she forcing Sean to prove his love to her?

"I didn't think about it like that. I'm sorry, truly. I was just as messed up as you were, if that's any consolation," Margaret admitted.

"Don't you think I could see that when you walked in? Your clothes all but hanging off of you? Why do you think I'm trying to force-feed you lunch every day?" Sean asked.

Margaret huffed out a laugh.

"Lord, we are quite the pair, aren't we?"

Sean leaned closer, his lips hovering inches from hers.

"Will you come to dinner tonight? I can take you out or have you over. I'd be lying if I said I didn't want you to come over," Sean said.

Margaret felt her stomach clench at the thought of going back to Sean's house – to what they'd left unfinished on the couch. She wasn't sure if she was ready for that emotional rollercoaster quite yet.

"Baron misses you," Sean said, further twisting the knife in her gut. Margaret pursed her lips.

"You can pick me up at my hotel and take me to a nice dinner, like I deserve," Margaret ordered.

"Yes, ma'am," Sean said as he brushed his lips across hers in the softest of kisses. "Now get back to work."

Margaret found herself laughing the whole way back into the warehouse, feeling lighter after their talk.

"'Bout time you put a smile on that man's face," David called from across the warehouse.

"Get back to work," Margaret shouted back.

But she couldn't quite wipe the grin off her own face.

CHAPTER 52

MARGARET COULDN'T QUITE calm her nerves as she paced her hotel suite, glancing at the nightstand clock repeatedly as she smoothed her dress. It was one of her favorites, a Diane von Furstenburg in a navy print with bold red flowers splashed across the fabric. It made her feel flirty and feminine. Checking her hair again in the mirror, she pondered whether the curls were too much and if she should pull it back from her face. Raising a nervous hand to her hair, she laughed at herself.

"It's not like this is your first time going on a date," Margaret said out loud. Sean had pushed her out of work early, with strict instructions that she meet him in the lobby no later than 7:30. Which meant she had another twenty minutes to kill. Groaning, Margaret contemplated calling Keelin to kill the time when a knock at her door made her jump.

"Coming," she called, wondering who it was. Peeking through the peephole, Margaret didn't see anyone. Curious, she opened the door a crack and poked her head out.

"Hello?"

And shrieked as a furry animal streaked past her. Whirling around, she brought her hand to her chest and laughed out loud.

"Baron!"

The dog wiggled at her feet, a rose in his mouth, a plaid bowtie on his neck. Leaning down, Margaret laughed and pulled the rose from his mouth, stroking the eager dog's fur. As soon as she touched him, Baron rolled on his back, his paws in the air, the bowtie at his neck making him look like a little gentleman.

"Oh, aren't you the charming one," Margaret gushed, scratching Baron's belly as he wiggled in delight on the floor.

"Ahem, might I come in?" a voice from behind the door asked. Margaret jumped up, laughing at herself. Of course Baron hadn't come to her hotel on his own.

Smoothing her dress again, she pulled the door all the way open, holding the rose in one hand.

Sean stood outside, with at least two dozen roses tucked in his arm, wearing a three piece tuxedo and black wool newsboy cap. Margaret gaped at him, then looked down at her dress.

"I'm not dressed for black tie," she said immediately.

"You look beautiful. You're perfect," Sean said, stepping forward to plant a chaste kiss on Margaret's cheek. "Flowers for you."

"Thank you," Margaret looked around for something to put the blooms in. "I need a vase. Let me call the front desk."

"I have it taken care of," Sean said simply and opened the door. "We're ready."

Margaret gasped as a line of men trailed into the room. One whisked the flowers from her hand and placed them into a crystal vase, setting them on the sideboard. Another took a table into the separate sitting area, proceeding to unfold the table and pull linens out of a box. More men poured into the room, and Margaret stepped back, scooping up Baron to keep him from getting trampled. In moments, her sitting room had been transformed into a five-star restaurant, complete with candles all over the room, even more flowers, and a violinist setting up in the corner. Margaret blinked as the next wave of suited men entered the room, proceeding to set up a different sideboard with covered dishes, complete with a chef standing behind a small portable stove with a chef's hat perched jauntily on his head.

A man in a suit with a crisply pressed white linen napkin draped over his arm approached Margaret.

"Dinner is ready, Madam," he said, bowing slightly with the words. Margaret raised an eyebrow.

"Thank you," she said politely, shooting a glance at Sean as he ushered her to her seat. Margaret laughed as she saw that a third stool, with a little dog bed for Baron on it, had been pulled to the table, allowing the pup to sit with them. A new bone was placed neatly in the pillow on the bed.

"You didn't miss a trick," Margaret murmured, shooting a smile at Sean.

Bending, she placed Baron in his bed. He immediately

sniffed at the bone, then happily began to gnaw at one corner.

"My lady," Sean said, pulling the chair out and waiting until Margaret sat before laying a napkin over her lap. Margaret caught herself almost giggling with excitement as the violinist struck up a soft melody in the corner by the windows. The setting summer sun cast a warm glow across the room, and Margaret swallowed against the lump in her throat.

Sean settled in across from her and nodded to the waiter.

"The first course is a cilantro shallot mussels dish, sourced from Grace's Cove," the waiter announced, pulling a covered dish from the chef's table and settling it into the middle of their table.

"From Grace's Cove?" Margaret asked, raising her eyebrow at Sean.

"Yes. Nothing but the best for you," Sean said simply, smiling at her over the steaming mussels.

"These look fabulous," Margaret agreed, feeling a rush of excitement as she and Sean began to eat, chatting lightly about work and other subjects. The waiter topped off her wine every time she took a sip, leaving Margaret feeling a bit light-headed from the wine – and from being swept off her feet.

"The main course is lobster from Grace's Cove, served with a warm butter sauce, and roasted potatoes," the waiter announced. Margaret looked at Sean again.

"Flynn's lobster?" Flynn's lobsters, caught from Grace's Cove, were legendary across Ireland; the waiting list to order any was six months long.

"I put in for a favor," Sean said.

"I'm beginning to feel that there is a theme to this dinner," Margaret murmured as the waiter pulled a silver lid from her plate with a flourish. Her mouth watered just looking at the lobster presented so beautifully for her.

"Grace's Cove was the pivotal point in our lives. I don't want to push that away or hide it. It's as much a part of the fabric of what we are as our children are," Sean said. Margaret blushed, feeling uncomfortable discussing such personal matters with the waiters hovering over them.

"I agree," she said softly, glancing up at the waiter.

"I have more to say…with dessert," Sean said, understanding what Margaret was saying with her glance at the waiter. "In the meantime, I'd like to tell you how happy I am with the website design."

Happy that they were back on neutral topics, Margaret devoured the best lobster she'd ever had while talking about work. She found it enjoyable to be able to speak freely about their shared goals in the business. She wondered if this was how married people felt when they came home from work and had someone to talk to about their day. It was a nice change of pace, she thought.

"And, for dessert, we have a molten chocolate cake with raspberry gelato on the side."

Margaret laughed as she leaned back and put her hand on her stomach.

"I don't know if I can eat all that."

"There is just one dessert, for both of you to share," the waiter said and Margaret felt a little trill of lust run through her at the thought of sharing a dessert with Sean.

"One moment," Sean said, standing and nodding at the

violinist in the corner. Margaret watched as all of the staff packed up and Sean thanked each of them individually with an envelope that she presumed had a tip in it. In moments, the room had emptied and it was just her, Sean, and Baron. Nerves kicked up her spine.

Sean settled back in his chair, his eyes heavy with meaning as he watched her across the table. Candlelight flickered over his face.

"Try a bite," Sean said, picking up a spoon and slicing a piece of the moist cake. Margaret opened her mouth as he spoon-fed her across the table. She moaned as the delicious cake melted in her mouth. Licking her lips, Margaret smiled at him. Being here with him felt right.

"This is amazing. Truly. Thank you for all of this."

"I'm so glad you like it," Sean said. He looked down at Baron. "Baron, it's time."

The dog jumped to alert, cocking his head at Sean.

"Go get the bag," Sean ordered and Margaret laughed as Baron jumped down from the bed and trotted across the room to a corner where a small black bag now sat on the floor. Margaret wondered when it had appeared, as she'd certainly not seen it earlier. The dog maneuvered his teeth around the bag's handles and trotted back over to Sean with his head held high to keep the bag from dragging along the carpet.

"Not to me. To her," Sean said, pointing at Margaret. Baron dutifully turned to Margaret, depositing the bag at the foot of her chair. Margaret laughed and leaned over to pet Baron.

"He's so smart," she observed.

"Open the bag," Sean said.

Margaret felt her stomach flip-flop as she reached into the bag and pulled out a black velvet jewelry box. Her mouth went dry as she ran her hand over the square box.

"Sean," she began.

Sean stood and moved to turn her chair, then knelt at her feet.

"Just open it," he whispered, the plea mirrored in his eyes.

Margaret gulped and nodded, easing the lid of the box open with shaky hands. She gasped at the ring that lay nestled in the white silk fabric.

It was blue. A stunning sea blue, the exact shade of blue that shone through the waters when the cove glowed with its legendary light. The stone had to be at least two carats, and was surrounded by a circle of icy white diamonds on a hammered gold band. Margaret's heart clenched and tears blinked into her eyes as she looked up from the box at Sean.

"I'm asking you to marry me, Margaret. I've loved you for my whole life. These past six months have been the worst time of my life. Having you again and losing you so quickly tore me apart. I know we haven't figured it all out, I know we have a troubled past. I'm asking you to take a chance on me. I don't want to spend the rest of my life wondering what if or worrying that you'll run away at the slightest argument. You're it for me. You always have been. I love you, Margaret O'Brien. Will you be my wife and make an honest pup out of Baron?"

Margaret laughed at the last part, though tears were streaming down her face. There were so many things she wanted to bring up – all of the past hurts that could rear their heads at any time – all of the ugly history that lay between them. How did she know it would be okay? How could she let herself be vulnerable to this man who had hurt her so badly in the past?

And suddenly it became crystal clear to her.

This was the lesson she was supposed to learn. A lesson of forgiveness – of following her heart – of taking a leap of faith. It was time for Margaret to break down her walls and let herself be vulnerable in love. Even if it meant that Sean would have the power to hurt her again.

"I…" Margaret began, and then shook her head, "Yes, actually, yes. I'd be honored to be your wife. I know we have a history and I know the past will come up in arguments again. But I don't want to be defined by my past anymore. Or yours. I want to look forward to our future. I love you so much, Sean," Margaret said, openly crying now. She found herself being scooped up from her chair, the box falling from her hands as Sean devoured her lips in a kiss.

Margaret felt the wave of love wash over from him, so powerful and pure that she knew she would never have to doubt his feelings for her again.

And in that second, the feeling winked out.

Margaret stilled for a moment, pulling back to look past Sean's shoulder at the ceiling. Testing, she put down her shields and reached out, trying to scan Sean's mind to see if she could read his emotion.

"What's wrong?" Sean gasped.

Her special ability was gone. Margaret could have crowed with glee. Instead, she smiled happily up at Sean.

"Nothing at all. Everything is exactly as it should be."

"Then it's time for me to give you your real dessert," Sean growled into her neck, beginning to carry her towards the bedroom.

"Wait! My ring," Margaret protested.

Sean slid her down his body, kissing her the whole time, and Margaret felt a little dizzy on her feet as he left her to walk over to where the box lay on the floor. Bending, he picked it up and came to stand before her, dropping to his knee again.

"You don't have to do that," Margaret said.

"I do. Margaret, will you marry me?" Sean repeated.

"I will," Margaret gushed, holding out her hand and laughing out loud as he slipped the ring on her finger, the weight of it cool and lovely against her skin.

"Now, about that dessert," Margaret said and laughed when Sean swooped her off her feet once again.

Throwing her head back in laughter, she gasped as she caught a glimpse of Grace O'Malley in the corner, petting a bemused looking Baron.

With a small lift of her hand, Grace nodded to Margaret with a smile before fading from sight.

EPILOGUE

FIVE AND A HALF MONTHS LATER

Margaret smoothed the white silk of her dress, her hands nervously repeating the motion.

"Stop it. You look beautiful," Keelin said from where she stood, one hand pressed to her back, her pregnant belly sticking far out from what used to be her waist. A maroon dress complimented her hair and brought out the warm tones in her eyes.

"You look stunning," Margaret said, smiling at her daughter as Keelin reached up to clip a circlet of flowers in her hair. "Just perfect."

"And as big as a house," Keelin grumbled.

Today was Margaret's wedding day, and she couldn't help but nervously fidget inside the small white canopy the men had set up on the beach at Grace's Cove. White panels unrolled from the sides, concealing the women from the small group of guests that waited on the beach.

It had seemed like the perfect place to have her wedding, Margaret thought, though nerves skittered up her spine now as she thought about all the potential things that could go wrong if the cove decided to get moody.

"Stop worrying," Fiona ordered as she ducked into the tent, a flowing greyish caftan with maroon trim making her look every inch the powerful healer she was. Flowers were also entwined in her grey hair and Margaret smiled at her, reaching her hands out to both her mother and her daughter, completing the circle.

"I'm trying not to," Margaret admitted.

"You look so beautiful," Fiona said with a smile, her eyes softening at the corners as she looked at her daughter in her wedding dress.

"You think? It's not too young?"

Margaret had been drawn to this dress even though it was a departure from her usual buttoned up style. White silk flowed in a single column down her body, with the smallest hint of lace to create straps at her shoulders. A circlet of white flowers was entwined in her hair and a sheer veil trailed behind her. She wore no jewelry, save the pearls at her ears and her engagement ring, sparkling where it rested on her finger.

"It's perfect. Elegant and simple. You look amazing," Keelin gushed, pulling away to walk slowly in a circle around her mother.

"Keelin. How are you feeling?" Fiona asked and Margaret whipped her head around to study her daughter.

"Is something wrong? Are you having contractions?" Margaret asked.

"No. Just an achey lower back today. I'm carrying a lot of weight, you know," Keelin said with a smile and Margaret met her eyes.

"You promise to tell me if anything happens? I don't care if we have to stop the ceremony."

Keelin waved her hand distractedly at her mother.

"Stop it. This is your day. Now, I hear the music starting. I'd better get ready," Keelin said, moving to the front flap of the tent. As the processional music struck up, Keelin hoisted her bouquet of white roses in front of her stomach and pasted a smile on her face, stepping into the sunlight.

Margaret turned to meet Fiona's eyes.

"Is she lying?"

"I can't be certain. But I plan to stay very close to her today," Fiona nodded towards the corner, where two boxes of supplies sat. "And I'm prepared. Just in case."

The thought of Keelin going into labor down on the beach certainly knocked the nervous wedding jitters from Margaret's stomach. There were clearly bigger things to worry about. She stepped to the front of the tent and held out her arm for Fiona, who was walking her down the aisle.

"I'm so proud of you," Fiona said, smiling up at her daughter.

"I love you, Mom. I'm so glad I'm home," Margaret said, feeling a little weepy.

"Let's get you married then," Fiona said, and they pushed through the tent flaps.

For a moment, Margaret was blinded by the warm sunshine of a perfect fall day in Ireland. She'd known it was a gamble, planning an outside wedding in fall in Ireland, but she decided to risk it anyway. And had been rewarded with puffy white clouds, warm sunshine, and just a hint of a breeze.

A makeshift aisle had been concocted with chairs and wooden walking sticks wrapped in ribbons and flowers. At the head of the aisle, an altar had been created of wood branches and ribbons, and draped in a canopy of flowers. Margaret's mouth went dry as she saw Sean standing at the front, looking resplendent in the same tuxedo he had worn to propose to her, a white rose at his lapel. His face broke out in a wide smile as he met her eyes and Margaret felt a rush of love wash through her at the sight of him.

These past five months had felt like a whirlwind to Margaret. It was like she had finally come alive again. Everything she did with Sean was based in passion. From their disagreements to their lovemaking, they argued, laughed, and talked endlessly. It was almost as though they were making up for lost time. Rarely did they spend time apart, and instead of being annoyed by his constant companionship, Margaret reveled in finally having a partner by her side.

Together, they had pulled Sean's business out of distress; it was now running so smoothly they were both taking off on a tour of the Mediterranean in December. For an entire month! Margaret could hardly wait.

But for now, she needed to focus on getting down the aisle without tripping.

Margaret smiled at her very intimate group of guests, all whom grinned cheerfully back at her as she and Fiona made their way through the sand. Cait and Shane held little Fiona on their laps, a flower headband and cute dress making her look like a doll, and not the mischievous baby

Margaret knew her to be. Morgan and Patrick looked young and awestruck by the concept of marriage, though Margaret could see them holding hands tightly as she passed. Aislinn and Baird leaned into each other, both smiling serenely at Margaret. Colin, Aislinn's twin brother, sat with his wife and their young son, Finnegan. Margaret had begun to establish a good relationship with them and was happy to see Colin nod at her before giving her a wide smile.

Margaret looked to her favorite people. Keelin wiped tears as she stood next to the altar, fulfilling Margaret's maid of honor duty. Flynn stood centered behind the altar, having happily agreed to the great honor of being the one to marry Margaret and Sean.

Margaret took a deep breath as they stopped in front of the altar, then turned to hug her mother and kiss her on the cheek.

"Thank you," Margaret whispered.

Fiona nodded and stepped to the chair waiting for her in the front row. Turning, Margaret stepped forward and reached out to put her hands in Sean's waiting ones. They both smiled giddily at each other, and jumped when Flynn cleared his throat.

"It is with great honor that I am brought here today to wed these two lovebirds in holy matrimony..."

Margaret giggled and found herself getting lost in the beauty of the moment. Flynn's words flowed around her and she found herself gazing out towards the water that gently lapped at the shoreline.

For a sliver of a moment, Grace O'Malley flashed into view.

Keelin gasped and Margaret turned to look at her.

"Nothing, keep going," Keelin said with a smile; Keelin must have also seen Grace, Margaret thought. It was comforting to know Grace was overseeing the ceremony with her own blessing, and Margaret turned back to Sean with a smile.

"Sean, do you take this woman…"

Margaret stumbled through the vows, so deliriously happy and in love that all she could do was smile at Sean and wait for the words.

"I now pronounce you man and wife. You may kiss the bride."

As the guests erupted in cheers, Sean brushed his lips across Margaret's in the most tender of kisses, and felt her heart cracking wide open with love. She shrieked happily when he scooped her up and dipped her, his lips following her in a kiss as he upended her towards the sand. As he pulled her back up, Margaret gasped as the cove shot out a beam of light, so stunning in its beauty that it all but blinded everyone on the shore.

Margaret felt her heart stop for a second; then she nodded at the water and whispered, "Thank you, Grace."

"I didn't run this time," Sean said at her ear, and Margaret broke into laughter.

Margaret thrust her bouquet high in the air as she walked back down the aisle, the guests clapping and laughing as Patrick flipped the switch on the CD player to begin their happy end-of-wedding song.

At the end of the aisle, Margaret and Sean stood for a moment and looked into each other eyes, lost in the moment, as they waited for Fiona and Keelin to proceed down the aisle.

Margaret turned, smiling at Fiona, and then looked past her to where Keelin stood, a horrified expression on her face, the damp sand at her feet a silent explanation for her expression.

"Mother! Get your supplies!"

Fiona reacted instantly, swiveling her head to see Keelin stood frozen in the sand. Flynn had already moved towards her, asking her what was wrong.

"Flynn, bring Keelin to the tent. Tell them to hold dinner – we've got a baby on the way."

The guests reacted immediately, the women jumping up and racing towards the tent. Margaret looked up at Sean.

"I have to go in there with her."

"I know. Keep us updated. Dinner will wait." Their dinner was being cooked and served at Flynn and Keelin's house, in his expansive dining hall.

Margaret moved to Flynn's side as he carried Keelin down the aisle. She reached out to squeeze her daughter's hand as they walked across the sand.

"This shouldn't be happening like this. We should be at the hospital," Keelin gasped out, her breath coming in short gasps as pain flashed across her face.

"Nonsense. Fiona brought supplies. She obviously suspected this would happen," Margaret reassured Keelin, holding back the tent flap as Flynn passed through.

Inside, Margaret was amazed to see what the women had set up in such a short amount of time. A large blanket was spread out on the sand floor, with pillows for support.

Two low tables were spread with various types of medical equipment, a basin, and towels. Rows of Fiona's bottles of elixirs and herbs were lined up, ready for use.

"Just put her down in the sand," Fiona said gently, her hands already encased in rubber gloves.

"Don't you think we should get her up to the doctor?" Flynn asked, worry crossing his features.

"If I'm correct, you won't have time," Fiona said serenely. "Now, Flynn, get behind Keelin and put your legs alongside of her so she can lean back into you for support."

Margaret knelt on the blanket, holding Keelin's hand as Fiona knelt between her legs, lifting her skirts and gently pulling Keelin's underwear down. Nobody said a word as Fiona peeked under the skirt.

When her head reappeared, her expression was grim.

"This baby is already on its way out. Another thing about the cove, it facilitates fast births," Fiona said easily and began instructing Cait and Aislinn to bring her herbs and salves. Laying out towels, Fiona looked up and met Keelin's eyes.

"You push when I say push. Grace is here with us today. You are completely protected. Do you understand me?"

Keelin nodded, determination shining through on her already sweat-soaked face.

"Remember that Fiona is one of the best healers this world has known. You couldn't be in better hands," Margaret whispered to Keelin.

"Push," Fiona ordered, and so Keelin pushed.

Margaret winced and held her daughter's hand as they

counted through contractions, yelled together through pushing. After what seemed like an exceptionally long time – but was probably only twenty minutes or so – Fiona met Keelin's eyes once more.

"Last one. Push!"

Keelin closed her eyes and pushed, gasping as her body delivered new life into the world. A flash of light startled them all, and Keelin screamed with her effort. In seconds, a baby's cry split through the tense silence in the tent, and everyone cheered.

"Towels and water," Fiona ordered, expertly cleaning out the baby's nasal passages and mouth before tying off and clamping the umbilical cord. "Finish cleaning her off while I finish the birth," Fiona ordered, handing the baby to Cait, who did as she was told. Margaret held Keelin's hand as she sobbed with emotion, finishing the birth with determination.

"My baby. Let me see her," Keelin gasped, holding her hands up. Cait put the swaddled infant in Keelin's arms and Flynn peered over her shoulder.

"She's beautiful," Keelin sobbed.

Margaret leaned in so she could get a better look, and her heart all but stopped. Turning, she met Fiona's meaningful look. The older woman shook her head and Margaret bit back what she was about to say.

But Margaret knew those eyes. The eyes staring out at her from the tiny bundle of blankets were those of none other than the great pirate queen – Grace O'Malley.

"I'd like to introduce everyone to Grace Margaret," Keelin said happily, and Margaret's heart swelled with the honor.

"She's stunning. You did such a great job. All of you," Margaret said, looking around.

"So is there a baby or what?" a voice called from outside, and Cait jumped up.

"Whoops!" Moving to the tent flaps, she pulled them open so everyone could crowd around.

"Awww, she's beautiful," everyone crowed in delight.

And she really was, Margaret thought. Though she had a sinking suspicion she knew what that flash of light meant.

And that little Grace Margaret was about to put her parents through the wringer.

"They can handle it," Fiona whispered at her side.

"That's Grace in there. You know that, right?" Margaret hissed back.

"I know. Keelin doesn't need to know. Not yet, at least. Grace had her reasons for coming back. She'll do wonders in this world. That baby is destined for greatness," Fiona predicted.

"I suppose that's all I can ask for," Margaret murmured.

Sean pulled her away from the tent, leading her towards the water.

"Look at all of this," he said, turning to gesture towards where their wedding altar stood, and back towards the guests crowding around Keelin and Flynn, congratulating them on their new arrival.

"I think we had to go through all of this to get back here," Sean said, pulling her to him so that she leaned into him, his body rock solid against hers.

"I think you're right. Everything in its own time. This was all meant to be."

In one final flourish of light, the cove lit up as the baby cried, and Margaret and Sean sank into a kiss, forever cementing their love and the circle of life on the shores of the mighty mystic cove.

Available now as an e-book, paperback or audiobook!!!

Available from Amazon

The following is an excerpt from Wild Irish Witch

Book 6 in the Mystic Cove Series

CHAPTER 1

"Don't go," Fiona whispered as she pressed her hand to John's cheek. She could all but feel the bristle of his beard under her hand, just as it had felt the last time she'd touched him. Two days out from a shave, his eyes a laughing blue, and his dark hair just long enough to curl.

They were always young in her dream. Well, it was the only way she'd ever known John. Young, full of life, yet tender-hearted and gentle with her in their most intimate moments.

He'd been coming to her in her dreams over the years, but they'd increased in frequency as of late. Even though a part of Fiona knew that she was curled beneath worn flannel sheets in her cottage, in her mind she dreamt of her happiest moments. After all these years, the loss of John still stung. Fiona wondered if she would ever get over the grief, but it had been almost half a century since she'd last felt his lips against hers, and the sting of loss had yet to go away. It might have dampened a bit, but it had never truly left her.

Fiona shifted as the dream slipped away, taking her beloved with it. She let out a soft sigh of loss, and stayed still for just a moment longer. In her mind she was still young, agile, and full of zest for life. As the years crept on, Fiona felt a bit bewildered by the chasm of time that separated her from the last time she had spoken to John.

It shouldn't have been this way.

And yet, it had been the only way it could be.

Fiona knew without a doubt that John wouldn't have begrudged her the choice she'd had to make.

But the pain had never faded for Fiona. Perhaps that was just her cross to bear. Shifting once more, she rolled over and forced her eyes open. Ronan slumbered at her feet, her constant companion. Though he was technically Keelin's dog, when Keelin had moved over the hill to Flynn's he'd decided to stay with Fiona.

She'd never admit how secretly pleased she was by his choice.

"Come on boy, we've got a big day ahead of us," Fiona said, and Ronan popped his head up to look at her.

"It's Thanksgiving! Come on, come on, sure and you know we've got to be helping in the kitchen."

"I CAN'T BELIEVE I'm cooking a Thanksgiving dinner! This is my first Thanksgiving," Fiona pointed out as she followed Keelin's carefully printed recipe card for preparing bread stuffing. Fiona had crossed the hills, blustery with November wind, to help Keelin prepare for her favorite holiday. Ronan had raced beside her, barking into the gusts and chasing away imagined intruders.

"Maybe it's dumb of me to try to continue the tradition in Ireland. I'm the only American here, really." Keelin bit her lip, her pretty brown eyes scrunched in concern.

"It's never dumb to get the family together for a nice dinner," Fiona said with a smile, winking at Flynn as he ducked his head into the kitchen, Baby Grace cradled in one arm.

"I've got a fire started. It should help ward off some of that chill," Flynn said.

"How's Gracie doing?" Keelin asked, her hands deep in a bowl of cranberry sauce.

"She's fine. You know how much she loves me," Flynn said as he left the room, at ease with being a father. Grace shot them both a look over his shoulder. Fiona winked at her, and sure and the baby didn't wink right back.

"It's true. I've never seen a baby take such a shine to her father quite so quickly," Fiona chuckled as she sliced an onion.

"Yes, well, you'd think she'd love her mother. I'm the one who gave birth to her, aren't I? Yet she cries like a banshee half the time that I hold her."

Fiona bit back a laugh. She'd known since the day Baby Grace was born into this world that she was going to give Keelin trouble. The baby was major magick, after all. "We'll just have to wait and see what sort of gifts this little one gets. I expect she's going to give us all a run for our money very shortly here. I'm sure her crying around you has to do with her trying to communicate something that you aren't understanding yet."

Keelin's head shot up.

"You think? Really? I've been worried that I'm missing out on something. I just don't know what she's trying to tell me."

"All in good time, dear. It'll work itself out," Fiona said gently, warmth racing through her at Keelin's concern. She was a good mother, surprisingly so for not having been raised with siblings or around other children. Fiona was proud of how she'd navigated her first few months of motherhood.

"I just keep worrying that I'm doing everything wrong," Keelin admitted as she checked on the turkey in the oven.

Fiona pulled a bowl of cream from the refrigerator and began to whip it, focusing on the repetitive task as she thought about her words.

"I don't think that ever goes away," Fiona admitted. "As a mother, you're going to constantly question whether you're doing things right. Sure and you'll never stop worrying, either. But I always feel that, so long as you come at your decisions through love, it will all work out. The best you can do is give your child love and direction. As they grow and change, you'll need to step back and let them make their own decisions. Even if it means failing. You think the crying is hard? Wait until she walks out the door and starts to make decisions on her own. It only gets more difficult from there."

"Like my mom. When she left you alone," Keelin said softly.

Fiona shrugged.

"Yes, but what do you do? You can't force a grown

adult to listen to you," Fiona said as she tapped the whisk on the side of the bowl. "Now enough about that. Pull out the whiskey I brought, will you? The coffee's just perked and I'd like a fine Irish coffee."

Fiona shook her head as Keelin left the expansive kitchen that lay at the back of Flynn's large house. It was a far cry from cooking in her own small kitchen at her cottage, and Fiona loved visiting here and whipping up batches of scones while Keelin nursed. She'd missed out on the opportunity to help when Keelin was just a baby, so she was determined not to miss out on anything now.

Fiona sighed as she looked down at her hands. Her skin there was thin, but just showing the wrinkles of age. She'd be lying if she said she didn't add a little charm to her anti-wrinkle creams to help keep the signs of age away. But some days she felt it. Like today, when she looked at Keelin and her baby, so young and fresh. She remembered those days with Margaret. She'd been so young and innocent, at least for a brief moment in time. In that time of simplicity and love, Fiona had been so carefree, so in love with her husband and her life.

Sometimes she wished with all her heart she could have those days back.

And her John back in her arms.

Fiona shook her head at herself. She'd learned long ago that there was no use living in the past. No good could come of it.

She smiled brightly at Keelin as she came back in brandishing a bottle of whiskey.

"I think I'll join you for a cup. It sounds perfect on a day like today," Keelin said, as she placed the bottle on the counter and reached into a cupboard for her coffee glasses.

"There's nothing like an Irish coffee in front of the fire. Food's all set. Why don't we go in the other room and wait for Margaret?" Fiona asked as she measured sugar into the bottom of the glass and poured a liberal shot of whiskey into each.

"Sounds perfect," Keelin said, giving Fiona's arm a squeeze. "And, hey, thanks for the advice. I know it hasn't always been easy for you."

"Life isn't always easy."

Read Wild Irish Witch today.
Available from Amazon

MS. BITCH

FINDING HAPPINESS IS THE BEST REVENGE

Available as an e-book, Hardback, Paperback, Audio or Large Print.
Read Today
New from Tricia O'Malley

From the outside, it seems thirty-six-year-old Tess Campbell has it all. A happy marriage, a successful career as a novelist, and an exciting cross-country move ahead. Tess has always played by the rules and it seems like life is good.

Except it's not. Life is a bitch. And suddenly so is Tess.

"Ms. Bitch is sunshine in a book! An uplifting story of fighting your way through heartbreak and making your own version of happily-ever-after."
~Ann Charles, USA Today Bestselling Author of the Deadwood Mystery Series

"Authentic and relatable, Ms. Bitch packs an emotional punch. By the end, I was crying happy tears and ready to pack my bags in search of my best life."
-Annabel Chase, author of the Starry Hollow Witches series

"It's easy to be brave when you have a lot of support in your life, but it takes a special kind of courage to forge a new path when you're alone. Tess is the heroine I hope I'll be if my life ever crumbles down around me. Ms. Bitch is a journey of determination, a study in self-love, and a hope for second chances. I could not put it down!"
-Renee George, USA Today Bestselling Author of the Nora Black Midlife Psychic Mysteries

"I don't know where to start listing all the reasons why you should read this book. It's empowering. It's fierce. It's about loving yourself enough to build the life you want. It was honest, and raw, and real and I just...loved it so much!"

– Sara Wylde, author of Fat

AFTERWORD

Ireland holds a special place in my heart – a land of dreamers and for dreamers. There's nothing quite like cozying up next to a fire in a pub and listening to a session or having a cup of tea while the rain mists outside the window. I'll forever be enchanted by her rocky shores and I hope you enjoy this series as much as I enjoyed writing it. Thank you for taking part in my world, I hope that my stories bring you great joy.

Have you read books from my other series? Join our little community by signing up for my newsletter for updates on island-living, fun giveaways, and how to follow me on social media!
http://eepurl.com/1LAiz.

or at my website
www.triciaomalley.com

Please consider leaving a review! Your review helps others to take a chance on my stories. I really appreciate your help!

THE MYSTIC COVE SERIES

Wild Irish Heart

Wild Irish Eyes

Wild Irish Soul

Wild Irish Rebel

Wild Irish Roots: Margaret & Sean

Wild Irish Witch

Wild Irish Grace

Wild Irish Dreamer

Wild Irish Christmas (Novella)

Wild Irish Sage

Wild Irish Renegade

"I have read thousands of books and a fair percentage have been romances. Until I read Wild Irish Heart, I never had a book actually make me believe in love."- Amazon Review

Available in audio, e-book & paperback!

Available Now

THE ISLE OF DESTINY SERIES

ALSO BY TRICIA O'MALLEY

Stone Song

Sword Song

Spear Song

Sphere Song

"Love this series. I will read this multiple times. Keeps you on the edge of your seat. It has action, excitement and romance all in one series."- Amazon Review

Available in audio, e-book & paperback!

Available from Amazon

THE SIREN ISLAND SERIES

ALSO BY TRICIA O'MALLEY

Good Girl

Up to No Good

A Good Chance

Good Moon Rising

Too Good to Be True

A Good Soul

"Love her books and was excited for a totally new and different one! Once again, she did NOT disappoint! Magical in multiple ways and on multiple levels. Her writing style, while similar to that of Nora Roberts, kicks it up a notch!! I want to visit that island, stay in the B&B and meet the gals who run it! The characters are THAT real!!!" - Amazon Review

Available in audio, e-book & paperback!

Available Now

THE ALTHEA ROSE SERIES

ALSO BY TRICIA O'MALLEY

One Tequila

Tequila for Two

Tequila Will Kill Ya (Novella)

Three Tequilas

Tequila Shots & Valentine Knots (Novella)

Tequila Four

A Fifth of Tequila

A Sixer of Tequila

Seven Deadly Tequilas

Eight Ways To Tequila

Available in audio, e-book & paperback!

Available from Amazon

"Not my usual genre but couldn't resist the Florida Keys setting. I was hooked from the first page. A fun read with just the right amount of crazy! Will definitely follow this series."- Amazon Review

AUTHOR'S NOTE

Thank you for taking a chance on my books; it means the world to me. Writing novels came by way of a tragedy that turned into something beautiful and larger than itself (see: *The Stolen Dog*). Since that time, I've changed my career, put it all on the line, and followed my heart.

Thank you for taking part in the worlds I have created; I hope you enjoy it.

I would be honored if you left a review online. It helps other readers to take a chance on my work.

> As always, you can reach me at
> info@triciaomalley.com
> or feel free to visit my website at
> www.triciaomalley.com.

AUTHOR'S ACKNOWLEDGEMENT

First, and foremost, I'd like to thank my family and friends for their constant support, advice, and ideas. You've all proven to make a difference on my path. And, to my beta readers, I love you for all of your support and fascinating feedback!

And last, but never least, my two constant companions as I struggle through words on my computer each day - Briggs and Blue.

Printed in Great Britain
by Amazon